JOANNA BARNARD

◆

PRECOCIOUS

Complete and Unabridged

ULVERSCROFT
Leicester

First published in Great Britain in 2015 by
Ebury Press
an imprint of Ebury Publishing
London

First Large Print Edition
published 2016
by arrangement with
Ebury Publishing
Penguin Random House
London

This novel is a work of fiction. Names and characters
are the product of the author's imagination and any
resemblance to actual persons, living or dead,
is entirely coincidental.

A catalogue record for this book is available
from the British Library.

ISBN 978–1–4448–2936–5

Published by
F. A. Thorpe (Publishing)
Anstey, Leicestershire

Set by Words & Graphics Ltd.
Anstey, Leicestershire
Printed and bound in Great Britain by
T. J. International Ltd., Padstow, Cornwall

This book is printed on acid-free paper

For Mum, with love

1

We meet again in the supermarket. The drone of the tannoy announcements, the bustle of people, all seem to pause for a second while I register that it's really you.

'You look great,' I say. *You look old*, I think. You're holding a bag of frozen prawns, and a basket. Good. I stare at the basket. No trolley equals no family.

You're looking at me and for a horrible moment I think you don't remember me. Then you smile, and the smile is fifteen years older but the same cloudy, wry smile as then, as ever. Your wrinkles, your teeth.

'Fee, fi, fo, fum,' you say.

We embrace clumsily. You have no hands free and I have only one, so we sort of clang together and I end up patting you on the back as if in recognition of a job well done.

With my head buried momentarily in your shoulder I send a wish skywards that when we separate my hair will look neater, my face fresher, my waist thinner.

Pulling away from me, your polite questions begin.

'So, what are you doing now?'

'Shopping?'

I'm doing that thing where I say everything like a question — it comes out when I'm nervous.

You laugh in that way you used to when I could never tell if you were making fun of me.

'I don't mean right now, I mean, in life — for a career.'

'Oh. I work in publishing.'

I tell everyone this. I sell advertising space in the Yellow Pages.

'Publishing,' you consider this for a while, 'and the writing?'

But you say it with capital letters. The Writing, followed by a question mark, heavy with expectation.

'Oh, bits and pieces,' I mumble. The truth is I haven't written anything except emails for eight years.

The last thing I wrote was a letter I never sent. A letter to you, when I was twenty-two. Years had already passed and I was angry. I tried to disguise it as defiance. 'I would eat you for breakfast now!' I wrote, daring you to come back. I put it in an envelope and sealed it and it stayed on my bookshelf, so unlike the notes and poems I used to put in your pigeon hole or on your desk to wonder all day if you'd read them.

I'm brought back to the present by your question:

'What are you doing for dinner?' I look at my trolley full of food.

'No plans,' I say, 'nothing that can't wait.'

'Great. You can tell me your stories.'

And you're back.

* * *

A small part of me has wondered, from time to time, whether you might have died. But somehow I felt that I would have known — not found out, not seen it in the newspaper, not been told by someone — I would have just known. I would've felt it, in my gut. I would've felt a hot pain behind my eyes. I would have known.

I didn't think I'd been obsessed with you all these years, but now that you're back, the terrain between then and today takes on a different geography. I've thought about you, perhaps not every day, but most days, for however fleeting a time. I thought I saw you — lots of times — which was always disconcerting, even though a second glance would prove it to be only a piece of you, the flick of your hair, maybe, or the curve of your ear, on an impostor's face. I've heard your voice: unmistakeably you, the lazy sound of your vowels, your bored drawl. And each time when I realised it wasn't you, in the back of my mind was relief, and further back still a strange certainty that one day it would be.

So you didn't die — today you reappeared, very much alive, somehow smaller and with thinning hair, but still you, holding a basket. And now I'm following your car, steering with one hand and texting my husband with the other.

I will be late home.

★ ★ ★

The restaurant is made mostly of glass. Floor to ceiling windows look out onto a rain-soaked street. You slice through your steak, metal scraping china.

'Tell me about him,' you say.

'Who?' I push my food around my plate. I always did feel uncomfortable eating in front of you.

You say nothing but motion towards my left hand. I glance down at the perfect diamond and, without thinking, spin it inwards with a flick of the thumb so that I only have to look at two thin gold bands.

'Dave,' I say simply.

'Tell me about Dave.'

'Dave is . . . a *grown-up*,' I want to say. I

4

realise how ridiculous a statement this is to make to a man who is now in his forties, and laugh to myself. But that's how I think of Dave. Or at least, he makes *me* a grown-up.

Dave is one of those people who is meant to be married. He got close, with the girlfriend before me. She left him three weeks before the wedding. When we met, it seemed like he was looking for a sticking plaster. He wanted me, yes, but only a fraction of how much he wanted to be married. It was as though the quicker he fell in love and got someone to love him back — the quicker he got married — the easier it would be to convince himself that his heartbreak had never happened.

He even has a husband's name. Dave. A comforting name, something about the warm sound of the 'v'. A big man's name, but not threatening big, just warm. Comforting, comfortable big.

I had once thought I would end up with an Alec, or a Holden, or even a Heathcliff, but they are only characters in books, not real men you can marry. I thought I might marry one of the skinny, glassy-eyed, long-haired wraiths who kept me awake all night in my teens, smelling of patchouli oil and brown ale, running their hands along my back and quoting inaccurately from *The Prophet*.

But none of them asked. The one who asked was a Dave, the Dave who brings me flowers, who smells clean, soapy even, who quotes old Genesis love songs, singing shakily while I look down at him through my hair.

I tell you all of this and you listen.

'So that's why you got married? Because he asked?' I nod; I don't tell you that I also felt a bit sorry for him. The rings on my third finger feel tight.

'Maybe. Why not? Why does anyone do it?'

'I don't know.' You laugh that dry laugh, like a cough.

'*You* got married.' I sound like a sulky teenager. You say nothing but keep chewing. To fill the silence I say, 'It's just what you do, isn't it? It's what people do. *Normal* people.' I wave my fork at you and all around, as though to demonstrate the difference between these normal people and you. A flake of salmon lands on the tablecloth.

'Funny, I never had you down as a traditionalist, that's all.'

'Well, people can change in fifteen years.'

'Hmm. Not everyone is as stubborn and set in their ways as I am, I suppose.'

I feel exposed, accused of a crime I don't remember committing.

'Get married, have a baby,' you pause, 'that's next, I suppose?'

'No.' A little too quickly.

'Why not? Isn't that what they do, these normal people you're so fond of?'

'I just never wanted to have his baby,' I say, realising too late that I've emphasised the word *his*.

You give a slow, reptilian blink and then say, 'Whatever happened to vegetarianism?'

For a strange, surreal moment I think you mean generally; in society as a whole. I finger my brain. Have I missed something? Has there been a widespread decline in concern for animal welfare, recently documented in the cleverer late night TV discussion programmes, or worse, in the popular press, and I have not noticed? How could I have come to dinner so unprepared to discuss topical issues?

I look at you blankly and you nod at my plate.

'Oh,' I look down, 'I had to start eating fish. Vitamin deficiency.'

'Glad to hear it. Always thought it was nonsense, you giving up meat so young. You can't be a vegetarian until you've tasted a really excellent rare steak. Until that point you're simply not making an informed choice. Oh sure, it's easy to see the reasons for becoming vegetarian — but what about the reasons for eating meat? Until you've eaten veal — or foie gras — you simply don't know enough. Some cruelty is worth it.' You look at me, pop a forkful of steak into your mouth. 'The end justifies the means.'

I could swear I see blood oozing out at the sides.

'So if Dan doesn't mind . . . '

'Dave,' I say; *you're not funny*, I think.

'If you don't think *Dave* will mind, can we go out again?'

'Are we becoming friends now?' I ask.

'Don't you mean again?'

'Are we becoming friends again?'

'Better late than never,' you grin.

'Fifteen years,' I say, 'that's late.'

★   ★   ★

I've had two glasses of wine. I don't drink and drive, as a rule; it isn't me. I like to feel in control. Something made me order the second glass and it's that glass, or that something, that I know is to blame when I reverse my car out of the pitch dark parking space and scrape the next car along.

Damn, damn, damn.

I get out, scribble my mobile number on the back of the supermarket receipt and leave it under the car's windscreen wiper.

From across the street I hear the thud of a

door, and footsteps, and now you are at my side, laughing.

'What did you do? Fee, Fee . . . '

'It's just a bump,' I say irritably. I feel like a child. I feel shaky, inadequate, and can't look at you.

'I just wanted to say goodbye.'

'You already did. It was good to see you.'

You say something that I hear but immediately forget, because at once your hand is in my hair, and now on my throat, and there is kissing. I can't say you kiss me, or I kiss you, only that there is kissing, because I am watching it from far away.

And all I can think about is what I ate, and therefore what do I taste like, and does it feel nice to you, and I shouldn't be doing this, and I should be doing this, and . . .

At last.

★ ★ ★

Tonight I will do all of the same things I do every night.

Come through the door, stroke the dog, murmur 'hellos', exchange perfunctory kisses with my husband, wash the breakfast things that weren't done in the morning, have a cup of tea. I will say 'no, I've eaten, but I'll do something for you' and I will put some rice or

9

spaghetti on to simmer while thawing out a sticky-labelled pot from the freezer. I do all the actual cooking at the weekends. I spend Sunday afternoons making chillies and stews and curries and broths and posting them, tightly lidded, colour coded, addressed to Monday, Tuesday and so on, into deep freeze.

Today is Wednesday.

Once I have thawed out, warmed up, talked about my day, I will put everything, including myself, away.

Tonight I will do all of the same things I do every night, but tonight is different. Tonight I feel like a ghost in my own life.

Dave often says: 'I can see right through you.'

It's one of his favourite phrases — he's said it for years. I used to take it literally, and I hated it; it made me look at the pale skin through which I can sometimes see my own veins. He would tell me, 'don't be silly', but all the while he would be absentmindedly stroking the fine purple lines on my inner wrist, my temple, my breast.

Then for a while I loved it: it made me feel completely *known*, and wanted. Safe.

Now it frightens me. What if he can? I feel high-pitched; a different, shiny version of myself. Does he notice?

I kick off my shoes and unpack the

10

shopping, sliding melted ice cream and car-boot-warmed cheese straight into the dustbin with a smile. I prepare a bowl of spaghetti for Dave and a piece of chicken for the dog.

'I saw someone today,' I say casually. 'I mean, I bumped into someone.'

'Oh yes?' He lifts the fork to his mouth. The bowl is balanced on his lap, his eyes fixed on the TV. I watch the blood-coloured sauce tipping, from left to right, towards his trousers, towards the sofa cushions.

'Mm-hum. An old friend.'

'Right.'

'That's where I was. I mean, that's who I had dinner with. In case you were wondering.'

'I just assumed you were with Mari. So where do you know her from?'

'Who?'

'This friend. Who is she?'

'Oh. From school. It's a he.'

'Uh-oh, should I be jealous?' He puts the bowl down and nuzzles my neck, jabbing at the TV remote, eyes never leaving the screen.

'He was my teacher.'

'Ah, that's a no then. If he was your teacher, what is he, about ninety?'

'Cheek!' I pause, as if mentally calculating, as if I don't know your age in years, months,

11

weeks and days off by heart. 'Forty-three.'

'Should I be jealous?' he says again.

'I don't think so,' I lie.

★　★　★

I lie awake: I, who have always been able to curl like a cat into any available space, any time, can't sleep.

You are replaying in my mind like a movie. How typical of you, to turn up like that, to put a spanner in the works, a cat among the pigeons, walking cliché that you are. I'm married. I'm happy. Finally I've put to rest the irritating feeling I've had for most of my life, the suspicion that I might be missing something, that around the corner, or tomorrow, I would find the thing that would satisfy me. I have done the done thing, and it is working. Has been working.

Then all of a sudden we were knocking each other over in the freezer aisle and I was hugging myself not from the cold, but for protection, and next I hugged you, and later there was the kiss.

Silence in the bedroom is an extra blanket: sometimes comforting, but not for long; usually too thick. Hot and scratchy. Through this deep cover my husband hears the sound of me rustling in his bedside drawer.

12

'Can't sleep?' he murmurs.

'Mmm.'

'Fee,' he lifts his head from the pillow, 'you had dinner with your forty-three-year-old ex-teacher?' Raises a quizzical, sleepy eyebrow.

'Like I said — he was kind of a friend. Aren't there any bloody pens in this house?'

Apparently satisfied with this response, he settles back into the pillow. 'Come back to bed.' Within seconds he is snoring softly.

I've always thought it is only when you spend the night with someone that you know whether you can love them. If you can bear their sour night-breath; if you can get used to their flickering eyelids and the knowledge that something is happening behind them that you can't know about; if you can lie and listen to their dream noises, you have a good chance.

I pad down to the kitchen like a thief, down to the bottom floor of our cavernous house. The dog barely stirs.

The kitchen takes up the whole of the basement. Copper-bottomed pans hang from the ceiling, so clean they look like they've never been used. In the windowless half-light they seem like weapons.

I pour a glass of filtered water (bottled is too expensive, tap too dirty, according to Dave) and attack the heavy oak drawers.

13

I need to find something to write with. The bill drawer — that's the one. On top of the neat pile of mail, a cheque book, a spiral-bound notebook and a rollerball pen. The itch in my head that I haven't felt for years is there, and I settle at the table to scratch it out onto the paper.

★　★　★

He was kind of a friend.

'If you trust me,' you used to say, 'I won't let you down.'

So I trusted you, and you did let me down, and later, you introduced me to your girlfriend.

It was the fifth year leavers' ball in 1994, that last summer before fifth year became known as year eleven at our school. There was a May smell of cut grass and keenly sucked ciggies behind the building. The fact that we were promised booze meant no one bothered to bring vodka in a Coke bottle. As it turned out, we only got one glass of watered-down wine each with dinner. I wore a pink and blue dotted puffball skirt and low-cut white top. I was carrying a 'proper' handbag for the first time in my life and was rummaging in it as I tottered into school and straight into the two of you.

14

You coughed in my cloud of Lou Lou.

When I say 'girlfriend', she wasn't a girl, she was a woman, of course. She had ash-blonde hair swept into a chignon and she wore her age like a badge pinned from a birthday card. It towered over me, gave her height.

'This is Fiona,' you said to her. 'The Genius.'

You both chuckled. She was not surprised — by my presence there, by your description. So you had talked about me.

I always thought teachers made fun of only the very dull (because they don't get it) or the precocious (who can give it back). Which was I supposed to be?

I left, and I left school, and until today I hadn't seen you since.

2

Tell me about Dave, you said. Okay, I'll tell you. About him, about me, about falling in love.

These are the things that did it:

The First Night Out. We argued. An amazing thing: to be relaxed enough to disagree instead of preening, lying and straining to impress.

The First Night In. The way we stayed up all night and talked and talked so urgently, desperate to *find out things*, and the way every uncovered shared interest or belief seemed incredible, natural, destined. Coincidence and magic in everything.

The First Morning After. He left, wearing stale clothes and shocked hair, drove round the block then came back, and stood on the doorstep, smiling.

★   ★   ★

It was about money. That first argument, that first night.

Dave never earned much, but spent less and borrowed nothing. I couldn't believe he'd

16

never had an overdraft; mine seemed to have lingered after university like a hangover. The thing is, it never really bothered me, but Dave was different. He was cautious; but then, he'd shelled out nearly fifteen grand for a wedding that didn't happen. That would make anyone err on the thrifty side.

'Most couples end up arguing about money anyway,' he'd said. 'Might as well start now.'

'You're assuming we'll become a couple,' I'd pointed out. I slurped up my spaghetti, I remember, not caring if I got sauce on my chin.

Dave didn't say anything but I think he knew, even then, that we would end up together. That's the way Dave works — and he's the same in every area of his life, there's no 'side' to him, no secrets — he sees something he wants and slowly, methodically, with no drama but with the utmost determination, he goes after it.

★　★　★

What is it to fall in love? Is it a different thing from being in love? At what point does falling become being? When do you land?

Some say love is security. It's a comfort thing. It was like that with Dave. It was

17

feeling utterly relaxed, melting into him the way a cat pours its every muscle onto a table or a chair arm, or someone's leg, moulding it to them. It's almost impossible to get up once a cat has sat on your lap, because they just make themselves belong there.

Love is: butterflies; a warm feeling; fear; jealousy; a grin you can't shake; sleeplessness; tears; hours of staring at the wall, staring at the window, staring at his photo, staring at his face; love is change. Security, insecurity. Passion, fights. Chatter, silence.

Love is chaos.

Dave and I didn't so much fall in love as stumble into it, both dazed and war-torn, like survivors of some disaster who cling to each other in their shock and find years later they are still holding on. He was stinging from the slap of the aborted wedding, I was tired and dispirited from a string of no-hopers, badly-suiteds and just-not-quite-rights.

I remember when it was just Love. Before it was Family, before it was Commitment, before it was *Arrangements*.

I remember wanting to say the word so soon but not wanting to say it first.

And when it was said, feeling strangely disappointed.

I love you.

Because it's the same thing as everyone else says, and I felt an odd sort of traitor to my heart, and cursed my own lack of originality, and thought,

I love you, followed by *(that's all).*

And I had, and still have, an uneasy feeling that once you've said 'I love you', the only way is down.

★ ★ ★

When I finally sleep, dreams bring the sea, and a replay of our first holiday together. The pebbles hurt my feet, but it was worth it when we got to the warm, bright blue. 'So, this is why they call it the Cote D'Azur then,' I murmured. I sat at the shoreline, half in, half out, my legs being lapped by the waves. Frothy tendrils crept up my thighs then shyly retreated, leaving my wet skin to sizzle in the late afternoon sun. All around, glossy heroines looked out from the covers of fat paperbacks strewn on sunbeds, were pored at through Dolce & Gabbana sunglasses. For a few moments I almost felt like one of them; I felt as though I belonged.

In truth, our Nice was a ten minute walk, four flights of unlit stairs and a world away from the shimmering seafront. The room we had secured with the help of Dave's barely remembered schoolboy French was high-ceilinged but narrow, with a worn-out carpet and a flickering shaving light over the sink in the corner (the sink had cost us an extra fifty francs). The bedding, at least, was clean. When we pulled back the plucked pink curtain we found we had a balcony. It was no more than six inches deep, we could barely stand on it, but we could lean out. I pressed myself into the black iron railing and breathed in the smells of the street below, from fresh bread and coffee to the over-ripe smell of the drains, and if I craned my neck I could see the sea.

Dave aspired to be the people on the seafront, in the impossibly grand hotels with white facades and cool marble floors. He wanted a pool (he never swam in the sea — too much salt), room service, doormen, à la carte dinner and fine wines. By the time of our honeymoon, the resort was different (Dave never liked to go to the same place twice — waste of money, he said), but we had all of the things he'd wanted.

★   ★   ★

So inevitably we ended up in the big hotels. Then we ended up in our own little hotel, our castle, our cabin, our casa, our so-called home. As love grows, dreams shrink. They get local. Instead of wanting to see the world together we wanted to make our own little world. After all, you can't just backpack forever. Can't keep 'staying over', like children, leaving a toothbrush there and just one drawer full of stuff. Eventually we were spending every night together anyway, and when I woke up late, again, with an extra half hour's drive to work ahead of me, and found I had forgotten to bring a clean shirt so had to scrabble on the floor for last night's crumpled top and spray it desperately with his deodorant, then the novelty of having two toothbrushes started to wear off.

This is how big decisions are made.

You can't have backstreet France forever.

You have to do the done thing.

★　★　★

Dave had bought the house with his ex-fiancée but they'd never moved in — they were waiting until they got married to start the renovations. Of course, the wedding never happened and the stately Victorian terrace sat gathering cobwebs while Dave stayed in his little rented flat. The ex continued to pay half of the mortgage for a while, perhaps out of guilt for leaving him, if not quite at the altar, then virtually en route to the church.

They had it on the market and when he asked if I'd consider moving in there, I think he was surprised when I said yes. I agreed to go and look at it, at least, and as it was the first time he'd seen it in months, he said he wasn't even sure whether he really wanted to live there.

'I was worried you'd think it was too full of ghosts,' he said as he put the key in the door and pushed it open with a creak, but as soon as we stepped inside I could see from the shine in his eyes that he *did* want to live there, that the house had been his choice, his dream, and I knew in a rush that he, that *we*, could make it a home.

'No ghosts.' I slid my arms around him, no idea why I was whispering the words except that I was afraid they would bounce too loudly around the high ceilings and cornices. As we crept from room to room, as if afraid to disturb the spiders who had been busily crafting their gossamer networks for weeks on end, I fell gradually in love with the possibilities of the place, its sad past receding like a wave.

★ ★ ★

We spent three days sleeping on the living room floor. The bed was going to be late, and we'd no sofa at this point either, so we sat cross-legged like squatters in the middle of the living room, eating Chinese takeaway and drinking champagne out of mugs. The glasses were who knew where, so tightly packed in newspaper and bubble wrap that the thought of locating and unpeeling them gave me a headache.

We had plans and a child-like giddiness, born out of a shared purpose, that we'd not felt before. For a couple of days we just wandered from room to room, dabbing tentative dots of tester-pot paint on walls, playing at being homeowners. It didn't seem real, more as though we were idling with a child's toy that we'd be giving back before long. I liked it when friends visited and I could repeat this tour, pausing here and there to give excited voice to our vision: 'this will be the kitchen . . . bi-fold doors into the garden . . . yes, these floors will be sanded and waxed.'

But all too soon, the play gave way to serious work and we found ourselves surrounded by seemingly interminable mess, noise and dust. Plaster dust, dust from the crumbling underlay we uncovered beneath the ancient carpets, dust that whirled and settled in corners and on windowsills and lingered in our hair and our lungs even weeks later.

★ ★ ★

Marriage, home, harmony. Even the patter of tiny feet — or paws, at least. Our shared love of dogs was one of the first ('amazing') things we'd uncovered about each other five years ago. And so as soon as we had a home-life we deemed stable enough, and solid wooden floors that could withstand muddy prints, we found a seven-week-old bundle of fur, eyes and paws and christened her Bella.

Neither of us wanted children; at least, that's what he said, then. It would change, later, but I couldn't have known that.

I definitely didn't want children and I was just grateful that he didn't press me too hard for my reasons. Of course, I realise now that this was probably because he assumed I would one day change my mind.

Funny how we can fall in love, claim to love everything about someone, and then set about trying to change them into someone else.

★ ★ ★

So this is what you do. You take the chaos of love and you weave it into a pattern. You make an Axminster of it. Put a ring around it. Sign for it. And I must be happy now, because I have someone to protect me from the catalogue of mini disappointments that has been my life so far.

But somehow in my dreams it is always that musty first room in Nice, and jumping on the bed swatting flies with the rolled-up porn magazine we found in the drawer, and leaning over that balcony perilously close to falling, and rubbing aftersun on his shoulders, and making tipsy love all night in the glow of that (blink, blink) shaving light.

*   *   *

On Thursday I go to see Mari. Mari lives in a flat above a music shop, not far from the estate where we grew up, and is my only friend from that place.

My friends are compartmentalised and the compartments never mix: school friends; university friends; work friends; friends of Dave's; friends from the estate — or technically, friend from the estate, since, as I said, this particular compartment consists only of Mari.

We met when she saved me from getting beaten up, when I was thirteen.

The houses we grew up in were grey, and pebbledashed. There was one park on the estate, but even that was more grey than green, its slides delivering children onto unforgiving concrete. There were horror stories: the girl who went so high on the swings that she went all the way over, fell out onto the ground and split her head open. Everyone said you could see her brains, right there, spilling out. Years later they would install a pit of wood shavings at the foot of the swings, but no one ever knew if the brain story was true, and back then, it was still concrete.

Depending on which crowd they belonged with, the estate kids hung around either on the park (the grebs) or the precinct (the skaters).

Grebs and skaters were largely defined by the kind of music they listened to, and each group looked on the other with the particular disdain that comes from *knowing* your taste is correct and everyone else's is wrong. Grebs listened to rock, mostly, sometimes heavy metal, sometimes goth music too. They bought albums from the kind of shop that also sold hemp and bongs and tie-dyed clothes. Skaters were about pop music, pure and simple, and they had picked up dance music in its late-1980s incarnation. It sounded tinny and trivial tip-tapping its rhythms out of their Walkmans.

As well as their place and their sounds,

each crowd had their uniform. The skaters wore baggy jeans, or long shorts, and bright colours. And of course, they each carried their board, like another limb; on the rare occasion you saw them without, their usual swagger would become a shuffle. They seemed most comfortable when their tricks and twists sent them air bound; the ground held no interest for them, except as a place from where they could set flight.

I'd thought I would find my place with the skaters until I became friends with Mari, who was high-ranking among the grebs. The grebs wore Doc Marten boots, a lot of black, and even the boys (some of them anyway) wore eyeliner. I was a little bit scared of them, they always looked so serious and severe, but actually when you got to know them they were a really good laugh. Mari was two years older than me and worked in a tobacconist's after school. It was from the window of the shop that she saw two orange-faced girls, their hair pulled so tight into hairbands that they looked as though they had extra cheekbones, their lips pinched, laying into me. Her plea wasn't particularly emotional: with her head and one arm dangling out of the window, gesturing as though swatting a fly, she simply yelled, 'Leave it — she's had enough,' and the two orange-faced girls with their flying fists ran away. After this, she just kind of carried on looking after me.

Mari said I reminded her of her kid sister, who had died when she was a toddler. I didn't understand how I could remind her of a two-year-old, but I didn't ask. Not having sisters myself, I liked the way she sometimes hugged my neck and called me 'sis' or, more commonly, 'doll' or 'babe'.

★   ★   ★

Coming back to the estate always makes me feel uncomfortable. They say the past is a different country; it's one I recognise less the further away I move from it. Everything looks smaller. There are street names I don't recognise, or don't remember. I am here because of the one thing that hasn't changed: the friend I can say anything to.

Mari's flat can be described as minimalist. Not in a contrived way, not in the sense of clean lines and a neutral palette — just in the sense that there isn't much *stuff*. Mari doesn't think much of possessions. She doesn't even have house plants, says they are 'too much responsibility'.

'Well, doll,' she says, appearing from her tiny kitchen carrying a bottle of whiskey and two mugs, 'to what do I owe this unexpected pleasure?'

'I need to talk to someone.'

I take a deep breath and pause for effect. I am ashamed to find myself excited to have something scandalous to tell Mari. She is my wild friend, the part of myself that never gets let out. She is usually the one with the stories, the one with the drama.

It comes out in a tumble.

'I saw Morgan last night, we went for a meal, we kissed.'

'Wait. Morgan? *Mister* Morgan? Henry Morgan?'

It's funny how, even as an adult, I still feel more comfortable using your last name. This was how I first knew you, after all; in school it was as though teachers didn't even *have* first names, or lives outside the classroom, or interests beyond the subject they taught and were defined by. Even when I got to know you, properly, I would avoid calling you Henry (you used to say Henry Morgan was a pirate's name, remember?). I avoided calling you anything at all, to your face, the way children sometimes feel awkward saying the first names of their friends' parents.

But I enjoy, now, hearing Mari say 'Henry Morgan' out loud. It proves you still exist, that I did see you, that this is really happening.

'You kissed?' She lights a cigarette. Hearing my confession repeated to me, I realise how small a thing a kiss is. I want to make it sound like more so I say it again.

'We kissed.' I am solemn.

In my head, in the space of fewer than twenty-four hours, the kiss has become epic. It is a movie kiss: sleeting rain, thundering heartbeats and the irrefutable proof that here you are, at the worst possible time, back in my life, fated to cause heady, passionate chaos. Your hands in my hair, my heart in my mouth — every nuance of the thirty, perhaps sixty, seconds heavy with meaning.

At other times I've had to remind myself that it was a minute, only a minute among the millions of minutes of my life, and what's more the further away the minute moves the more shadowy and intangible it becomes. In these moments I'm plunged into gloom — it was nothing, a mere brush of the lips, perhaps you were just being friendly and I've completely misread the situation. One thing's for certain: you won't be obsessing about it the way I am.

I stop myself from saying all of this to Mari, who is pulling a face having taken a large swig of whiskey.

'Well, a kiss is nothing really,' she says airily, waving her cigarette around. To be fair,

Mari routinely kisses complete strangers.

'It is when you're married.'

'Hmm. So what happens now? Did he take your number?'

I look at her. Somehow, stupidly, I hadn't thought of that. No — you didn't. You didn't ask for it, I didn't offer. I am never going to see you again. Why didn't you ask me for it?

The kiss-minute moves away another mile.

'No.'

'Well, no harm done then. I mean, as you say — you're married. And more to the point, why would you want that old perv back in your life?'

'Listen, I know what you think of him, but . . . '

'No buts, babe. Let it go,' she pauses, exhales, 'let *him* go.'

Let you go.

It was nothing.

No harm done.

We drink, and talk, and bitch about which of our friends has put on weight and who has lost weight, and laugh about old times, and I ring Dave to slur goodnight, and I fall asleep and Mari covers me with a prickly old blanket.

* * *

I am too old to drink whiskey in the week and crawl to sleep on other people's sofas. Mari brings me tea. I grimace.

'I hope that isn't the same mug as last night.'

'Of course not,' she says, but I'm not convinced. She runs her fingers through her scarlet hair, rubs her eyes. 'How are you feeling this morning?'

'I'm not gonna lie, I've felt better,' I rub at my temples, 'and listen, about what I told you. I feel a bit daft now. Ridiculous, actually. Thanks for listening . . . and for putting me straight. God,' I laugh, 'you can tell how boring my life has become when I make such a drama out of nothing!'

'Nothing wrong with a bit of boring, babe,' Mari smiles, and for a moment it's like I'm thirteen again, and she's fifteen, and I feel like she has all the wisdom of the world.

The beeping text alert actually makes my head hurt. It's from a number I don't recognise.

Mrs Worthing. Please call me re: collision on Weds night.

Could it be . . . ?

'What is it, doll?'

'Um . . . you know I told you I scraped that car. I left my number on the windscreen. It's . . . I guess it's them.'

32

'Uh-oh. Too honest as usual, kid. Well, your insurance will cover it, won't it?'

'Yep, I suppose. I'll call them from the car.' I gulp down my tea. 'Thanks for having me, honey, sorry to rush off but I'd better get to work.' I wink. 'The oily wheels of capitalism won't turn on their own, you know!'

She hugs me at the door.

'Any time you need to talk, just call,' squeezes me tight, 'and, give my love to Dave.' This is the first time in five years she has ever said that.

Mrs Worthing. Please call me re: collision on Weds night.

Has to be. I take a deep breath and dial the number. A voice reverberates through the car speakers.

'Ah — Mrs Worthing.'

I know immediately of course that it is you. I'm surprised by how much I dislike hearing you use my married name.

'Mr Morgan,' I laugh. From married woman back to schoolgirl, in a breath. 'You took my number from that car's windscreen? Neat trick.'

'You knew I would, that's why you left it there. Neat trick.'

'No wonder they haven't called me about the damage.'

'It was only a nudge. Practically nothing.

33

You got away with it.'

'Are we still talking about the car?'

'Of course.'

'Well, it was careless of me. I shouldn't have had wine with dinner.'

'No, probably not. Very naughty. What are you doing?'

'Going to work . . . but I can be late.'

3

Diary: Thursday, 1 October 1992

The fourth white shirt of the week hangs on my wardrobe door. It's the first thing I see, bright and ironed to stiffness, delivered by the Laundry Fairy, aka my mother. Every night she comes, swift and stealthy as Santa, gathering up the grubby and bestowing clean, pressed replicas.

It's the first day of a new month (white rabbits, etc.) and the first page of a new diary so I thought I should start with a suitably descriptive opening paragraph. I was told recently, while doing work experience for a local newspaper, that I suffer from 'verbal diarrhoea'. The editor was a woman, the rest of the small staff men, but not a trace of sisterly solidarity. On my 'report' all she could do was complain about the level of my neck/hem lines. Anyway I don't care: I want to be a writer, not a journalist.

I'm going to hide this diary better than the last one, which got read 'accidentally' (how do you read a diary accidentally?) and naturally led to all sorts of scenes, even though I'd gone to the trouble of omitting certain details, using codes, abbreviations and general red herrings. It's a strange thing, writing a 'secret' diary in the knowledge that it will probably be read. Anyway I will keep you with me, to be on the safe side.

I proceed to cover my body in regulation grey, and stand in front of the mirror. I look the same as every other day. Why wouldn't I? Mousey hair, fair skin, grey eyes. Unremarkable. I leave the house, looking the same as every other fourteen-year-old girl gathered at the bus stop on Wellbeck Street: grey sweater, striped tie, white shirt, grey skirt, white socks, black shoes.

It's a good job I know I'm different.

The school bus is a marvellous thing, especially for a writer. I watch boys flick various small inanimate objects at each other, their faces too red, their voices too loud. I watch Helen Taylor, Jo Maloney and Claire Smith studiously rearrange themselves. Their shin-length flannel skirts become thigh-skimming with a dexterous flick of the waistband. Sleeves are rolled up, collars opened, ties discarded. There is a blast of hairspray and they are done.

Me, I don't have to work to achieve disarray. I'm naturally untidy-looking. However neat I look when I leave home, somehow on the bus I invariably spill something, lose something or tear something. By the time we get to the school gates I always have a shoelace undone, or a button missing, or a loose thread trailing.

He told me to read a poem: 'Delight in

Disorder'. *I was flattered, I think. Was I supposed to be? Meant to be me, I suppose. He compares me to great literary heroines: Cleopatra, Lady Macbeth . . . it makes me laugh although I don't really understand.*

Today nothing wants to stay where it is. My skirt is wriggling around my waist, my shirt working free, one sock slipping continually down my shin. As if some invisible, inexpert hand is trying to undress me.

The bus empties. Our Lady of Compassion smiles down on us from her breezeblock throne. Sister Agnes glides among us as we file into the pupils' entrance. She's the head and unlike Our Lady, never smiles. She taps some girls on the shoulder and those chosen trot automatically to the toilets to wash off their recently applied mascara and lipstick.

I have a letter, in my bag. From the minute I stepped off the bus I've been looking for him. It is the usual formula.

The bell rings and people rush towards and around me.

I don't know if I have friends. At school I have followers; at home I have accomplices.

It was autumn, I was fourteen going on twenty-five, according to you, and I was having a perfectly ordinary day until you gave me your phone number.

'Fee, Fi, Fo, Fum,' is all you said when I came into your room after class. You were used to seeing me there, of course, so you barely looked up. I didn't mean to be a nuisance, I just liked being there. I liked the rows of books, the views out of the windows and the smell, and the old-fashioned chalk board (yours was one of the few rooms that didn't have a horrible squeaky white board), and the glimpse into your office where I could often see the back of your head and the steam from your kettle.

You drank a lot of coffee back then. Sometimes I could smell it on your breath when you leaned over me and looked at my work. You also smelled of Aramis; I knew this because I scoured department stores, unscrewing bottles, sniffing so hard I felt faint, until I found the scent that was yours.

I sat on a table, swinging my legs, looking out of the window, looking at my nails.

'Where are your followers today?' you asked as you meandered between the room and the office, shuffling papers, humming, running your hands through your hair. I laughed.

'Oh, I've escaped them. It's really a bind to be so popular, you know.'

'No, I wouldn't know!'

'Oh yes. Sometimes even the famous and

terribly gifted need their privacy. Anyway, I came to talk to you about that last story.'

Then I held my breath, as I always did. Often at this point you would say you were too busy right now to talk, or have been too busy to read it just yet, and you would say, 'I'm sorry, kid.' On those occasions I had to wait for the deadline, and the red pen, like everybody else. Or sometimes you gave me your unbridled critique, verbally, there and then, and were always honest, and sometimes made me flinch, embarrassed, but cleverly always finished on a compliment.

But today was all new. Today you seemed to want to *chat*.

'Coffee?' you called, stirring, not waiting for my answer. You brought me a mug and pulled up a chair. It occurred to me that I never saw you sitting down. I saw you striding down corridors, fast and purposeful, detached and superior but at the same time mindful of all errant behaviour, issuing sharp commands ('Chewing gum — bin'; 'Tie — on'; 'Class — NOW'). I saw you standing, in front of the board, in front of your audience, high above bobbed studious heads.

But today *I* had the vantage point, looking down from my table to your chair.

'What a day,' you said, leaning back and resting your head into your interlaced fingers,

39

'God, I hate school.'

'You're not supposed to say that,' I laughed.

'It's after 3.30 so it's allowed. I think I might leave and become a bus driver.'

'I don't think you have the people skills for that.'

'Gee, thanks.'

'If you hate it so much why do you always stay so late?'

'Why do *you?*'

To try and talk to you, I thought.

'I like it when it's quiet,' I said.

'Yeah, me too. Hmm, maybe it's not school, maybe it's the kids I hate.'

'Thanks!'

'Well, some are okay. All children are equal in the eyes of the Lord, as Sister Agnes would say. But clearly some are more equal than others. Speaking of which . . . ' You reached over to your desk. My story. 'Your story.'

I bit my lip as you scribbled on the back page, shuffled the papers together then handed them to me.

'Well?'

'You'll have no trouble getting an A with that. But you knew that already.'

'Cool, thanks.'

'But is that enough?'

'Er, yeah. I need to pass to do A levels, don't I?'

40

'What I mean is, you should be aiming for more than that.'

'More than an A?'

'An A just marks you out as better than the herd.'

'More equal than others.'

'Right. But again, you know that already. What you should be aiming for is to be better than *you* think you are.'

'I think I'm pretty good.'

You laughed. 'Of course. Anyway this all feels like more school,' taking a gulp of coffee, 'and we've already established we both hate school. Let's talk about something else. How are things in your world?'

'Oh, you know,' I shrugged, 'dramatic and fascinating, as ever.'

'Ah, to be fourteen. Things get so much less exciting as you get older.'

'I'm sure they do. I could use a little less excitement, to be honest.'

'Problems?'

'Oh, the usual rubbish at home.' You smiled your crooked smile. '*I'm* fine, it's everyone else that's the problem.'

'Mere mortals. Don't let 'em get you down, kid. Remember,' you got up and took your cup into the office, calling over your shoulder, 'you're extraordinary.'

For once I didn't have an answer. That

almost sounded like you meant it.

'I should go.'

'Do you need a lift?' You came out of the office shrugging on your jacket.

'No, I'll walk, it's fine. Ta, though.'

'Suit yourself. See ya, sunshine,' and with that you were whistling down the corridor.

So I walked home holding a story that, when I flipped it over, had your phone number on the back, in red pen, but no other comments, no marks, nothing. I kept trying to replay the coffee conversation in my head, but it shrank minute by minute, step by step.

★　★　★

Ring, ring. Click.

'Hello?'

I said nothing.

'Hello?' Your bored voice.

'Hello,' I tried.

'Who is this?'

'It's me.' *Who else could it be? Who else calls you?* I wondered. You laughed.

'Hello, kid.'

I laughed too. Thank God, you knew.

'Hello, older person.'

'Well?'

'Well, you said to call.'

'It's 11.30. Almost my bedtime.'

42

'Everyone here is asleep.' I was sitting on the stairs, curling into myself, hugging my knees, the receiver squeezed between my head and my shoulder, my lips almost touching the mouthpiece.

'You sound muffled,' you said.

'You sound tired,' I said.

'That's what happens when you get to my age, kid. You're tired all the time.'

'Your age!' I scoffed. 'You're only . . . '

'I'm twenty-eight. Nearly.' I smiled to myself; this was new knowledge, and you'd offered it easily. What else could I find out?

'Shall I let you go then, if you need your beauty sleep?'

'Not just yet.'

'What do you want to talk about?'

You laughed again. 'You called me.'

'You gave me your number.'

'Fair enough. Okay.'

We talked about more or less nothing until 11.49, then we both went to bed, I in my room at the top of the house, you in your house, I wondered where.

*   *   *

The clatter of regulation inch-and-a-half heels down the hallway. The paralysing drill of the bell. Everyone stops where they are,

43

what they're doing. An instant of quiet, then . . .

Clamour. Books stuffed into bags, bags lurched over shoulders, move on. On to the next hour-long slice of day.

The school building was a mix of old and new. The red-brown brick, climbing ivy and crumbling high windows gave way hopelessly to a square of breeze-block and UPVC that clung like a tumour.

In the old school there were places to hide. It was once a convent, and along its dark corridors you could feel the ghosts of solemn nuns hurrying, heads bowed, to prayer. By 1992 they wore calf-length skirts and navy sweaters, small crucifixes and neat hair. They had to raise their voices like everyone else in vain attempts to be heard above the teenage cacophony. They were teachers now, touching the world in ways their predecessors wouldn't have dreamed of; I wondered if they looked back wistfully to a time when their existence wouldn't have been blighted by acne-covered despots and hysterical five-foot Delilahs.

The new school had no nooks or alcoves. It was resolutely straight-lined and primary-coloured.

In Physics Laura and I passed notes to each other, as usual. We would take a piece of A4 paper and fold it over, once, and once more, making a little book, and number the pages. We wrote in different coloured ink so we could see at a glance who had written what, although our handwriting wasn't similar. I sometimes felt guilty for distracting Laura in this way, since I knew I would pass the exam without having to pay attention; she on the other hand might regret the sheets of folded-up A4 and the empty exercise books when June came. But it really was the only way to get through the tedium of protons and neutrons and blah blah blah.

Miss Danson was as dull as her subject. She had receding hair and a monotone voice a bit like a man's.

'Next week we are going to dissect a bull's eye.'

She didn't blink when she told us this. She breathed heavily, patrolling the desks in her leaden shoes. Most days she was preoccupied on these rounds with preventing Sean Brady from turning on the gas taps, or telling Martin McLoughlin to get his jumper sleeves OUT OF HIS MOUTH. Debbie Smith was painting something intricate in Tipp-Ex on the desk across the room from us, so I thought we were safe.

'Miss Palmer.' I wasn't expecting the dry voice so close to my ear, or the talon swoop that snatched up our carefully folded note.

She unpeeled it as though unwrapping a gift.

'What do we have here, ladies? Hmm?'

I shrugged. Laura stared at her feet as though she had never noticed them before.

''Andrew Partington is FIT,'' Miss Danson read aloud. The muffled giggles presumably encouraged her that she was being funny at our expense because she continued.

''Beautiful eyes,'' she huffed, ' — very insightful, I'm sure — 'and what a sexy bod.''

'Miss, isn't he a bit young for you?' A voice across the room, then a nervous laugh, then the full bleating eruption of twenty-nine teenagers. As she realised what she had said, the colour rose up Danson's throat.

'Right. Outside, both of you.' En route to the door I caught sight of Andrew Partington's beautiful, mortified eyes. 'And this . . .' she held up the closely written paper by its corner as though it might contaminate her, 'will be going straight to the Head of Year.'

Oh, fantastic.

★ ★ ★

'What are these notes about anyway?'

'She didn't show you?'

'I didn't think it polite to look.'

'Oh, you know, the usual. Who's in love with who.'

'With *whom*.'

'Yeah, yeah.'

'Love is over-used and over-rated.'

'The word, or the emotion?'

'Ha ha. Both.'

'Such cynicism. Such a shame. She must have really messed you up.' The words were out before I could stop them. I looked at your face, trying to read you.

'Who, exactly?' You smiled, thank God. When you smile your eyes crease.

'You know.'

'Ah, you mean the W — I — F — E?' You spelt the word out in a whisper as though disguising it from a small child.

'Uh-huh.'

'Technically it's E — X — W — I — F — E of course. And I'm sure you're right.' This much was a revelation: I wasn't sure if you were divorced yet, or even separated, but you hadn't worn your wedding ring for some weeks now, which of course I'd noticed. 'Need a lift home, kid? You can psychoanalyse me some more if you like.'

'Nah, I'll get the bus. But thanks.'

'One of these days I won't offer. A man can only take rejection so many times, you know.'

'Whatever!'

★ ★ ★

47

The journey home was when the change would take place, from one version of me to the other.

I don't mean the physical things that everyone did, like rolling down the skirt, rolling up the socks and wiping off the lipstick. I didn't worry about those anymore. You would think my mum and dad would be too busy ignoring each other to ignore me too, but somehow they managed it.

Whereas at school I was Top Group, everyone's friend and good at everything (well, except PE, but my creative skills came in very useful for writing weekly excuse notes), at home it was a tougher job to be noticed. By 'home' I don't just mean my house, I mean the estate. On the estate there were no points for being clever, in fact it meant you were viewed with suspicion. There weren't even many to be had for being popular. You could be too popular, especially with the boys.

The bus route told a story. Looking out of the window was like watching a reverse film reel of social evolution. Double-fronted semis with their bulging bay windows and effusive gardens rolled by. The streets narrowed as the houses shrank and moved closer together and some cleaved into flats. Oak trees mutated into lamp-posts and vandalised phone boxes.

The driver took the sharp turn by the pub and I pressed the bell for him to stop.

★   ★   ★

'Look — it's raining — you can't walk home in that.'

I was in your room again, drinking coffee. It was becoming a habit, at least once a week. It was a Friday, so there was hardly anyone left in school. Most people were out of the door at half past three with astonishing alacrity.

Out of the window, the rain was coming down in sheets, blurring the trees, the cars in the car park, the newsagent's across the road. It was late October rain: half-term rain. I looked at my bare knees and flimsy shoes and shrugged.

'Okay, okay,' I said, 'I'll *let* you take me home. Especially as you won't see me for a week!'

'I know. How will I cope?' You locked the office and we walked the empty corridors, side by side. I tottered to keep up with your brisk strides, the movement of which occasionally wafted aftershave vapours over me.

'You should wear a coat, you know,' you chided as you hurried me to your car, your

49

own coat held stretched out over my head. I felt a bit like a criminal being shielded by police, and at the same time felt this was the most gallant act anyone could perform for me, imagining that an observer would see a kind of reverse Queen Elizabeth-Walter Raleigh tableau.

Feet splashing, hair dry, I bounced to the passenger door of your Honda.

While you drove, I had the chance to look at you close up. Not in a classroom, not in a corridor or on stage, you looked smaller. I studied the short perfect scar on the side of your face, etched out in a life before you met me, little me, one in 800; maybe you fell from a tree, or off your bike, before I even existed. When I was born, you were already a teenager.

I could look at you for hours, I thought. The hair: sandy, scruffy. Chalk-dusted, in the week. The face: always tanned, the face of someone who is outdoors a lot, the wrinkles around your eyes whiter than the rest of your skin. That scar, a sudden hyphen just below your cheekbone.

'What do you want?'

The question shocked me. I felt defensive. Had I overstepped the mark? Been hanging around too much? Did you mean, what did I want from *you*?

'What do you mean?'

'What do you want to do with your life? What do you want to *be*?'

'Oh. I don't know.'

'Yes you do.'

'Okay,' I was surprised to hear myself say, 'I want to write.'

I had never said that aloud before. It had been a thought, a dream, an itch in the back of my head that I paid no attention to. But in the car with you, I suddenly felt as though I could say anything. Perhaps it was because you mostly had your eyes on the road, casting me only occasional sideways glances. I could speak, to no one, looking straight ahead, or into the passenger window, where I could see your reflection.

And I liked watching you drive, your square hands smoothly turning the wheel, tapping on the dash. You were almost too casual, irritatingly assured, but in a contrived way. Your sleeves were rolled up to the perfect point of insouciance, midway between wrist and elbow; I imagined you in front of the mirror, adjusting them until they were just right. You were calculatedly ruffled.

'What about the second question? What do you want to be?'

'Hum. A writer!'

'And I'm sure you will be. Let me put it

another way. What do you *not* want to be?'

I thought about it for a moment. We stopped at traffic lights. You hung your right arm out of the window, and as you pulled up the handbrake you turned your head and looked at me.

'I don't want to be ordinary,' I said finally.

'I've told you before,' as the lights turned green, 'and I'll tell you again. No fear!'

Outside the house, you said: 'I want you to write something for me.'

'I write stuff for you all the time!'

You fell quiet, looked hurt. What had I said?

'For me,' you repeated. 'You don't write for me, you write for examiners. You write for grades.' Looked at me with those concrete eyes. 'Write something for *me*.'

'Thanks for the lift,' I mumbled, pulling my bag out of the footwell.

'Bye, sunshine,' you called, arm still hanging out of the window, sunglasses back down, smile on, accelerator whirring, without looking back.

* * *

I could see my breath the next time you took me home. It had suddenly started getting dark at four.

'I have to rewrite *A Christmas Carol*,' you said.

'You have to? Compelled to improve on Dickens, eh?' I clicked my teeth with my tongue. 'Wow, it's true what they say — you *are* arrogant.'

'Who says that?' you smiled.

'Everyone.' I looked at your profile. 'You must know everyone hates you!'

'Nah,' you said, 'not the girls, anyway — they all love me.'

I made a gagging sound. 'Oh, please. Sick.'

'And come to think of it — the boys all want to be me.'

'And you say you aren't arrogant! Oh wait — I get it. Ha, ha. Very funny.'

It was true that most of the girls loved you. In the unofficial hierarchy of fanciable teachers, you were definitely in the Top Three. Mr Hill, Biology, was up there; he was newly qualified so didn't look much older than us. He had pale skin, a fluffy blond beard and piercing blue eyes. He was skinny; he looked like a boy, to me. He always looked a bit stressed and would blush uncontrollably when the girls flirted with him, which they did, often. Some girls liked Mr Dawson, the Art teacher. He had a dark, brooding look about him and was prone to fits of temper, throwing board dusters across the room and roaring when he felt people weren't listening to him. He *was* very good-looking, in a square-jawed, textbook kind of way, but he didn't do anything for me.

The girls who liked you were generally the cleverer girls. You had none of the shyness of Mr Hill or the fieriness of Mr Dawson. You were cool, and calm, and responded to cheek from boys and flirting from girls in equally laconic tones, unruffled. And when you held someone's eyes, you made them feel like they were the only one in the room.

When I heard them cooing over you and voicing their childish fantasies, I wanted desperately, even then, to shout that I *knew* you, I had more of you than they did. I'd been in your car; we'd talked, and not just about school work, about all sorts of things. I had your phone number. I was special.

'So anyway, getting back to me being a better writer than our friend Mr Dickens — '

'As well as being universally adored.'

'Along with that particular burden, yes. Sister Agnes, in her wisdom, wants me to rewrite the story of Scrooge, in time for Christmas, *and* — wait for it — make it a musical.'

I pulled a face.

'Wait, aren't The Muppets doing that?'

'Are they? Anyway, I've only got four weeks

to do it. And stage it.'

You rounded the bend into our cul-de-sac and I started to gather my things from the footwell and wrap my scarf around my chin.

'So I need your help.'

'Me?' I laughed. 'How can I help?'

'I'll pick you up on Saturday at eleven.'

'Saturday? But — '

'Didn't you hear me say we've got four weeks?'

'Yes, but . . . ' I had the car door open and one foot out, and I stopped, confused, 'where are we going on Saturday?'

'My house.' You winked. 'Bring your first draft.'

4

We have arranged to meet in the hotel by the orange canal.

I do the thing I hate when others do it: I make the call to work and put on the sick voice. It's not convincing, and my boss sounds annoyed; it's Easter week and lots of people are already off. 'You're leaving me short-handed,' he mutters. I croak 'sorry' and he hangs up.

I don't know what I'm doing here.

I'm early. I check my face in the rear-view mirror, regretting last night's whiskey. I slick on lip gloss, blot it off again with a crumpled tissue from the glove compartment. I don't want to look as though I'm trying too hard. I walk into the hotel carrying my laptop. If anyone sees me, anyone who knows Dave, I can say I was having a meeting. It's not that big a city.

I still have ten minutes. I open my laptop in an attempt to look busy. Order tea. Push my hair behind my ears, bite my nails. Sit on my hands.

I've always felt that hotel lobbies are in-between places, for in-between people. The

56

scuffed tables are too low to eat or work from comfortably, so all around me people are hunched over. The chairs are school uniform colours of grey and burgundy, and clash with the well-trodden carpet's hotel logo of royal blue and gold. Beleaguered waitresses tote cappuccinos and scalding pots of tea, and a man in the corner complains loudly about paying £4.50 for a round of toast. He demands Marmite.

This is a place for men on their own. Men in suits, all with square black cases, all with the same slightly rumpled look. Thoughts of the long weekend, thoughts of home, a wife, maybe a football game, are flickering in their eyes as they stare at their screens. A girl walks in and nervously asks two of these men 'Are you Mr Peterson?' before a third stands up and extends his hand. Perhaps it is an interview. She smooths down her skirt and sits down, smiling. She looks like a twenty-one-year-old me, filled with hope.

I wouldn't say I hate my job; that would imply some kind of extreme feelings towards it, and I don't have any. That's just it; it's the banality that gets me.

I have to admit I had a certain perception about sales, and specifically sales people, before I was one of them — hence my publishing 'lie'. But most people in sales are basically good — there are the players, and the bitches, but they're everywhere else too, so I'm told. The one thing that binds 90 per cent of us, though, is the fact that we didn't mean to end up here. We all had other ambitions. I'm used to feeling out of place — at school, at university — not in the sense of being a major outcast, just in a subtle, indefinable way — and now I'm in a job where it's practically a requirement.

You arrive and the whoosh of the automatic doors brings in a burst of cool air mingled with car-park dust. I see you before you see me. There is no hurry in your walk; it carries the absolute confidence that anyone would wait for you. Despite the threat of rain outside, you wear sunglasses, your rolled-up sleeves exposing a heavy watch and your weathered hands.

You sit down and help yourself to tea.

'Good morning, sunshine.'

You push your sunglasses onto your head and fix me with your steely eyes. Something inside me flips over.

'I bunked off work,' I say.

'I'm honoured.'

'Don't be — I don't like it much.'

'So why the laptop?'

'A prop, I suppose.'

'Shame. I thought you were tapping out

your masterpiece.'

'Yes, well . . . not quite got around to writing that yet.'

'Again, shame.' You look at me, unblinking. 'I always thought it was in you.'

I feel my throat start to colour. 'Maybe it still is,' I shrug, 'I don't know, just . . . life gets in the way.'

'I know. Tedious, isn't it?'

Your grin makes me want to move nearer to you, want to touch you. It is lopsided: your imperfect teeth, your pale lips and the wrinkles that frame them, deeper on your left side. (I wonder whether that's because you always blow out cigarette smoke to the left? Is that how it works?) It rarely reaches your eyes, but it does light up a face that otherwise would seem hard, with its scar, its angular nose. I want nothing more than to be the cause of that grin.

I want to say 'Why are we here? What is this?', but I know what your response will be: 'you tell me'. So I say brightly, 'So what shall we do today?'

'We'll drink tea,' you grimace as you take a slug, 'correction: *weak* tea, and then we'll go for a walk. We'll talk.' You check your watch. 'I only have an hour or so.'

'Oh.' I feel a little knot in my stomach tighten. I'd assumed we would have all day. I had thought . . . I don't know what I had thought. 'If I'm sick, I have to be sick all day.' I can't suppress the petulance in my voice. I look at my laptop.

You laugh a cold laugh. 'I'm sure you have better things to do than hang around with an old man like me anyway.'

'Of course.' But the knot is twisting, and rising in my gullet. I'm suddenly conscious of the thudding tick tock of the oversized hotel clock. I wonder what you are doing later, what it is that will take you from me, but I can't ask. I watch you yawn, lean back, stretch out your legs. The humming conversations, the plinking of computer keys, the clashing hotel colours and the suits, cases and phones are making me claustrophobic. 'Drink up then.'

★　★　★

You are pleased to be outside, because you can smoke. You wave your cigarette hand at the canal.

'Do you know why it's orange?'

I laugh. 'I don't, actually. I've always just sort of accepted it. It's weird, though, isn't it?'

You stop walking, look at me, take a drag.

'What is it?' I ask.

You exhale; it's like sighing. 'I want to give

you a good story now. Want to tell you some magical reason why it's orange. But the truth is fairly pedestrian.'

'Oh?'

'Yep, something to do with iron ore, or something. Even more depressingly, there's a big project underway to clean it up. Make it . . . I don't know, the colour of every other canal. Dirty grey. *Not* orange.' You suck on your cigarette again, offer me a drag. I decline, but watching it slip back in between your lips wish I had accepted.

'That *is* disappointing.' I pause. 'Did you know there is no word in the English language to rhyme with orange?'

'I think you told me that, years ago. Or maybe I told you!'

'Ha! Memory failing, is it?'

'Sunshine, everything's failing.' You reach over and grab my hand, squeeze it, then immediately let go.

'Speaking of memories,' you say, 'whatever happened to that friend of yours . . . Lorna? Laura? Laura.' You nod decisively.

'Laura, yeah.' I choose my words carefully. 'We're still friends. I still see her, but we're not as close as we used to be. But I suppose that's normal?' I know I'm rambling now but this knowledge only seems to be making it worse, and bringing with it a nervous giggle, and when I try to take the rising inflection out of my voice I seem to replace it with a kind of bellow, the mad holler of someone speaking in exclamation marks. 'I mean, it's been fifteen years, after all! We've both changed!'

You look at me, click your teeth and make a 'tsk' sound.

'Must be a man. Shouldn't let 'em come between you. I told you that when you were fifteen and fighting over boys. They're not worth it, kid.'

I don't remember ever fighting with Laura over boys back then and I'd love to say you're wrong about this, now, but you're not, of course.

'Matt,' I say miserably, 'Laura's fiancé.'

You nod. 'A charmer, I suppose.'

Charm is knowing precisely what to say to make a person feel good about themselves. *You* have it, and it's all the more powerful for how infrequently you bestow it. Since you, I've been looking for that in everyone I meet and I haven't often found it. Matt could do it; it was as though he had a little window into the specific part of me that was feeling insecure that day, and he could open it up and like a modern day miracle worker, make it right.

(On the other hand, people who know what

62

to say to make you feel bad about yourself — they're called husbands, and wives.)

It was at their engagement party that I realised I had feelings for him. Laura was beautiful in a green dress, and they had a swing band — everything was perfect. As for Matt — he took my hand in the opening chords of 'Fly Me to the Moon' and led me to the floor.

I dreamt about him every night for three nights after we danced. It was a mystery. He had the accent (Scouse) I had never liked. A face I found more inoffensive than attractive, plainly okay-looking but not striking. A nice height — maybe that was it. But there are thousands, millions of men that exact same height and they don't all kiss me in dreams.

It was his charm that did it, the charm and then the hands. I have a thing for hands. He held me firmly, one hand in the small of my back, the other grasping my hand, intertwining fingers. His eyes were red from drink, shining, and they seemed to be telling me a secret. I couldn't look at them for too long. *She's my best friend*, I kept saying, stupidly, to myself.

The only conversation we had that night was started at every point by him, and every sentence started with 'if':

'If you weren't . . . '

'If I wasn't . . .'

'If only . . .'

But I am, and you are, I told him, and chose those moments to turn around and let him spin me. I was glad I had worn my 'dancing shoes'. Afterwards I told myself that I had imagined it, that these words were part of the dream, like the kiss, but they weren't, they happened.

Never trust a man who can dance, Mari told me once.

'Fiancé?' you're saying. 'So, when's the wedding?'

I unfurl my fingers as though counting out weeks.

'Let me see, one, two, ah — never.'

'Oh really?'

'Yeah, he got her the diamond, they had the party, but somehow I just don't see it happening. It's almost as though he enjoys keeping her waiting.'

'Well,' you say darkly, 'some men are just like that.' You stop walking, glance at your watch, light another cigarette. I want to tear the watch from your wrist, stop time. Chattering birds sweep down and graze the surface of the canal. You lean over the graffitied railings and flick ash into the water. 'I need to leave soon, you better hurry up and tell me about the rest of them.' I frown, but you wink, nudge me playfully. 'Come on, I want names, occupations . . . vital statistics! I'll try and keep up.'

So although I want to protest (there haven't been *that* many), and don't want to think about the men who punctuated the thousands of nights between you and my husband, I am mindful of time, and wonder if by holding your attention I can buy some more. I remember how you used to like my stories, my characters. I list them as you ask me to; I try to keep it light, and witty, and am sometimes even cruel about them, to try to make you laugh, while mentally I say sorry, sorry, to these blameless ghosts.

We kick stones into the canal.

Every now and then you make a show of getting their names confused.

'Hmm. Jason? Which one was he, again? The tennis coach, or the junkie?'

'He wasn't a junkie. He just smoked too much weed. It made him kind of — moody.'

'Hmm. You liked the little weed smokers when you were at school, as I recall.'

I ignore this.

'Anyway, that wasn't Jason, that was Spencer.'

'Spencer? What kind of name is that? Isn't that a surname?'

'At least it's not an old man's name, Henry.'

'Was he the one with the snakeskin shoes?'

'*That* was Jason.'

'So which one was the tennis coach?'

'Adam.'

'Who did you have the most fun with?'

'Tom.'

'Whose heart did you break?'

I laugh and look you in the eye. 'What do you think? All of them.'

'And which one broke your heart?'

'That story's for another time.'

'Who is the man you have been most attracted to?'

'Are you hoping that *you* will be the answer to one of these questions?'

'Absolutely not.'

We wander in companionable silence for a while. I keep glancing at you, trying to photograph your face. I want to ask when I'll see you again.

'And now you have Dave.'

'Yes. Now I have Dave.' I touch my wedding ring.

'And he's perfect?'

I laugh. 'He is. It's me I'm not sure about.'

'What do you mean?'

'It's just . . . I feel like he's always trying to change me.' Even as I hear the whine in my own voice when talking about Dave, a little electric shock of guilt runs through me. But I continue, 'I mean, he's always trying to improve me.'

'Not possible!' you smile.

There it is. The nearest thing to a compliment I know I am going to get, and I am going to hold onto it if it kills me. So many of your words I've let whisper away.

Not possible. I am un-improvable. I could cheer. Of course, it was a glib, throwaway comment — not meant, not literally anyway, and as quickly said as forgotten (especially with your ailing memory).

Suddenly we are at your car, and those two nice words, and the fact that you held my hand momentarily — I suddenly know I can live on these for weeks. As we say goodbye, without so much as a kiss on the cheek, by the canal that won't be orange for much longer, I know I may have to.

★　★　★

I drive for a while, through the city I thought I couldn't wait to get away from when I was eighteen and couldn't wait to return to after three years in London.

I think about the canal, watch buildings loom whose histories you've chronicled for

67

me, from the cathedral to the town hall; disused mills and designer hotels. You know about things; I love that. You know about wine and architecture. Politics and art. You're so unlike me, with the butterfly mentality that always made you laugh.

On one of what seemed like hundreds of shared car journeys back then, as part of my continuing efforts to get you to open up to me, I quoted John Donne at you.

'No man is an island,' I said sagely.

'Ah. Getting into the metaphysical poets now are we, my little bookworm?'

'Yes, as a matter of fact I think, as a group, they infused new life into English poetry.'

'Hmm. Tell me more about that then.'

Long pause.

'I can't. I have absolutely no idea what I'm talking about.'

You leaned over then, and playfully tickled my neck.

'You'll be fine when you go to university,' you said (I noted the 'when', not 'if'; your confidence in me always gave me a thrill). 'So full of curiosity.'

★ ★ ★

It was the summer of the bomb when I went to university, and when I came back, a new city was rising. Somehow the fact of its having been wounded made me protective towards it, as though towards an injured (but still scrappy) puppy.

Manchester has always been a bold sort of city — cocky, even — mistrusted by the mill towns that surround it. A city born of industry turning its back, turning towards industry's flashier, better-looking cousin, commerce; a city in a race with itself to become something else, especially now. It was a pretender; too big for its boots. And I loved it. I liked its confidence, its style; always wished a bit of that style would rub off on me.

Not long after coming home, of course, via Spencer and Tom and all the others I've told you about, I found Dave, who was every bit home, who was old school northern town, and 100 per cent reality.

We met through friends of friends of friends, on one of those nights out populated by a gaggle of loose acquaintances with little in common except the threads of past work or college and an empty Saturday evening to fill.

I was in recovery from a messy break-up and was of the opinion that men were best used for drinks and sex and not much beyond that. The prospect of finding intimacy again was unwelcome to my newly armoured heart, so when he asked me if I'd like to meet one evening that week for 'a date', I'd scoffed and called him old-fashioned and pressed him instead to come back to mine for some 'no-strings fun'.

I don't suppose I looked like the greatest purveyor of fun, my eyes tired from weeks of crying and not enough sleep, my mouth a hard line no longer open to flirtatious chat and soft kisses. I think I said something like 'don't be a bloody misery, just take me home and fuck me'. I remember he said nothing, just squeezed my hand, wrote his phone number on a beermat and when I refused to take it, slipped it into my bag.

He left the pub shortly afterwards and I went home, placed the beermat on my bedside table, looking at it for three nights before calling him and saying a halting 'okay' to the date.

★ ★ ★

Now I have the rest of the day to do the thing I can't do when Dave is here — to visit the past.

Under the bed in the guest room I keep a suitcase full of diaries, photos, letters and 'souvenirs' (mainly from bars, here and abroad: beer mats, cocktail parasols, match-books, menus and even a couple of ashtrays).

The diaries are illuminating in what they leave out. The days the teenage scribe is most effusive are actually the average days. I recognise myself just trying to be clever, can see my younger self poised with the pen touching her lips, spending long minutes thinking of just the right word. Writing, even then, *performing*, for an invisible reader.

The extremes, the ups and downs, are harder to read — literally. On the good days, a large hurried scrawl reading 'Good day, censored' followed by a flurry of exclamation marks and a row of words coyly interspersed with asterisks. Bad, black days are never identified as such but are marked out by empty pages. Nothing to say.

I skim through them impatiently.

'Which one broke your heart?'

I always think everybody has only one major heartbreak in their life. If you think you've had two, you can't have. The big one just mustn't have happened to you yet — so watch your back. If you'd had it, you wouldn't mistake it for anything else.

* * *

In the past, some people exist in pictures, some in words.

I smile as among the photos I catch a

71

glimpse of the black-haired, black-eyed boy who came as close as was possible, after you, to breaking my heart. He is best remembered as a visual: his smile, his unbuttoned shirt, his tan. His words, as pretty as they were, dissolved like the smoke rings he blew around them.

★ ★ ★

I have kept your letters, of course. For all these years. For every ten I wrote to you at the time, you perhaps responded once, or twice.

I always keep things that people write for me. I printed out and kept all the emails Dave sent me in the first few weeks after we met. They weren't particularly lyrical, but they were warm, and funny, and full of promise. And he could spell — I liked that about him and I suppose I've kept the emails partly as evidence. Friends laugh when I list that as one of Dave's qualities, but it's important to me — I don't know why.

I find this, dated only a few weeks after I met him:

You think too much, but I like that about you. You make me laugh, as well. You make me more fun, more interesting. I don't understand you; not yet.

72

Don't know where you go when you get that weird look in your eyes, but I like that, too, and I'm in no hurry to find out. I've got time.

And this is me: I give everything away. You may as well have it all upfront.

Here are the things I love:
Laughing
Crime novels
Those foam sweets shaped like bananas, even though they've been the direct cause of at least three fillings
Ginger biscuits
Dogs, of course
Rugby (as a spectator, not a player — not anymore — dodgy knee)
Oh, and
You.

I prefer letters to emails, though.

Your letters were good. Unlike Dave, you never gave too much away, but the letters gave me something of you that I could hold on to.

'You cannot imagine,' you used to say, 'how much of a strain writing letters is for me. I think I have a limited number in me and each one is a countdown to death.' And then, because I always teased you about your age — which seems strange looking back, given that you were younger then than I am now — you said, 'There can't be many left.'

73

When you did write, though, you wrote eight or ten pages, plain paper covered in your perfect, lilting handwriting. I studied your lines and loops; your capital 'G' that looked like a treble clef; the way you sometimes crossed your 't's twice.

I paid at least as much attention to the way you wrote as to what you wrote, because it wasn't about the content of the letters, not really. I wasn't naive enough to think that in those pages I would ever find a declaration of wild, tumescent emotion, or a sexual tension that might have given my adolescent libido a tremor.

What I loved was to think of you in the act of writing, to imagine you at your desk, or on your sofa, or sitting up in bed, leaning on a book, pen in hand, moving it across the page, creating something only for me. What I loved was that for those few moments, I was in your mind.

I find them, in a bundle, bound in the back page of a hand-written story, a fifteen-, sixteen-year-old page with your phone number on it. Red ink, and a blot like a bloodstain.

★ ★ ★

Every day, Dave comes through the door at 6.45 p.m. I don't know why I wait until 6.35

to try your old number. It rings twice.

'Yes?'

'It's me.'

'So soon?' There is a smirk in your voice.

'You still live there.' *I've been looking for you all these years, I think, and you were there, all the time.*

'It would seem so.' You pause. 'What's up, sunshine?'

'Why didn't you kiss me again?' I blurt it out, squeeze my eyes shut and wait for your answer. Seconds feel like minutes.

'You're married,' you say simply.

'So — what? You're a good guy now?'

'Like you said, kid. People change.'

I hear footsteps on the drive. He's early.

'Can I call you again?'

'I'm not sure that's a good idea.'

'Why not?'

'You're married,' you say again. 'Look, I've got to go. Take care, sunshine.'

Dave's key in the door, the click of you hanging up in my ear.

The same as every day, he calls out, 'Fill many pages today, babe?'

The same as every day, I say, 'Hundreds.' I take a deep breath then trot out my line, 'Sell many shoes today?'

'Oh, thousands.' He slips his arm around my waist from behind and kisses the top of my head. Just as I slide my phone into my pocket, it beeps, vibrating against me. My stomach lurches.

'What's for dinner?' he asks into my hair.

'Chicken casserole,' I murmur. 'Could you take Bella out while I warm it up?'

At the sound of her name and the word 'out', Bella bounds into the room and starts nudging her head into Dave's hand.

'I have to now, don't I?' he laughs, bending to stroke her. 'Come on, girl. No rest for the wicked.' He kisses me again before grabbing the lead from the sideboard.

I smile but all I can think is, *Go, go, go*, feeling the phone in my pocket like heat.

As soon as he leaves I pull it out and stare at the little envelope icon. I click it and there it is, your number, no name attributed to it but memorised by me already.

You're not the kind of person to have an affair, the message reads. I move my thumb rapidly over the keys.

What kind of person am I?

Don't ask me that, don't make me say it. It's not fair.

So of course I fill in the blanks for you, and wonder what your words would have been, and this makes my heart feel light, and dark, all at once.

5

So this is how the lies begin, and how they spread, like bacteria. They need only themselves, and air, to breed and multiply.

They begin as lies of omission. That black-haired boy who almost broke my heart (I can't even say his name, so I suppose he must have been close, very close) was adept at this technique; I now know I must've gone through all that pain with him so I could learn his cheating skills.

'How can I have lied to you when I haven't said anything?' he used to say. 'Not telling you something is not the same as lying.' It's an irresistible argument, and one I now keep in my armoury in case I am found out.

Of course, I know from experience that I will only be able to 'not tell' for a limited time. Sooner or later I will create entire stories, I will fashion them in my head while driving away from you and back towards him, and I'll recite them with an unblinking eye and busy hands.

So this is where my creative skills will come in useful.

It is two weeks since our supermarket

collision, our dinner. Two weeks of phone calls, of texts, of brief daytime meetings. Nothing more than that, not yet.

Dave is becoming an irritant. The wet munching sound of him eating breakfast. The way he leaves the tap running while he brushes his teeth. Who would do that, waste water like that?

Criticising him, I hear your words coming from my mouth.

Example: you have accused me of caring more about things than about people. 'Face it — you got married for the gift list,' you said.

On an innocent Sunday, Dave asks me if I think we need a new dishwasher. Every time the door closes the power switches itself off and his incessant tinkering has done nothing to improve the situation, in fact we now appear to have a leak. A creeping puddle is forming on the kitchen floor.

'Your problem,' I sniff, 'is you care more about things than about people.'

He blinks, looks confused, continues struggling with the door and mopping up the spills with tea towels.

I don't care about damned dishwashers, and new tiles and carpets, and whether this picture or that one looks better hanging over the sideboard. Everything is unbearably neat, and clean, and feels stifling.

I want to be outside, in a field or on a beach, carefree as a child. I want to be drunk, or better yet, high, laughing uncontrollably.

I want extremes.

I don't want a twenty-minute debate about whether we should have sofa cushions in mocha or cappuccino. None of that matters. What matters is living.

The 'beep, beep' of a text gives me a getaway.

'It's Mari,' I announce, 'some crisis or other. I don't know how long I'll be.'

And I'm gone.

* * *

It's a strange and intoxicating thing, seeing someone again from the past. You can step across years as though crossing the street, oblivious to the detritus at your feet. You summarise thousands of minutes into pithy sentences. It's an editing job. It makes everything look simpler, and prettier, than it really was.

I drive to your house, my quickening heart thudding out the risks one by one. Risk One (da-dum): you have someone there. Someone else. A woman. Risk Two: you just won't want to see me. Risk Three: you *will* (which is worse?) want to see me, and we'll be alone for the first time, without the safety of streets and public places to cover us.

I swing the car into a petrol station and do something I haven't done for years: I buy cigarettes. I drive ten yards off the forecourt, make a U-turn and go back in to buy a lighter, and mints for later, to disguise the smell of the cigarettes.

I pull over, two or three streets away from your house, musing on the fact that the last time I was here I didn't know how to drive.

('When you're old enough,' you used to say, while my hand idled on the handbrake, 'I'll teach you.')

Company cars are funny things. Even the phrase summons images that aren't entirely positive and don't match up with the way I thought my life would be. Mine is a 'pool car'; there are a fleet of them, all lined up, all the same, outside the offices. They let me choose the colour. I didn't care, but I knew that Karen, who started at around the same time as me, wanted the silver one, which of course made me want it just for devilment. We'd stood in the car park, looking at the identical grilles, headlights, bonnets. There were three we could choose from: silver, red, black. Karen's eyes were hungry. She wore fake fingernails and a pout, except when smiling too widely, maniacally, at the boss.

He was playing fair; I started at the firm two days earlier (only because, as she repeatedly pointed out, Karen had had a holiday in Marbella which she couldn't possibly cancel) so I could choose first.

'Or we could draw straws,' he was saying.

I shrugged.

'I'll take the black one,' I said. Karen looked as though she would hug me, if it didn't entail the risk of smudging her make-up. She took the keys triumphantly, like a prize.

But all I could see was a car in a row with a dozen others. I wasn't being ungrateful; it was clean, and functional. But it wouldn't feel like mine.

I love those corny magazine articles: 'What does your car say about you?' Mine says I'm a cog in a machine.

I always look enviously at people in old bangers that they've lovingly brought back to life. I love seeing things hanging from rear-view mirrors, even though Dave thinks it's 'tacky'. I notice these things. Air fresheners, often; fluffy dice (which is probably what Karen has in her silver Mondeo, now); once, a rosary. Once a photograph. People just want to personalise their space, I tell Dave. I love that.

I turn off the radio, light a cigarette, hang

my arm out of the window. I look at the 'No Smoking' sticker on the dashboard; all pool cars have them. It gives the impression of being in a taxi: being in transitory, borrowed space, governed by someone else's rules. Dog walkers pass by. A man helps a much older woman (his mother? Grandmother, even?) down the steps of the church opposite. A lilac tree overhanging the pavement sends a rush of scent into my car; I feel decadent, polluting it with nicotine. I eye passers-by boldly, as though anticipating a challenge, but none of them look at me. There is nothing extraordinary, to them, about a thirty-year-old woman pulled over on a suburban street, smoking.

★　★　★

You answer the door with a glass in your hand and a tea towel thrown over your shoulder. You're wearing shorts and a linen shirt.

'His name was Peter,' I say. 'The one who broke my heart. Or nearly did. If you must know.'

You raise an eyebrow.

'You didn't say you were coming. I might not be alone.'

'Are you?'

'Yes.'

82

I brush by you, holding out the cigarettes like a backstage pass. You laugh and I feel heat from your smile.

★ ★ ★

Lying on your sofa, leaning into you, your hands resting on my shoulders, I tell the story.

Peter was what they call a ladies' man. Or a man's man — they amount to the same thing. He was smooth. The first thing I said to him was, 'If you ever call me a lady again, I'll give you a black eye.'

He came from a different world to the one I knew. At the weekends he would go sailing, or to watch polo matches. His friends all had the straight teeth and shiny hair of the wealthy. Not many of them worked, but he did, and that was how we met. He was destined for success, even though he used to wind up our boss by calling her 'babe' all the time.

He stood out. People wanted to be near him — he was magnetic. This is a definite advantage when you work in sales.

On a team night out, tired of the trail of low-lit, overpriced bars where everyone watched everyone else and no one seemed to ever smile, I sneaked him off to a place I

83

knew with dirty carpets and music so loud it hammered in your chest like a heartbeat. He loved it, and in a taxi kissed me for seven whole miles while the blinking red light ticked over the cost.

It was a classic and predictable trap. He was a rogue and I thought I could change him. It all happened faster than it should have. We lived together and, for a while, it was intense and fun and curious.

'Isn't Peter supposed to mean rock?' I asked him once.

He laughed.

'I'm the opposite,' he warned me. 'Don't try to hold onto me. I'm more like,' trailing his hand over the side of the boat, 'water.'

Or air, I thought. *Always there, surrounding me, but impossible to fix myself to.*

Then what happened? What everyone said would happen: he got bored, I got jealous. Before long, he was kissing other girls in taxis.

'I was never enough for him,' I tell you now, 'nor him for me.'

I couldn't give him enough attention — no one person ever could — and he couldn't give me enough security. We both came out of it a little worse off, but I don't tell you that part, because I want you to believe I am wiser, better, now.

'Where is he now?' you murmur. Your breath in my hair.

'Married. She isn't enough for him either.'

'Oh? How do you know?'

I twist around from the waist, look into your eyes.

'How do I know? How do you think?'

'Ah,' you say slowly, 'I see. Revenge. When was this?'

'A while ago. After we split up, but before I met Dave. It was only . . . it only happened once.' This part a lie; it was a messy affair that went on for weeks.

'And did it make you feel better? Or not?'

'It did,' I shrug, 'for about five minutes. I mean, at least I knew it wasn't me . . . I wasn't the only one he cheated on. It wasn't anything I did wrong. I certainly didn't feel bad about it.'

'And now?'

'Now I don't feel anything.'

'I don't believe you.' Your hands squeeze, hard, too close to my throat. Another inch and I would be choking. I hold my breath. 'I wish I did, though,' you say, your voice like metal.

The reality of your touch hits me like cold air after a fire.

I jump up, smooth out imaginary wrinkles from my clothes.

'I have to go.'

'Okay.'

You don't care if I leave or stay. I can be there, or not. I could disappear for another fifteen years. It wouldn't upset you, or please you; it would be irrelevant. I am dizzy, overwhelmed by a need to affect you.

What is the best way? With stories, and words? With indifference? (But this was always your forte, not mine.) I lean forward and kiss you, uninvited. I want to stake my claim, leave a print on you.

Your lips are still, and soft. You taste of smoke. I touch your hair, run a fingernail down the back of your neck. You don't move, and pulling away wordlessly, the threat of tears stinging my throat, I leave but know I'll be back.

* * *

I'm not surprised to find the drive home gets to me. Cars can be lonely places. I try to distract myself from where I've been, and from where I'm going.

I follow a young guy in a blue Clio for a while. Funny, I always thought a Clio was more of a girl's car. Those 'Nicole' adverts. Still. Perhaps he thinks the same, because he has tried to beef it up a bit, with big tyres and something resembling an egg-box stuck to the back.

People flip their lights on. Some as soon as the cloud starts to drop, cautious souls, not to be confused with the Volvo drivers whose sidelights are on permanently due to the car's country of origin, country of no light. Some take much longer, maybe enjoying the gamble, having little bored bets with themselves, how near to home can they get before they have to switch on, every day they get a bit nearer, that means spring is coming. Maybe some are enjoying that fast, anonymous feeling of driving in the dark, like flying.

Metal boxes buzzing up and down tarmac, everyone in their little worlds. That slice of time you don't have to account for, In The Car. People driving home from Sunday lunches with families. People talking on mobiles, reps like me in Mondeos and Vectras with handsfree, heartsfree. The Wife thinks you get up, go to work, come home, but when you're In The Car, she doesn't know where you are.

No one knows where I am.

But although a car covers you, it can also betray you.

I watch the trip counter wheels click forward, forward, forward, with the unsettling feeling that I'm being clocked.

★ ★ ★

This is how life works. You go to work, you get married. You pay the bills, do the shopping. It's an endless cycle. Maybe you have babies. Some people do. But not me, not us.

I stand at the checkout, listening to the 'beep, beep', in a daze. *This is my life*, I think. *I'm on the conveyor belt*. But so is everyone else, says a smaller voice, and what's so bad about it?

And in these endless arguments with myself, as I pack the bags and hand over my card, punch in my number, the overriding question is always:

What if I just jumped off?

★ ★ ★

There are secret ways I can have you near me when we are apart. I start taking your sugar in my tea. Run my shower colder because I know that is how you like it. Play music I have heard in your car, in your house. Drink your drink — rum and coke. Stop wearing a seatbelt.

You are everywhere.

HM. Your initials. I see them in car registrations and my heart skips a beat. I seek out the letters H and M in newspapers and draw them together with my eyes.

HM.

Him. Him, him, him. You, you, you. Parasite of my thoughts.

Hmm. A thought; a consideration.

Hum. Music. A throb, a buzzing, a beat.

Humbert. Humbug.

★   ★   ★

I take every opportunity to be alone — taking a bath, popping out to the shops — just so that I can have my thoughts of you without any interruption. So that if a faraway look passes across my face, I don't have to explain it, won't have to lie to that most intrusive of questions: 'What are you thinking?'

Dave and I aren't used to arguing; haven't done it for years. It's a foreign country to us; we can't speak its language. We fumble for words and end up spewing out half-syllables and slamming exasperated doors.

When he asked me to marry him I cried and cried. He did everything you're supposed to. He'd done it before, after all. Location: smart French restaurant. Candles . . . even a

violinist! Champagne. Ring: solitaire, naturally. Just as I'd wanted. He always seemed to
know what I would like. Never asked, though.
Down on one knee. Expectant, hopeful eyes.
The little tell-tale box. Subdued rounds of
applause from the other diners. Streams and
streams of tears and the promise he would
always look after me. Then the ring was on
my hand and hasn't moved since, except to
make way for its partner, the gold band.

Thinking about it — I never actually said
yes.

This has been the anatomy of our
marriage: he has made decisions, I've gone
along with them. So it comes as a surprise to
both of us that there is fight in us.

It seems those who love the hardest fight
the hardest. And not just for each other but
against.

And that ability we have to finish each
other's sentences — I use that as a hammer.
Kill every word I don't want to listen to, snuff
it out. It goes like this:

'I know what you're going to say.'
'Why do you always interrupt me?'
'I know what you're going to say.'
'Maybe you don't.'
'I do.'

(I had been surprised to find out only a few
days before the wedding, at the rehearsal, that

during the ceremony you don't actually say 'I Do'. You say 'I Will'. Makes sense, really. It has a greater air of permanence. 'I Do' sounds like 'I do at the moment, yeah', or 'Well alright then — for now'. 'I Will' has another word hiding in there somewhere: it has 'always' under its breath.)

Fights don't fit patterns. Do they?

We try to contain them in rounds. We put them in a ring, which is actually a square, with a bell and a referee and a barely dressed girl flashing up numbered cards.

When we were first married, Dave had a failsafe way of deflecting arguments just as they were about to begin. He could see me coming. He would distract me into laughing, by shouting, 'Ding a ling a ling: Round One!'

But now there is no laughter. Looking around our home all I can see are *things*. Washing machine, vacuum cleaner, fridge freezer, dishwasher. I'm surrounded. I'm a housewife in a 1950s TV commercial. I feel applianced in. Everything has been bought together or bought by parents-in-law, sitting looking at me whitely, quietly, waiting to be divided, fought over, split. All the work we did on this place, the paint colours, the sanded floors, the carefully chosen mirrors and vases and blinds, they're reminders I don't want, can't look at.

I'm starting to fill with an irrational hatred. He's the block, the barrier to me living the life I was supposed to have. I curse the vanity and greed that led me down that stupid aisle. Dazzled by diamonds and the promise of nothing more than the same kind of life as everyone else has. Why had I gone along with it? How could I not have known that this day would come, when I would be bored and he would be frustrated, and in you would swagger to rouse me from my anaesthesia?

I hate Dave.

You start off seeing everything that's there in a person, *wanting* to see and know everything. Next you see the faults, the pieces that don't quite fit. Then you start looking for what's not there.

I found a You-shaped gap, unfillable.

'I always feel there's a little bit of you that's unknowable,' Dave said once, in a matter-of-fact way that made it seem like this didn't trouble him.

I shook my head at it but he was right. The only bit of me he couldn't have was the bit where you still lived. You carved a nook inside me that no one could see.

Language is unpeeling from me. How is it that these lips, this tongue, all the apparatus of kissing, that once formed the words 'You are my angel', now struggle to generate anything but lies?

Each lie is smooth and round, like a marble in my mouth. And it isn't just the words: my clothes are a lie. The laptop case I bring through the door and set down with a sigh, implying I have been working late. The mints I eat to mask the smell of the cigarettes he wouldn't approve of. The baths I know I will take to wash you off me, when the inevitable happens, as it must.

I'm planning for it. I find myself in a department store, under unforgiving lights, buying lingerie for a man I've barely kissed (this time around, anyway). *Adultery underwear*, I think to myself, laughing in a giddy, guilty way, swinging the bag on the way back to the car, sneaking its contents into a separate drawer, away from my usual things (white and black only; cotton, mostly; utilitarian), as if to prevent cross-contamination. I touch the new satin and lace reverently, bury the violent jewel-colours — ruby, emerald, amethyst — under innocuous towels and sheets. For now.

I'm preparing for something that is coming towards me, unstoppable as a train. Separate drawers, separate lives; these are the necessary precautions and I perform them with the cool precision of a surgeon. I'm almost certain Dave won't find out, and if he does, my only defence will be, pathetic as a shrug: 'I couldn't stop it.'

Lies, arguments, silence, secrets. This is the new anatomy of our marriage.

6

Diary: Wednesday, 11 November 1992

I phoned HM, he'd just got out of the shower (there's an image), we talked for a bit. He said he's got a letter for me, he's had it for a week and kept forgetting to give it to me! I remember now seeing him at the play rehearsals the other day and he dropped an envelope, then shoved it back into his jeans pocket. I had a feeling it might be for me. He says he'll give it to me on Saturday — nudge nudge, wink wink, etc.

When I think about it, I have really sort of worked on him, and I feel like I'm getting somewhere. In the space of about a year, I've decided I would get close to him and I have. I wonder if this will always work for me? I know I'm not exactly good-looking, so it's not like I attract loads of boys, but I think I have a good mind and once I set it on someone, I get them.

I have got a tiny piece of HM — but it gives me hope. I will get all of him some day.

No one at home questioned why I was going to Mr Morgan's house on a Saturday, although I didn't give them the opportunity to. I only told Alex, who muttered, 'he's a pervert', but then, he said that about everyone. 'Pervert' was his new favourite word. He even shouted it at Dad once, who just blinked at him as though he didn't know what it meant.

I was up early, twisting my damp hair into knots to make it curl, humming, slathering cocoa butter onto my skin until the smell made me feel dizzy. Mum was busy 'cleaning'. Contrary to initial appearances, she wasn't very domestic. She made a martyred show of housework but was terrible at it. She would spray polish without dusting first, leaving sweet-smelling balls of hair and mites mummified on the furniture. She vacuumed only the centre of rooms, so that the edges turned grey while a central circle of carpet buzzed with colour.

The soundtrack to what she called cleaning was always The Musicals. She loved them all. You could tell what mood she was in by which record she was playing: today was *Phantom of the Opera* so was obviously going to be dramatic. Her quivering voice fought with the vacuum cleaner.

As I edged towards the window she saw me, narrowed her eyes and shouted, 'Why are you wearing so much make-up so early in the day?'

'I'm going out,' I yelled over Michael Crawford. I stood at the window watching for your car, and immediately its blue-green nose rounded the corner I was down the path.

'See you later,' I called, my bag swinging behind me.

Even though I hoped I would be staying all day, I ran my eye greedily over every detail of your bungalow: a square, welcoming hall and five closed doors. You opened one of them, to the right, and motioned for me to enter the lounge. Its terracotta walls looked freshly painted. A sofa and matching chaise-longue showed no signs of wear. I looked down. A bold, diamond-patterned rug was positioned in perfect alignment against the polished dark wood floorboards. Even your scatter cushions were *organised*. Reluctant to sit down for fear of creasing something, I retreated and found you in the kitchen (spotless). I watched you from the doorway and laughed when you filled the kettle from a little jug rather than just yanking it from the wall as we did at home.

'What's so funny?' you said without turning around.

'You are,' I said. Typically, you didn't respond to this.

'Do you like the house?' you asked, spooning Douwe Egberts into a chrome cafetière.

'Mm.' I continued my unguided tour, gently pushing doors open and leaving them that way. In the bathroom was the Aramis I smelled on you every time you leaned over me in class. Toothpaste, cap on. Towels, impeccably folded. I couldn't find a single thing out of place. Everything was coordinated, not just in each room but from one to another. The colours and textures flowed perfectly, testament to your artistic eye, I supposed. On the walls of your hallway, I was surprised to see your initials at the bottom of three watercolours.

I didn't recognise the scenes in the paintings. I wondered where and when you did them.

'Where did these come from?' I called out. 'The depths of your murky memory, or your even murkier imagination?' I jumped as I realised you were standing next to me, holding out a cup of coffee. You laughed and said,

'Most people — '

'I'm not most people.'

'On that we're agreed. Most people just say they're good.'

'Well, I expect they're just being polite.'

'So that's my attempts at art critiqued. Sit down and tell me what you think of the rest of the house, since you've had a good nosey.'

'I sense traces of an ex-wife,' I lied, because it sounded interesting and as far as I could gather you'd not been separated long, so it seemed a pretty safe bet that the former Mrs Morgan might still be hanging around.

'Where?' you asked, puzzled. 'Everything's been completely changed since she was here. Well, almost everything.'

'Exactly,' I said quickly.

'What do you mean?'

'I think you know,' I deflected, trying to be cryptic because I didn't know what I meant. You laughed.

'You think I've tried too hard to cover her tracks.' I nodded gratefully. 'You might be right. Your little psychoanalyses are really very impressive.'

I was glad you'd noticed, because for months I'd been working on persuading you that you were seriously repressed and needed to 'unburden' yourself on a sympathetic ear, i.e. mine, although now that I was here and listening I didn't feel so sure.

'I like that wine rack,' I said, and then moved away and started to rummage in my bag. 'I've got something for you.'

'Oh?' You raised an eyebrow. I tossed your dog-eared copy of *Lolita* to you, announcing that I'd read it in two days flat. You looked pleased.

'What did you think of it?'

'Well,' I said tetchily, 'it's not exhaustive on the subject.'

You'd set us some work a couple of weeks ago, 'a story of no more than 2,000 words about wanting something you can't have'. You had directed a surreptitious wink towards me as you said this, to which of course I scowled.

As I sat in front of a pile of blank white paper the night before it was due in, I knew exactly what you would expect me to write: a none too subtle piece about being in love with an older man, hmm, a teacher perhaps? There was no way I would give you that satisfaction, so I decided to do something different. People like my mum and the nuns at school maintained that a 'grown' man couldn't possibly be attracted to a fourteen-year-old girl. But I knew life wasn't like that.

So I wrote a fast-moving, and I thought extremely touching, monologue narrated by an ageing, frustrated teacher nursing a tender, secret desire for his most precocious pupil. I called the pupil 'Jade', because that was the kind of name I wanted — exotic-sounding and sophisticated — and because in my imaginings she had bright green eyes, so unlike my own which were dishwater grey.

(I didn't come up with that on my own, by the way — it was my mum. She was really good at pulling these rare stunts of affection, like a bear hug in the middle of the kitchen when you were trying to wash up, or a soft stroke of your hair while you were watching TV. They'd take you by surprise so much she'd then be able to insult you and disguise it as a compliment. 'Poor love,' she'd murmured, stroking my hair I think it was this time, yes, must've been, 'dishwater-grey eyes and mousey hair. Good job you have a lovely personality, eh?')

Anyway, the story. Jade's story. It came back with 17/20 (a poor mark for me) and the comment, 'Interesting, but it's been done before; see me.' I waited behind after class and you gave me *Lolita*. It had old, yellowed pages and a picture on the cover of a child wearing heart-shaped sunglasses, sucking a lollipop.

'Oh alright, it's a pretty good book,' I admitted now. 'Anyway, I'm almost too old to be a nymphet, so you'd better get a move on!'

'I'm no Humbert,' you protested, leaning forward.

'Humbug,' I laughed, and picked up the script.

★ ★ ★

Over lunch I invented a serious love interest for Scrooge.

'You have to bring sex into everything,' you complained, almost whispering the s-word, which made me smile.

'I just don't think it's realistic to have this man who's so completely cold and unfeeling.'

'Why not?' you said, draining the last of your wine. I wondered if you were planning to drive me home. 'Look at me!'

'Don't try to pretend it isn't important, because it is,' I said in a low voice.

'No it isn't. You just ignore it, and it goes away. Not a problem at all.' But you were watching my fingers on the stem of my wineglass.

'The iceman cometh,' I laughed.

I wished there was someone I could tell, later: 'He gave me *wine*!' It seemed like a big thing, not only because the only wine we ever had at home was Mateus Rosé, at Christmas. I was always allowed a drop with lemonade. This was real wine, and I wasn't sure if I liked the taste or not, but I liked the fact that you were giving it to me. It told me you saw me as an equal.

You insisted on doing the dishes and told me there was more wine in the car. I took the keys, spotted the carrier bag on the back seat and as I clambered, from habit really, into the passenger seat, the glove box sprang open.

You're so tidy, there was disappointingly little in there: the Honda's manual and service history; a box of tissues; a couple of cassettes; a pen; a photograph. A photograph, face down. I pulled it out and turned it over.

A girl smiled up at me. She was wearing jeans and her knees were drawn up towards her chest. I recognised the diamond patterned rug she was sitting on. And I recognised the girl.

It wasn't the former Mrs Morgan. It was Helen Platt. She was three years above me at school; she was at college or uni now. Some people said Oxford. I didn't really like her; I suppose a lot of it was envy. She was pretty, in a fresh-faced sort of way. She was bright. She was talented, too; in her fourth year she had played Nancy in our school production of *Oliver!*. I was a first year then, I'd been in the chorus, watching her, wishing I could sing like that, being hardly surprised by your appreciative coos and smiles and the way you squeezed her hand before she went on stage on the first night.

I looked at Helen before putting her back. She must have been about fourteen when the photograph was taken.

I went back into the house.

I may have been young, but I had experience — mostly thanks to Mari's parties.

Mari's mum was a nurse who worked nights. We rarely saw her, so we all sort of had the impression that it was Mari's house and her mum just lodged there.

Sometimes when I called round after school she would be there, bleary-eyed, in a dressing gown, having her 'breakfast': a cup of tea and three cigarettes. On the odd occasion, she would boil a couple of eggs in a tiny saucepan and mush them up in a cup, with butter, as though for a baby, then eat them with a teaspoon, standing by the cooker.

Mari's mum never seemed to inhabit any room other than the kitchen, which added to the impression of her not being a full-time resident. She always lit her cigarettes off the hob; I don't know why she never bought a lighter, or how she never singed her eyelashes when she leaned over the flame. The whoosh of gas, the click of the ignition and the rhythmic knocking of eggs against the side of the saucepan: these were the sounds of Mari's kitchen at tea/breakfast time.

When Mari's mum went off to work and dusk arrived, things changed in the house. As with the outside, the world got darker.

I was thirteen when I had my first drink at one of Mari's gatherings. Vodka and orange in a pint glass, followed by a bottle of brown ale. I was sick in a wastepaper basket, but I was back the following weekend, and almost every weekend after.

The crowd didn't vary much. A procession of long-haired boys in black trench coats and Doc Marten boots. A trio of girls whose friendship with Mari made me feel possessive: they all wore thick eyeliner and their hair was backcombed; Gina's was dyed an unnatural shade of black that was almost blue. She rarely spoke and never smiled; Mari said she had had a tough childhood and took years to trust anyone. The girls just seemed impossibly glamorous and knowing; I preferred the boys.

My favourite was Todd, who always carried a little plastic biscuit box: it was full of weed, he called it draw; sometimes magic mushrooms. He had soulful eyes and smelled of autumn.

We would sit on cushions on the floor instead of on the furniture. We talked: about music, about religion. 'Do you believe in God?' and 'What do you think happens when you die?' were favourite conversation openers. We talked about what we would be when we 'grew up', although I was the youngest so most of them already seemed adult to me. We made wild plans: we could foresee no barriers to running off to live in New York, Marrakech or (my personal favourite) Paris.

I thought I was going to be a bohemian poet, drinking coffee all day and roaming the streets with wild hair and scuffed shoes, notebook in hand. Everything in my existence would be tawdry but beautiful, and I would live in a tiny flat on the Left Bank filled with battered antique furniture and dusty books. I would have a pair of lovebirds in a silver cage.

We mostly drank the hours away, but sometimes tiny tabs of paper decorated with strawberries or stars would get passed around, and those who took them would spend hours marvelling at the patterns on the wallpaper or the veins on their own hand. This bored me; I was more interested in drink, or smoking weed. I liked the gradual warm feeling, and the rolling laughter that felt as though it lasted for hours.

I didn't actually know much about the kids in the group, apart from Mari, and yet there was a strange intimacy between us; the kind you only get in a dark smoky room where everyone is inventing themselves.

Inevitably, there was drunken fumbling. It would start with Truth or Dare, or Spin the

Bottle, then we would pair off and I would be led into a dark corner, or sometimes into a bedroom. It just seemed like something you did, with your friends, after a night of drinking and talking and getting stoned. If it went on too long, I would get bored — with their wet kisses, with the mechanical rhythm of fingers and palms — but I would always do it, because for the first few moments, those very first seconds of touching each other in the dark, I felt like someone who mattered.

So because of the parties, I knew what to do — up to a point — with boys. I wondered, was it the same with men?

I stood in your bathroom, looking at myself in the mirror. I knew things from books, as well: about body language, for example. I knew that women wore lipstick to make their lips mimic what other parts of their body might look like when sexually excited, and that this was why men found it attractive. I knew that if someone pointed their feet towards you, or played with their hair (usually women) or put their thumbs in their belt loops (men — to accentuate the groin area, apparently), or if their pupils got bigger when they looked at you — all of these things meant they liked you.

★ ★ ★

When I went back into the living room, you were leaning over the sheets of paper we had scribbled all over. I felt a strange thrill seeing my handwriting next to yours. Mine was small, neat; yours looping, artistic. Our words seemed to be dancing together on the page.

Taking a slug of wine, I told myself: *it's now or never.* I sat next to you and used my most practised move: I put my hand onto that dangerous point in your lap that is between thigh and groin. There is only a fraction of possible ambiguity in this touch, and a movement of my fingers of less than an inch would remove any ambiguity altogether.

You looked at me, raised a quizzical eyebrow, and in that instant I crushed my lips onto yours.

It all happened quickly. You shifted, my hand brushed your fly, then was stopped, my wrist caught in your grasp. Your other hand held my chin, gently pushing me away. Something flashed in your eyes. For a second I thought you looked angry.

'What are you doing?' It was a demand; your voice hoarse.

'I . . . I thought . . . ' I was suddenly terrified. I recoiled from your grip and you released me. I wanted to curl in on myself, disappear. I scuttled like a crab to the opposite end of the sofa.

'Fee,' you said softly, 'look at me.'

Somehow I found the strength to lift my head.

'I like you.' You reached out as though to take my hand again, then apparently thought better of it. Clearing your throat, you said decisively, as though on stage, as though in school assembly, 'I like you, but I can't like you like *that*. Do you understand?'

'Why can't you?' I heard my whining voice as though it was coming from someone else.

'You know why. We'll have to just be friends.' You paused, searched my face with your eyes. 'A hug?'

I wanted to stay stubbornly at my end of the sofa, but I wanted the contact more. I sank into your chest, circled your waist with my arms. I rubbed the small of your back with my fingers and pressed myself hard against you, trying to feel a response from you, a movement, anything.

Gently, you unpeeled me, planted a chaste kiss on my forehead.

'Come on, kid — let's get you home.'

★   ★   ★

On Monday morning I closed and locked the bathroom door against the bustle of the house.

I dressed slowly. A button left undone, then another. Black tights instead of socks, today. Skirt rolled up, sleeves rolled up. As little of me covered by uniform as possible.

I stared at myself in the mirror. Looked at my dimples, my snub nose, my stupid wispy eyebrows, all the features that made me look young, pale, insignificant. Took out my make-up bag and plunged my fingers into the pot of foundation. Honey beige.

I smothered and smeared until you couldn't see my pores anymore, until my face was a seamless mask. Smoothed on layer after layer, carefully, raising my chin, observing the line on my neck and blending it downwards like they said in the magazines. My finger nudged the collar of my school shirt, leaving a rusty streak, but no matter, I was covered. I took out a brush and dusted myself with powder, setting the layers I had made beneath golden dust.

I pulled out a black eyeliner and got to work lining and circling my eyes, the way I'd seen Mari do hers. Made my lashes heavy with coat after coat of mascara. Little clumps fell onto my cheekbones like tiny spiders and I picked them off carefully with tongue-moistened fingertips. Blinked. One more coat. Just at that moment,

Bang, bang, bang.

Sudden impatient thumping at the bath-room door and I nearly poked myself in the eye with the mascara wand.

'WHAT?' I yelled.

'Come on, *loser*,' Alex droned.

'Get lost, pig,' I shouted. 'Mum! Tell him!'

I heard muffled voices and then a lighter knock and my dad's gentle tone. 'You *have* been in there nearly half an hour, Girl. We all need to get ready.'

'Fine! Whatever.' I swung open the door and left the room with a scowl at the triumphant Alex.

'What have you got on your face?' My mother was nibbling her toast, leaving the edges, blowing on her fingernails which were still wet, maroon-coloured.

'Make-up?'

'Oh, very droll.' She stood up and poured the remains of her coffee down the sink. 'Now, do you want a lift to school, or what?'

'*What*. I'll walk.'

'I'm taking Alex to college.'

'So? I'm walking. I don't want to get in the car with that *pig*, anyway.'

'Please yourself.' She swung her jacket around her shoulders. 'But wash your bloody face.'

* * *

111

'Fiona, could you stay behind please?'

I gave a brief nod and sat rooted behind my desk while the other kids stirred up a whirlwind of coats and bags and scarves, rushing from the room as though in a race to make the door before the bell's wail expired. I heard somebody mutter, 'Oh dear, looks like the teacher's pet's in *trouble*,' someone else snigger and Laura call, 'Talk to you later, Fee,' but I just stared straight ahead.

Once they'd all gone you closed the door quietly, sat down beside me, and said, 'I think I might have given you the wrong impression.'

I felt as though the heat from my face might melt my make-up. I was suddenly conscious of it caked over my pores, gathering in a greasy orange crease at my hairline, dry and flaky around my nostrils and lips.

You went on without looking at me, 'I hoped we could be friends . . . '

'We can, we can!'

' . . . and if I've given you the idea we could be anything else, I could get into a lot of trouble.'

'But it wasn't your fault,' I cried. 'It was me. I'm sorry.'

'No, I was responsible, Fiona. I'm the . . . '

'Don't say it!' I shouted. 'Don't say you're the adult! Don't you dare!' I jumped up, pushed the desk away from me and ran from the room without looking back, hot tears forging cracks down the contours of my painted mask.

★ ★ ★

I held the receiver for a long time before I dialled your number.

'Hello?'

'I know you'll say I shouldn't have called . . .'

'No, it's okay.'

'It's just, I felt like we couldn't really talk, before. Not properly. At school.'

'Well, maybe we should stick to school.'

'I need to ask you something.'

'Go ahead.'

'What do you . . . ' I took a deep breath. 'What do you think of me?'

'Wow. It's very brave of you to ask that.'

'Is it?'

'Of course. That's all anyone ever really wants to know from anyone else, isn't it?'

'I suppose so.'

'But most people don't have the courage to ask, so they go around wondering.'

'Sister Agnes says courage should be rewarded.'

You laughed. 'She means in heaven, probably.'

'I can't wait that long.'

I heard you take a gulp of something. Coffee? Wine? The physical sound of you swallowing made me shiver.

'I think you're . . . different. Extraordinary, in fact.'

My heart fluttered in my chest.

'So can we be friends?'

'You're also very persistent.'

'Only when something matters to me.'

'Okay, sunshine. Friends. Just friends.'

'Just friends.' *For now*, I thought, and I climbed the stairs to bed and fell asleep with a smile still on my lips.

7

My two best friends are as different as the two sides of me.

Laura has always found me fascinating in my 'worldliness', especially when we were teenagers, but it was really only ever a coat I borrowed from Mari — I presented a toned-down version. If Laura had ever actually met Mari, or any of her crowd, I think her head would have exploded. For example one guy, Cole, used to flip out his own eye with a dessert spoon, then pop it right back in again. He hardly ever had to go to hospital as a result of this party trick.

These were not the kinds of circles Laura moved in.

In return, I was desperately jealous of Laura and her 'normal' life. Her mum actually baked. Their house always smelled of biscuits, and flowers.

When we were younger, she loved that I lived on an 'estate'; I think she associated it with a country estate, which was about as far as it could get from the reality.

One thing that living on an estate implied that was actually true was a sense of community. Wives shared fags over garden walls; husbands were members of darts or cards teams at the local pub. Everyone knew everyone's name, and people were usually referred to in conversation by both names: Doreen O'Farrell, Sharon Keene, Angela Horrocks. I wondered when all the introductions had happened; I couldn't imagine my mum, having just moved in, taking a freshly baked pie or a bunch of flowers to the neighbours and brightly offering a potted biography of her family. And yet everyone knew us; it just seemed to have happened by osmosis. People in the street knew me, if not by name, then as 'Charlie and Tina Palmer's girl' or sometimes 'you know, the clever one'.

While there was camaraderie, as with any community there was also always gossip and mistrust. Anyone who got anything new, for example, was regarded with open envy, sometimes suspicion: from a car ('how can *they* afford *that*?') to a privet hedge ('what have *they* got to hide?').

No one ever moved away, and no one was allowed to move up. It would have been seen as a sort of betrayal.

As far as my mum was concerned, there was 'common' (us) and there was 'posh', and there was 'nowt in between'. She thought Laura was 'posh', with all the associated mistrust that that brought. Of course when we were really little, still at primary school, we had no real understanding of class, but I was vaguely aware that the area Laura lived in was more well-to-do, and that their house was bigger than ours, even though Laura was an only child.

She had two rooms: a bedroom, and what had been a playroom and was now a dressing room, with rows of jewel-coloured clothes lined up like sweet jars. Necklaces and bracelets hung from hooks on the wall as though from invisible throats and wrists.

'If *I* had two rooms,' I would tell her, 'I would have two bedrooms.'

'Why?' she asked.

'I don't know,' I shrugged, 'it would just be cool to be in your own house, but pretend you were sleeping over somewhere else.'

Of course, the other big difference was that Laura's family owned their home — ours was owned by 'the corporation', who seemed to me to be a shadowy organisation whose purpose was to demand money and give nothing in return. Some families on the estate had bought their houses, but it was beyond the reach of most, us included.

'What would I want with a mortgage?' my dad would mutter, as though the very fact of it being possible were an insult.

'It's about time the corporation gave us a new kitchen,' Mum would complain every time the cooker went on the blink. 'The corporation haven't done the grass for a while,' she would say, looking out of the window at the small green that faced our house.

★ ★ ★

Kahlil Gibran said, 'your friend is your needs answered'. Right now I feel I need both of them, to balance me out. They are light and shade; if one is the angel on my shoulder and one the devil, first of all I need the devil.

'I need to talk to you,' I tell Mari when I turn up at her door, bottle of wine in hand. 'About Dave. And about Morgan.'

She knows, of course. She can see it in the tilt of my head, the way I walk, the tell-tale shine in my eyes that you have put there.

'It's happened, then?'

'Yes. God.' I sink into the sofa.

It happened, like the first time, because I led it. You resisted me, this time even said it was 'wrong', and I repeated 'how can it be, how can it be', kissing your neck, stroking your back, until you gave in.

I wasn't going to tell anyone, but not telling Mari almost feels like a bigger betrayal than the thing itself.

'So how was it?'

I pull a face, groan. 'Come off it,' I say. From the kitchen I hear the heavy 'pop' of a cork being removed, followed by the comforting sloshing of wine against the sides of a glass.

'That's why you're here, isn't it? To talk? So, talk.'

There's something new and unrecognisable in her voice. I look up.

'Mari, what's up? You sound . . . are you being funny with me?' She says nothing. 'Are you *mad* at me?'

There's a pause briefer than a heartbeat before the familiar grin spreads across her face.

'Course not, doll.' She ruffles my hair as though petting an errant puppy. 'Rough day, that's all. So tell me — what happened? What was it like?' She looks at me meaningfully over the rim of her glass. 'Better than Dave?'

'No.' I shake my head firmly. 'No, not at all. It's just — different.'

★ ★ ★

How can I explain it? With Dave, I know what to expect. In bed, we move like well-rehearsed dancers, perfectly in time. I know the landscape of his body; I know the meaning in every sigh.

I always imagined sex would be the first thing to go once a relationship, a marriage, starts to turn stale. But it isn't the sex; it's the kissing.

Kissing requires effort, patience, sensuality. Sex can be performed mechanically; kissing can't. It's an imprecise art, whereas I had come to view sex as cold biology.

You spent a long time kissing me.

You were familiar and unfamiliar all at once. There is more hair on you, than him and than before, and now it is grey in places; I traced its line from your collarbone down to your stomach, fascinated.

Dave and I undress quickly, automatically. There's no sensuousness in it anymore; it is a practical act. We fold our clothes before folding ourselves under the duvet and into each other.

You undressed me as though unwrapping a gift, layer by layer. I felt exposed, as though you might finally unpeel my skin, take my bones, leave only soft, beating organs.

You made me lie still.

'Control freak,' I tried to say, but you put your hand over my mouth. I bit your fingers, but you seemed to feel nothing, your free hand holding me down at the hip, your eyes

120

turned away as you moved in me and I let myself be taken over.

★ ★ ★

'Don't get me wrong,' I tell Mari, 'Dave presses all the right buttons. Every time. But with Morgan it's . . . exciting. Dave satisfies me, but . . . '

'He doesn't surprise you.'

'Exactly.'

Slightly drunk, she says, 'So what you're saying is this. Morgan is like lobster. Dave is like a McDonald's.'

'Ha! Here we go.'

I love Mari's McDonald's analogies — my favourite was a lengthy exposition on how McDonald's is the one-night stand of food: you crave it, it feels great while you're doing it, but immediately afterwards you're filled with remorse. Or wait, was it the other way around, that a one-night stand is the McDonald's of sex? Anyway, she's warming to this familiar theme.

'I mean, with a McDonald's you know what you're getting, it's the same every time. And it satisfies your appetite — '

'For half an hour or so!'

'Half an hour, right, you always feel hungry again half an hour after a Maccy Dees, I'll

121

give you that. But the good thing is, it's the same every time.'

'But the trouble is,' I say, 'it's the same every time.'

'Good value though,' and she starts to laugh. Suddenly I feel sorry.

'You're supposed to like Dave,' I say. I can't believe I'm telling her off for doing exactly what I hoped she'd do; for making light of it. *Defend him*, I'm thinking. *Don't make fun of him. Someone has to protect Dave in this.*

'Yeah, well,' she drains her glass, 'you're supposed to be married to him.'

'Lobsters mate for life,' I say.

'In that case,' she says, 'Dave's the lobster.'

Something in me sinks, because I know she's right.

'I just wasn't prepared,' I say slowly, 'for how happy this would make me. How good I would feel.'

'Yeah, well,' Mari takes a long drag of her cigarette and breathes out a dramatic plume, 'that's the big secret no one tells you about adultery.' (I wince at the word.) 'What? You'd rather I called it screwing around? The secret no one tells you, and the reason people do it. When people say, 'God, how could he or she do that — they had so much going for them — how could they risk it, blah blah blah' — it's obvious, isn't it?

Because it feels bloody good.'

'Morgan once told me a story. I think it was *called* 'Happiness'. It was French. '*La Bonheur*'. Something like that. A man has an affair.'

'It's always the man in the stories.'

'Don't interrupt. You see, he loves his wife but he also meets this woman, he has an affair with her, and she's wonderful, and she makes him feel so . . . *happy*. The thing is, he can't bear to keep it from his wife. He decides to tell her, not out of guilt but just because he has to share how happy he is.'

'Nice! Doesn't sound like a great plan.'

'Right. Anyway he tells the wife everything. They are in a park, by a lake, on a bench, and as I remember it after he tells her, she says she'll forgive him, they make love, and they get back all the passion and intensity they ever had. He's so incredibly happy, and drifts into a blissful sleep.'

'He might well. Smug pig.'

'The thing is, he wakes up later to a huge commotion, people all gathered around the lake. His wife has thrown herself in: she drowned.'

'Shit. Sad story, babe. Is there supposed to be a moral in there, or something?'

'Yeah. Never confess, I suppose. Give me one of those.' I lean forward and slide a long menthol cigarette out of Mari's packet and into my mouth.

'What, you smoke now as well? Dave wouldn't approve.'

'Ha! I know. It's the least of his worries though, don't you think?'

It's a strange thing. Once you take one big risk — with your life, your happiness — other risks seem meaningless. You feel more alive, sort of invincible, but at the same time you know it could all blow up at any moment so you feel permanently on edge. Vulnerable. It's an addictive sort of tightrope.

It's the beginning again that does it. It's the talking, and inventing yourself, getting to know yourself as much as the other person. Everybody likes the first weeks of a relationship the best; no one admits it. Everyone says: love changes, yes, but it grows. It gets even better. And everyone agrees, but knows they are lying.

'This shit'll kill you.' Mari lights another. 'So what are you going to do?'

'I need to be with him. That's all I know.'

'And two years from now? What then? Ten years? Twenty?'

'What do you mean?'

'Who's to say you'd be better together than you and Dave are? I'm telling you, two years on, same shit, different pair of shoes under the bed. When you eat lobster every day, eventually it'll taste like a Big Mac.' She pauses then says again, 'I'm telling you.'

* * *

Laura and Matt's house is like the houses you see in magazines. It's like ours, really, but without that underlying sense that it might be teetering on the edge of chaos. In our house, if you open a cupboard, it might be uneventful, or you might suddenly be rained on by shoeboxes; a badly placed ironing board; old videos; the plastic bags we keep meaning to recycle.

In Laura and Matt's house, there are always lilies, and candles that are never burnt down. It feels like being at a spa. Even Dave, who likes things to be tidy, never feels quite comfortable there and always gently insists we eat out whenever they ask us for dinner.

I still get a warm feeling when I think of the four of us together, especially the first night I took Dave to meet them. I remember watching him laughing with Matt in that easy, relaxed way he has, and feeling the glow of relief that my friends liked this new boyfriend. It was the moment I knew that not only were we safe, the two of us, but that that safety now extended to a network, a support crew, a circle. That was probably when I knew I would marry him, if he asked.

Laura is on a health kick, as usual, so we sit on her perfect cream sofa drinking pomegranate juice. I hold my glass nervously with both hands.

Even though we've known each other for so long, there's always a preamble when we get together. A few minutes of feeling our way into the conversation, getting the polite chit-chat out of the way, sizing up the other's mood. An outsider might think we barely knew each other, but actually the opposite is true. It's as though when we talk about the mundane, we can see each other's deepest secrets. I'm here to show her mine, but I sense something brittle in her voice almost immediately. I don't say 'what's wrong?'; I say, 'Tell me.'

She takes a deep breath and in the same tone she just used to talk about the gardening, says, 'It's Matt. He's cheating.'

I feign surprise; it's not as though I didn't know first-hand that he's the type. I think back to the way he touched me when we danced.

'When? Who is she? How'd you find out?'

With a bitter laugh she replies, 'Oh, I don't think there's anyone in particular. That would require commitment. I think it's more of a habit. His little hobby.'

'But how do you know?' I ask again. 'I mean, how'd you find out?'

'The usual,' she sighs, 'he's not exactly been careful. His phone, his email . . . there are so many ways to catch people out these days, you know? I know all his passwords . . . I know him inside out, Fee.'

Dave's voice is ringing in my ears: 'I can see right through you'. I shake my head, attempting to empty out the words. Concentrate on Laura, on what she's saying. She's still trying to be matter-of-fact but her voice is low.

'Of course, he knows me as well. So he's gotten more careful. Now his phone never leaves his side. He deletes his call history, his messages. Why would he do that? I think he knows I know, but he can't exactly say anything.'

'Jesus, Lau. You seem pretty calm about it all.'

'The thing is,' she says miserably, 'I don't blame him. Who doesn't want to be wanted again? I mean, wanted in the way that only a stranger can want you. Someone who doesn't know your faults . . . '

I look at her and in this moment I cannot imagine what faults Laura thinks she has. She is truly beautiful, in the way that only people who are not can appreciate: in jogging pants, hair scraped back, no make-up, she is stunning. She needs no accessories.

I feel a blush rising up my throat. I mumble, 'But . . . you and Matt. You've always had a great sex life. That's one of the, oh, ninety-six reasons the rest of us have always been so jealous of you.'

She looks at me, and suddenly something about the way her hands are cupping her belly flicks a switch in me. *Of course.*

'Yeah, but it changes when it's all about making a baby.' She sighs. 'I guess you can't have everything. Not forever. And now — *especially* now — I can't say anything. There's too much to lose.'

'First things first,' I say softly, 'congratulations. I know how much you've wanted this.' Laura has longed to be a mother all the time I've known her. 'But . . . Lau, let me get this right. You're pregnant, and Matt's going to carry on being unfaithful to you, and you're going to carry on pretending you don't know?'

'Well, yeah.' She looks defeated. 'Providing, of course, my disco-dancing hormones don't make me stab him or something.' A weak laugh. 'Like I say, I don't blame him. I might have done it myself, except for two things.'

Two things? I raise an eyebrow and she

holds up two pretty, manicured fingers.

'One: we were trying for a baby. If I'd cheated and I'd got pregnant, well . . . I wouldn't know whose it was, would I? And that would be *bad*. Two: don't laugh.'

Laugh? I have never felt so serious. I can't speak. She goes on, 'Two: I haven't . . . I haven't got the guts for it. I had a chance, you know. But I couldn't do it.'

'Of course you couldn't,' I say softly, and then, 'Bastard.'

Who am I kidding? This is me, this is what I'm doing. I may as well *be* Matt, the cause of her hot tears, her crumbling self-esteem. I feel sick.

I want to find Matt and kill him.

In my mind he is the source, he is the inventor and root cause of all infidelity, adultery, that's what they call it when you're married — ha! Nothing adult about it, especially not in my case, it's all about being that dopey-eyed schoolgirl again.

I hug Laura tight, but when I leave here I call you, and immediately delete the call history, covering my tracks, just as I cover myself with perfume to mask your smell when I go back to my husband.

129

8

You've announced you can spare a 'whole day' for me. You're uncharacteristically excited when you tell me this and we spend ten minutes on the phone, like teenagers arranging a first date.

'What do you want to do?' I ask.

'What do *you* want to do?'

'We could go to the seaside. Blackpool!'

'Oh, please.'

'Okay, your turn.'

'I was thinking a stately home . . . a picnic.'

'Snore!'

'A museum? Art gallery?'

'No, no.'

'You used to like that kind of thing.'

'Well, I was trying to impress you then. Besides, I want fresh air.'

'Okay, you win. Blackpool. I'll pick you up at nine. The usual place.'

★   ★   ★

I don't know what made me suggest it; I find British seaside towns, especially Blackpool, kind of sad. It's not the same place that was

130

captured in muted colours on our childhood photographs: boy posing next to his sand-castle; me in a flowery hat, licking an ice-cream; Mum's bikini seeming to be evidence that summers really *were* hotter then. The Tower imperious in the background against an improbably blue sky.

Everything looks tawdry now. Even though, being half term, it's busy with families, who mill through the arcades and bustle on and off trams just the way we used to, the sour, hung-over taste of stag and hen parties, of bloody fights and half-eaten kebabs, lingers in the air.

'Look at the donkeys,' I frown, 'they don't look happy.' We're walking along the front, the famous Golden Mile, hand in hand, anonymous in the crowd. Slow pressure of your thumb across my knuckles.

You laugh, 'I shouldn't think they are, endless tourists dumping their fat kids on their backs and forcing them to trot up and down all day.' Peering at me, 'I do hope you didn't think you were going to get *me* on a donkey?'

'You, the animal lover? Hardly,' I squeeze your hand, 'but I do think we should get fish and chips.'

'Nah, not fish and chips — mussels. Cockles and mussels. Come on,' and, whistling the song, you pull me to a nearby van where a man in a blue-and-white-striped hat cheerfully takes your money in exchange for two polystyrene cups of unidentifiable seafood bobbing in nostril-stinging vinegar.

Miraculously we find a bench and, looking out over the choppy grey sea, I feel the happiest I've ever been.

★　★　★

'I've told you my stories,' I say when we're walking again. 'Why don't you tell me what you've been doing these past fifteen years?'

You take my hand to your lips and kiss it.

'Nothing as important as what I'm doing now.'

It's not an answer, really, I know this, but I like it and I accept the silence you obviously want to offer, because it gives me the opportunity to really look at you. You've put on weight, of course, in fifteen years, but you still have the shape of a swimmer: broad shoulders, narrow waist. Your clothes hang on you in a way I've never seen on another man, clinging to your shoulders and chest, loose around your flat stomach, which I glimpsed when you stretched after getting up from the bench. A neat line of hair snaking to your waistband. You still have a body that I ache to touch, giving me a physical, smarting sensation made all the more acute by the fact that you permit it so infrequently. You're not a 'touchy-feely' person, you told me this all those years ago, so when you do bestow contact, affection, I'm pathetically grateful to receive it.

Everyone has one feature, I think, that makes them attractive in a way unique to them. Yours is your eyes: the colour of dull steel, of stone, of the undulating Irish sea. One minute impenetrable, the next, flickering with mischief, glinting. I want to make it my life's work to put light in those eyes. To make them burn.

★ ★ ★

The wind has blown sand into our hair and our skin is covered in a film of salty spray. You suggest a shower, but we'll have to go back to yours for that, of course (said with a wink). In the car I trot out my feeble married-woman lines ('I can't, I shouldn't') and this time you're the one doing the persuading, in your calm, logical way. 'You've done it already. What difference does one more time make?'

But your driving isn't calm, it's fast and erratic, and when we reach your house, as soon as the door closes we fall into each other.

★ ★ ★

There are things to do, at home. There is cooking, and paying bills, and touching up the paintwork on the skirting boards, and there is always, always cleaning to do.

When we argue, I clean. When I feel guilty, I clean. At least I can be a good wife in this one way, if in no other, is what I tell myself. But then I catch myself wiping a work surface and shying away from the very back, or hoovering around the sofa but not under it, or brushing crumbs into the air, and I realise, I am like my mother after all. All show, and no real effort.

So I scrub and scrub until my hands are raw, deliberately using bleach although I am allergic to it. No gloves. My hands swell and turn red, angry. I look at them: scarlet woman. My eyes stream. The bathroom gleams.

★ ★ ★

There are no things to do, with you, except philosophise, posture (we make each other and ourselves laugh with our grand ideas

— our plans for world domination — the sweeping pictures we paint with words), look at art, talk about books. We drink wine, we drink coffee. We lie silently listening to music: Dylan, and Janis Joplin, and Tchaikovsky. We watch *Manhattan*, and *Annie Hall*, smoking and crying and laughing.

You ask me to move in with you, but you 'won't be the reason' why I leave my marriage. I tell you you're not, it's on the rocks anyway. But I'm unsure, in my heart, how true this is. I think you've watered the seeds of decay that were already there, that exist in the soil of any long-term relationship — the petty disagreements, the small daily grievances and irritations — most people leave them covered and get on with managing the surface; you've just turned everything over and brought them to light.

I wonder aloud if this craziness that is you and me can be sustained.

(Mari's words in my ears: 'Same shit, different pair of shoes under the bed.')

'Who cares?' you shrug. 'Why not try?'

The answer to 'why not', of course, is Dave. His pleading eyes. Even when we argue, when I deliberately provoke him in my vain efforts to get him to do or say something that will justify the way I'm treating him, his eyes are always saying 'please'. I stop being able to look at them.

The trouble is that love comes as a deceiver, a flatterer, a cheat. It makes you believe you are the only two people in the world who have ever felt it. Felt *this*. Okay, other people have been in love, you might say, but no one has felt *this*. No one feels like we do.

The trouble is, everyone is saying that. You may have said it yourself several times, but by the next time you've forgotten.

Love is a great eliminator of memory.

I love you.

That's all.

*   *   *

Guilt infects my sleep. In my dreams, Dave is flicking through photographs and he finds one of you. I move to cover it, but I can't reach.

In the photograph, your back is to the camera and your head is turned over your shoulder, as though someone has just called your name. There is a surprised look on your face. Dave's fingers rest on this miniature version of you, his hand bigger than the whole of you. He touches your shoulder as though trying to unpeel you from the picture, turn you around, see you front-on.

My heart pounds, full of excuses and lies, but nothing comes out of my mouth, and I feel as though I'm drowning, and then I wake up with a sudden feeling of having been winded.

The realisation of what I've done is heavy in the pit of my stomach. And small and dark, the realisation that it can't be undone.

★   ★   ★

The times before you arrived again are a distant country, filled with innocence.

There was such an overwhelming sense of relief when you reappeared that I never stopped to think what the effects on my normality would be. It was as though for years I'd been holding my breath without realising it, and finally I was allowed to exhale.

In the intoxication of release I saw only magic, nothing sinister, nothing that could do any harm.

When you convince yourself that something is 'meant to be', when something feels so good that it can't possibly not be 'right', it absolves you of some of the guilt. In some strange way you also imagine that it could not possibly hurt the other person. The Other Person, The Husband, suddenly relegated to

Third Party status. It — The Thing, The Feeling — is ethereal, other-worldly: surely it can't touch your husband, and all the base matter of your earthly life.

But it's foolish now to continue to believe that you don't affect my everyday existence. When an ordinary evening on the sofa descends into tears; when Dave's concerned, if slightly irritated 'What's *wrong* with you?' elicits only an animal cry that he can't understand the meaning of, or doesn't want to.

I try to tell myself that he hasn't noticed anything, but he's started getting up earlier. They say getting up excessively early or staying up late means you're avoiding your bed and what it represents, and ours has been the scene of, apart from the obvious, some of our most important conversations, our closest cuddles.

I, on the other hand, although struggling with sleep, lie in; avoiding reality, I suppose.

Some days I'm jaunty, springing around the house unable to stop myself from whistling Dolly Parton's 'Here You Come Again', a foolish grin on my face. Other days I'm morose, I either rattle about, a bear in a too-small cage, or sit on the sofa for interminable minutes, staring at the wall.

Dave mostly ignores the bad moods and

tries to take advantage of me when I'm cheerful. Sometimes, I let him. I lie under him while he makes love to me in that way you never do: with tenderness, with hand-holding and hair-stroking. He makes love to me so *considerately* it makes me want to cry. And when he rolls away, sometimes I do cry, snuffling secretly into the pillow, because I've realised that the pendulum has swung and I feel as though I'm being unfaithful ... to *you*.

★ ★ ★

He asks me why I don't read in the bath anymore. How could I read? I'm in a trance, letting the water wash over me, sink into me, make grooves in my skin. Watching myself change. My hands, my feet wrinkle. Like ageing.

I visualise scenarios, each one unbearable. Leaving Dave seems impossible, him finding out about you even worse. But letting you go now is unthinkable.

I hear him down in the kitchen, running water, rattling pill bottles. Does he have a headache? Every morning?

Do I only feel guilty because your mark is on me? Under my hair, under my clothes, on the soft part of my shoulder, just above the collarbone, waiting to be discovered or to disappear, whichever comes first. Loitering on me, heavy with risk. A purplish mark with no other explanation. Look closely, see teeth marks.

I look at it obsessively every time I pass the mirror. Am I checking that it is fading, or hoping that it isn't?

Because it is proof of you: proof that you were here, that for a few seconds you abandoned your control.

* * *

Unable to sleep, I try a trick Dave once told me. Deep breaths, in, out. Count backwards from 300 in threes. Used as a memory test, but also a good relaxation aid apparently, although I'm sure it works better for people like him who are maths-minded. 'The word woman and the numbers man', he used to call us when we first got together. 300. 297. 294.

Grunt. Creak. He rolls over.

291.

Behind my squeezed-shut eyes, reversing trios of sheep stumble over fences.

Concentrate. If you make a mistake you have to go back to the beginning.

288, 285, 282.

Slow down; the aim is not to get back to zero. I should be asleep before then.

Count the days, weeks, months, since we — what? Restarted? Is that the word for what we've done? What do I use as zero? The first time we slept together? Or that first supermarket collision, that dinner, that kiss?

243. 240.

Count back to countless instances of wishing for you. Do they count? Delirious with half-sleep, words and numbers whir in my head.

Dave's soft snoring. The shape of him under the sheet.

Who am I kidding, I don't have to strain to think of it — I know the dates, I know the days, weeks, months. I know the years. I know your number. Your phone number, postcode, birthday and car reg (then, and now). They're imprinted on me, my brain the tattooed wrist of a prisoner. Marked for life.

Hurtling towards zero, no sign of sleep. 37, 33, 30. Thirty, my age, that pivotal age imbued with meaning. A conversation with you, lying in a bed not like this one, playing our own game with numbers.

'Remember when you said I was fourteen going on twenty-five? Does that mean I'm now thirty going on . . . forty-one?'

You laughed at the barely perceptible

141

pause. 'Maths never was your best subject.'

'Cheek. Well?'

'I don't think so . . . I think you've caught yourself up.'

'Seriously . . . have I turned out how you thought I would?'

'To tell you the truth,' (whenever you start a sentence like this, I always get the unnerving feeling that everything you've said before was a lie), 'I never really thought about you growing up.'

Thirty. My brother Alex passed that milestone, two years ago. He's grown old disgracefully, as the saying goes. He doesn't know how to be in his thirties; it feels wrong to him, he says, like wearing someone else's clothes.

Once, when he was drunk, Alex slurred to me that he'd always secretly assumed that he would die at the age of twenty-nine, if not before. I didn't want to tell him that in a dark place in my mind I'd thought the same thing. He didn't seem the type to ever grow up. He told me that when he woke up, aged thirty, he felt some small relief but mostly disappointment. He felt lost.

30, 27. I think about you at twenty-seven and me at fourteen.

24. Wait. Go back. Ticking off fingers under the covers. Days since that afternoon in your

bed. Days since I . . . stop. Count weeks. I sit up. There'll be no sleeping now.

Late. It's not a word Dave was ever fond of.

I'm going to be late.

It's too late.

I'm late.

I'm not keen on it in its present context either.

I'm late.

Late, the word welling in my head, in my mouth; its connotations with death, with history, unavoidable. *The late Fiona Worthing*, I think.

I don't know what makes me tell him, and I instantly regret it, but it just feels too big a word, a concept, to contain.

'Dave,' I shrug him awake, 'Dave. I've just realised . . . I'm late.'

'Late?' he repeats. 'You mean . . . ?'

When we've talked about children, we've always brushed them away under another holiday we must take, or something we decided we desperately needed for the kitchen. The shining hopefulness that the word 'late' puts into his eyes fills me with surprise. And it finds no reflection in mine.

While my heart is sinking, while my insides are all churned up, he is smiling. The ghost of a child that to me is just cells, cells and blood, a problem to be dealt with; for him it has eyes, and a name. Oh God. He is visualising it, feeling it, he already has the child in his arms, on his knee, in the garden kicking a ball. Jesus. I feel like I can't breathe.

This is how the distance between us is illuminated, but still only I can see it.

★ ★ ★

'You should do a test.'

I'm making tea in the morning and the kettle is loud, so I pretend not to have heard him. I pull my dressing gown tighter around my stomach.

'I said, you should take a test,' he repeats, coming up behind me and squeezing my hand even as it clenches around the edge of the worktop.

'Mmm.' I make as non-committal a sound as I can muster. 'Well, you know, I'm not *that* late.'

It becomes one of those conversations that you think is finished but then starts again, later, exactly where it was left, with no preamble or warning. Ruining a perfectly good Saturday.

'Five days is a long time for you, though, isn't it?' he says, suddenly, while we're in the garden reading the newspapers. I raise the arts pages so he won't see my frown. *For me?* I think to myself. Since when does he know what's normal and not normal for me and my menstrual cycle? I suddenly resent that this man knows anything about me, let alone such personal information. It's as though he's not my husband, it's like he's someone I've just met.

Eventually, when he brings it up again while I'm parking the car at the supermarket, I snap.

'I'll buy the bloody test, okay? I'll do it in the morning.' I look at his face and feel sorry, so I say more gently, 'It's better to do them in the morning, that's what they say. We want to be sure, don't we?'

What's weird is that he doesn't question any of it. He doesn't bother to count the days, for example, whereas I do this obsessively. I can see my cycle as a bold, bright diagram emblazoned across my brain and there, right in the middle, you, me, bed. It wasn't him, on that day. It was you. You, me, tangled bodies, wet hair, bed.

It doesn't seem to occur to Dave to even wonder aloud about the fact that he and I are always careful. Oh yes, I use condoms with my husband. Not with you, but with my husband, always.

I'm annoyed at him for not hurling these

things at me. And I'm annoyed at him for wanting this baby real.

★ ★ ★

That night, I dream. Underwater.

Swim towards you with bloodied hands, wipe them on your face. *You did this.*

In the morning, I wake to pain, and warmth, like comfort.

Red.

I find myself weeping with relief that Dave still can't read; mistaking it for grief, he holds me. Sitting in our bed, in my blood, I sob harder. I can't have this kindness.

'There'll be other times,' he whispers, 'other months. We have all the time in the world.'

With a deep breath, I push him away.

The next few days make it obvious I need to leave. The 'non-baby', as Dave has taken to calling it bitterly, has become a block between us, a boulder we can't get around.

'You knew what you were signing up for,' I tell him. 'I was clear from the start.'

'Yes, but I never knew why. Maybe it would help me understand if I knew why.'

'But you didn't care! You didn't ask then, and it's too late to ask now. You've married me now — it's not fair to ask me to change. Sold as seen.'

I haven't had to tell him about you. I'm glad, for selfish reasons, that I don't have to say: 'I've been having an affair.' I don't want to admit to myself that that's what it is. That that's all it is.

We talked about it once, about how we would feel if one or the other of us were unfaithful. It's only a suitable subject of conversation for a couple in the very early stages, when it seems the most remote possibility. It's an 'in the pub' conversation, along with 'what would be the first thing you'd buy if you won the lottery?' and 'which of my friends do you find most attractive?' — another one that can only be had very early in relationships, and even then it's risky.

It was the classic debate: which is the worse infidelity, a one-off dalliance or an ongoing affair? A drunken, 'it meant nothing' fumble or falling in love? We'd disagreed, but amiably, because either seemed so unlikely to happen to us. To other people, but not to us, lacing our fingers together across the table in the pub, by the fire.

Dave: 'It would be worse if you'd fallen in love.'

Me: 'Nah, the one-nighter is worse.'

'How'd you figure that?'

'Because that would mean you'd risked everything we have for something that didn't even mean anything.'

'Yeah, but it's just physical. It's the heart stuff that really hurts.'

★ ★ ★

When I do try to tell him how I feel, that too is selfish. An honest voice inside me lists my reasons:

I want him to understand. To *pity* me.

I want someone else to feel the great gaping loss that I feel, of loving and not being sure of being loved in return.

I want *him* to leave *me*, want *him* to break us up.

★ ★ ★

He's not going to let me get away with that. He won't let me get the words out.

'I know what you're going to say.'

'Why do you always interrupt me?'

'I know what you're going to say.'

'Maybe you don't.'

'I do.'

'I don't — '

'You don't love me anymore.'

'You're putting words in my mouth.'

'I can say you don't love me but I can't hear you say you don't love me.'

'That doesn't make — '
'Sense? I know. So?'
'But I do. I do — '
'Don't. Don't say that either.'
And that is all the talking.

★ ★ ★

I've told him I'm going and that it's 'for the best', but I'm not sure. His confused face says it's not best for him. I divide my belongings into two sets of boxes: one for Mari's, which is to be my 'decoy home', the place Dave thinks I'm going, the address my post will be redirected to, the home Dave will call if he needs me; and one for your house. I want to bring as few things as possible to yours because it is complete as it is. I don't want to crowd you, at least not with things that hold traces of the life I had before.

All my things are touched in some way by Dave. I can almost see his prints on them. But your prints are on me, and everything has changed, and no shower or bath can make me clean, now.

★ ★ ★

There is a photo of the two of us at Aphrodite's Rock in Cyprus. Dave is

149

squinting in the sun, and we are clinging to each other as though afraid that the same foam that gave birth to the goddess of love might jealously snatch one of us away. When I look at photos of the two of us, from holidays when it was just us, I often try to remember who took them. Who Dave waved the camera at with 'please?' in his smile. Were they English? German? Greek? What did they look like? Why didn't we ask their name? Someone we didn't know pointed the shutter at us, snapped us, shot us. Some stranger created an image of us.

We exist — together — only in someone else's line of sight.

★ ★ ★

I spend almost an hour cuddling Bella, while Dave waits upstairs.

I hadn't really thought about the fact that leaving Dave means leaving Bella. Taking her with me is not an option — I know how *you* feel, or rather don't feel, about animals — and besides, Dave thinks I'll be living in Mari's little one-bedroom flat.

When we adopted Bella, she looked more like a lamb than a puppy. Her fur, which would later grow long and golden, lay in white curls tight against her tubby body.

Taking her home was the only time Dave ever criticised my driving.

He sat in the back seat with her box beside him, one hand resting protectively on top of it, while she scrabbled around inside.

Mostly he spoke to her, in soothing tones: 'It's alright, baby', 'Soon be home'.

★   ★   ★

Dave has made his face vacant, that's the only way I can describe it. He doesn't really drink, never smoked, but he takes pills, sometimes. I downplay it, don't think about it, because he downplays it.

The first time I saw him do it, we were getting on a flight. We drove to Nice (hours upon hours of French motorway, wind skimming our hair through the sunroof, listening to Dave's Genesis and Pink Floyd CDs on rotation) so it must have been Cyprus, I think that was the first time we flew together. To calm his nerves, he said. I was a little spooked but he was blasé about it. 'It's not always tranquillisers,' he said, 'not often even, mostly painkillers,' as though this was okay.

Dave put his back out at work. He was a get-stuck-in kind of manager, so even though he didn't need to lug boxes in the storeroom,

151

that's exactly what he would do on delivery day, sleeves rolled up and beads of perspiration decorating his face and neck.

Following this injury, when it became obvious neither rest nor physio was really working, he was prescribed strong painkillers. He'd just kept taking them, he said.

They made him numb, and he liked it. As our marriage progressed, it became one of those facts: he had his pills; I was numb anyway.

I remember thinking, and I think it now, how typical it was of Dave. Even his worst habit, the closest thing he had to an addiction, was legal and on prescription. Or at least, it used to be; I don't know where he gets the stuff from these days. I can't question him because he just gives me that pointed look that says considering the chemicals Mari and I ingested in our teens, I should keep quiet. Its purpose only to make him even more placid than he is by nature. I suddenly feel angry, and cruel, and pity him, and then I feel more angry at myself for feeling all of those things. It's time to leave.

★　★　★

I push my face into Bella's fur, murmuring in her ear, just in case she can understand. 'I'm sorry,' I whisper. 'I love you.' She smells of grass, and warmth. She licks my ear, her snuffling breath covering my face.

'Baby, baby,' I coo, hugging her neck, tickling her tummy, stroking each paw carefully in turn. 'Be good. Look after him.'

Is this my idea of fair? I wonder. I get you, so I leave him the dog?

I want him to shout at me. Beg me to stay, maybe, even though we both know I won't. He is breaking me up with silence.

As I wrench open the door to put the last box in the car, he appears at the bottom of the stairs. When he speaks, it is quiet but clear, and after so much silence hits me like a thunderclap.

'Fiona,' he says, 'I'll always be here.'

9

Even when your life is on the brink of change, when nothing feels normal anymore, you still have to go and do the things that normal people do. You have to go to work. You have to get in your car and make the familiar short drive, weaving in and out of lethargic traffic, in the knowledge that stuffed into the boot is a case, like a secret, and inside the case are the pieces of your world that you're ready to transport to a new place, a new normal.

I'll bring my stuff over tonight. The message I sent you this morning, depressingly pedestrian. I wanted to add kisses or say 'can't wait!' but it seemed wrong, somehow, like laughing at a funeral.

Great. I'll cook Chinese, you'd responded, and I'd wanted something else, expected more, but what?

Our office is open-plan and I'm glad of the noise and distraction, the presence of others that means I have to work, or at least appear to, stabbing at computer keys, eyes fixed on the screen, making calls, scribbling notes in my diary. Surrounded by the usual chatter and activity, I can move through a day that looks to outsiders like any other, instead of The Day I Leave My Husband.

It's a standard office, white desks and black chairs, a study in monochrome uniformity and impersonality, but we have this embarrassing system whereby every time someone makes a sale, a bright yellow balloon is tied to their desk. I'm so industrious that by lunchtime there's a bloom of them obliterating my view of the person opposite me.

Dan, the facilities guy who occasionally mans reception, approaches my desk, pushes the balloons to one side and peers at me. In his disinterested monotone he announces: 'There's a visitor for you.'

'What?'

'You're not expecting anyone?'

'I don't think so.' I flick through my diary, a superficial gesture since I know there's nothing in it. 'Who is it? A client?' But clients rarely come to the office.

'She didn't say. Didn't look like a client.'

I feel a rush of relief at the word 'she' — for a moment I'd thought it might be Dave, making some grand gesture to persuade me against what I'm going to do. A huge bouquet, sad eyes, and everyone here would coo and tilt their heads and think I was heartless if I didn't fall into his arms.

'Old or young?'

'Young.' Could be Laura, or Mari? But they'd call, wouldn't they? I stand up, straightening my skirt and tucking my hair behind my ears, and head for the lift with an irritated sigh.

At the clicking of my heels across the marble floor of reception, the girl hunched on the visitors' bench looks up.

The young woman is about twenty-three or twenty-four, judging by her complexion, the way she is dressed and a certain awkwardness in her movements as she stands up. But her eyes look older. Her eyes, which were fixed on the floor, now swivel towards me.

'Can I help you?' I start to walk towards her, hugging a notebook to my chest.

'Are you,' she looks back at the ground as though reading my name from it, 'Fiona?' She swallows. 'Fiona Palmer?'

It's a long time since anyone has used my maiden name, and perversely it brings an image of Dave swimming before my eyes. I can feel colour rising in my throat.

'Why?' I demand. *What is this?*

'Are you?' There's desperation in her eyes. Hands stuffed in her jeans pockets, legs twisted over one another, she kicks at her own heel. She's thin and fragile and for a second I'm afraid she might knock herself over.

I nod slowly, then say, 'Well, I used to be.

Why?' I look carefully at her eyes, pools of dirty grey water. 'What do you want?'

'You used to go to Our Lady of Compassion?'

'Yes.' I motion for her to step away from the reception area, into the quiet, narrow side corridor. I move to steer her by her skinny elbow but think better of it.

'I need to talk to you,' she whispers, 'I need your help.'

'What's this about?'

'Henry Morgan.' She swallows and looks at me carefully. At the mention of your name, as always, my heart dances in my chest but there is something new there: fear. She starts to speak quickly, eyes searching my face. 'Did he . . . were you taught by him? Have you seen him since?'

'Look, I don't know who you are, but — '

Before I can say anything else she thrusts a piece of paper into my hand and starts to walk away, slowly, backwards, as though from a predator. As I unfurl the note she says,

'Alice.'

★   ★   ★

You're in your conservatory, painting, when I arrive, letting myself in through the side gate. I stand in the garden for a moment, a small

157

suitcase in my hand, watching you. You are stunning to me in your self-sufficiency. I've never seen anyone who looks so entirely comfortable in their own skin, or so pleased with their own company. Even my little bag feels superfluous to this scene, and I hold it behind me, willing it to shrink.

Classical music is streaming from a digital radio in the corner; I don't recognise the piece, but you know it, because you are softly whistling along. There is so much you know that I don't; I wish I could climb into your brain and plunder it, taking out all the pieces that are there that would make me richer, make me more like you.

A glass of white wine stands on the side table, droplets of condensation glinting in the late afternoon light. You are frowning with concentration, making broad, sweeping strokes with your brush; the easel looks like an extension of you, or a mirror, reflecting your brilliant white shirt, your wide-legged stance.

I tap on the glass and you look around and break into a smile. There is a spot of paint on your nose, and one on your sleeve. Your hair is too long, the ends curling over your collar.

'Hello, hello,' you beam, opening the conservatory doors to me, and then you are lifting me up, suitcase and all, and holding me so high that your face is pressed into my stomach. I feel like a doll; I feel light as air. I laugh and run my fingers through your hair, resolving to cut it, but first, imagining washing it, sitting in the bath with you, or standing in the shower, hands full of soap, bodies pressed together.

You put me down and kiss me, easing the suitcase from my hand. There is a rolling rhythm to our kisses that is missing from the staccato kisses I've become used to in marriage. Our kisses begin slowly, softly, then there is urgency, then one or both of us pulls away, then we start again, and there is a sense of moving higher each time. In our kisses I am always conscious of myself, and always trying to impress you.

It's not that the rest of the world, of my life, matters less when I'm with you; it's that it actually ceases to exist.

So when you whisk a blanket off the sofa and lay it on the conservatory floor; when you push up my shirt, dip your fingers in paint and trace them over my stomach, smearing me with your initials; when you hold my hands above my head and kiss my throat; surrounded by glass, and the illusion of open air, sunlight bathing our movements but with only the birds as witness, nothing exists anymore, not even myself. Only you.

My closed eyes, my lips, my body become a hymn: *only you*.

When I come to from a hazy sleep, wrapped in a blanket, stomach sticky with paint and sweat, the last of the sun is kissing the roses at the back and the front of the house is in gloom.

You are industrious in the kitchen, your hands deep in some blood-coloured marinade, pulling out strips of meat and dropping them with a flourish into the sizzling wok.

There's an ice bucket; champagne; two chilled glasses.

'For when you've unpacked,' you grin.

'Oh, and Fee?' as I back silently out of the room. You hand me a flower, picked from the garden, its heavy head lolling on a delicate stalk. I cup it in my palm as one might a baby animal. Its petals are a perfect, blush-coloured pink. Woven around the stalk is a piece of Hessian string and carefully attached to it, a key. A front door key.

'Welcome home, sunshine.' You kiss me softly on the forehead and turn back to your cooking.

★　★　★

It's harder unpacking a few things in someone else's house, than moving your entire belongings to an empty place. You have to work out where things *fit*; what the rules are around here.

I start with the clothes, because I know this is where I will struggle to make things look right. Your wardrobe is so masculine, and ordered. There is no place for my scarves and belts and cardigans. Neatly pressed shirts hang in blocks of white, grey, Oxford blue. Then trousers: I run a finger along their perfect creases. A jacket; a raincoat. And at the back, under wrapping that crackles to my touch, a tuxedo. *When did you last wear that?* I wonder. *Who were you with?*

I feel as though I am finding out secrets, and with this thought comes an itch, an urge, that I try to put to the back of my mind.

I have *never* pictured you ironing a shirt. The thought of it makes me laugh, but also feel sad. Your clothes, without you in them, look different. They could be anybody's clothes. I think about the hours you must spend making everything so neat, only to then roll up your sleeves in that way you do, only to end up crumpled.

Our colours clash. I try hanging up a navy-blue shirt dress, the smartest thing I own; it makes the whole wardrobe look untidy. Taking it out again I turn to the drawers, looking for the one I know you'll have left empty for me. I know the drill; I have done this before, after all. First there is a drawer, and a shelf in the bathroom; in time, possessions merge, the lines of two people's histories blur and they meld, like their things, into each other.

But each drawer in turn, from your balled-up socks to your folded T-shirts to your jeans laid out flat, one pair on top of another, one fold at the knee, right down to the predictable drawer left empty, each makes me realise how far away that day is.

I hurriedly roll up my clothes and squeeze them in, underwear, shirts, pyjamas, everything, and press down tightly so I can close the drawer. I stand back and look. It's as though I was never there.

Now for the book shelves: some things we own are the same, and these are the things that make me smile. At first I leave my (invariably newer, less dog-eared) versions of books and CDs that you own too in the box, but then I take a couple out and put them on the shelf, just to see how they look.

The Beatles' *White Album*. Yours, and mine.

The Catcher in the Rye. Yours, and mine.

They sit next to each other like long lost twins reunited. It's satisfying, like finishing a jigsaw, or arranging flowers in a vase with perfect symmetry.

But these are just pieces, neat corners in a thousand-piece puzzle whose final image is a mystery. I'm surrounded by evidence of a life you had before I came, before you knew me.

I'm suddenly aware that I'm holding my breath, and I lie carefully down on the floor, staring up at the ceiling. *Don't*, I tell myself. But a familiar temptation is creeping up on me; I feel heat in the roots of my hair and behind my eyes. I hear your soft whistling from two rooms away, listen to the pottering sounds of the kitchen, and calculate how long it would take you to get from there to here.

Carefully, quietly, I begin.

I don't know what makes me start. Insecurity? Curiosity? Habit? It's a habit I've had in all my relationships since Peter, except Dave, and Mari tells me all people (or maybe only all women) do it, only some admit it to their friends and some don't. We call it Investigating. I don't even remember how it started back with Peter, only that it became as much a part of our relationship as sex, as arguments, as cooking and walking and drinking and laughing. It was a sickening thrill: all the more exciting when he was in the next room, or could come home any minute.

I am adept at investigating. I leave no traces; I am methodical, and memorise every item's exact place and angle. The giveaway tilt of a photograph album; the dull green flashlight of a recently thumbed mobile phone; these clues can be enough to spark a question, and while usually easily discharged, questions are not to be desired by The Investigator.

It's a crazy thing to do, of course: there is no right outcome. If you don't find anything, there's relief but it's overwhelmed by guilt for snooping; if you do find something, there's the brief victory of vindication followed immediately by the sinking stomach and the rising taste of bile you get when you're about to be sick.

What am I searching for? With Peter, it was simple: evidence of his infidelities. I'm not sure now which came first: did I start my investigations after his first indiscretion or did I find out what he was up to as a result of one of these searches? It doesn't matter, really; the spiral became addictive. In the part of the stomach where butterflies are felt, there was always something. It hurt, but it was a *feeling*. It was like a mental challenge, a game of attack and defence. I always felt like I was on the edge of a cliff, but God, it was exciting.

With you, it's more complicated. I thumb pages of books; flit through photos, noting the location of ones I might revisit later when alone with more time. But I don't know what exactly it is that I hope for and dread in equal measure; only that I'm looking for pieces of you. More bits of the puzzle.

A memory rises in me of seeing my mum without her make-up. Another, of Peter in the mornings, his hair soft before he put gel in it and went into the world. Dave, being himself, almost from the start. No investigation needed, with him; everything on show.

This is what I want: to know you, under your layers.

There are yearbooks, lined up neatly, in chronological order. This was a trend that started after I left school. I'm surprised you've kept them; I would've thought you'd have found them a vulgar Americanism, like Trick or Treat at Hallowe'en or leaving the 'u' out of words like 'colour' ('It's just lazy,' you used to say. 'How lazy do you have to be to need to write five letters instead of six?').

I flick through the pages, some of them signed, which doesn't surprise me. You were always a 'cool' teacher, after all, and most of the comments reflect this. Am I looking for a comment in girlish handwriting, loaded with meaning? Am I looking for something, someone, in the pictures? I scour the faces but they all look the same. It strikes me how a uniform isn't just clothing, it doesn't just affect the body, it somehow reflects onto and permeates the face, the whole being. The regulation pullovers in their bottle green (in later years, sweatshirts; in later years still, grey with yellow stitching) cast a sickly glow over hundreds of faces: some smooth, some pockmarked; all bored or embarrassed to be photographed.

In every class picture, each separated by a year, you look the same. The same pose, leaning slightly forward while everyone else is upright; forearms lolling on your knees, tie loosened. Unsmiling, staring out the camera. You look like the class rebel.

'Fee,' you call; I jump as if snapped back into the present. A hot, sweet smell, chillies and soy, suddenly fills my nostrils.

'I'll be there in a sec.' I carefully but quickly put everything back in its place. 'Just a couple of bits to finish up.'

I go back to my cardboard box and take out the book that you gave me years ago. Before homing it on the shelf I slip between its pages the note from my pocket: 'Call me — A' and a phone number.

10

Diary: Saturday, 12 December 1992

Morning!

Getting ready to go to HM's house. I've reassured him that I won't repeat my previous bad behaviour, ha ha. I'm wearing a burgundy top, my black Lycra skirt, black tights. He says I've got nice knees. We're supposed to be having a 'committee meeting' about the play, which happens next week. But really he's going to be cooking me lunch and hopefully we'll have a nice chat. God I've actually got butterflies! What does this mean? Every time I hear a car, my heart skips a beat. Waiting . . . bored . . . but excited.

Much, much later!

I've just got back! I'm knackered. Well what can I say? I've had a very nice time. Firstly we had lunch, which was very nice (what a stupid word 'nice' is!) We did a lot of talking, as usual. I've had three or four glasses of wine, with the meal, which is probably why I'm tired. But then again I've had an equal number of cups of coffee, and some biscuits and a Cadbury's Creme Egg. We ended up looking at old photos — God, he hasn't changed a bit! Anyway we were lying on his front room floor for ages, then at some point he put his arm around my shoulders (he says I've got nice shoulders, that is a good compliment coming from him because he's got a bit of a thing about shoulders!), my head was resting on his arm, my hand on his chest and he was kind of making little circles with his fingers. We just kept on talking as normal though, and it was really nice (aargh! There it is again). Our foreheads kept touching and we'd kind of look at each other, laugh, then go back to the original position. We just lay there, and looking back I can't imagine what the hell was going through my mind, or his, come to that. I just know I could have fallen asleep there quite comfortably!

'An 'A' just marks you out as better than the herd. You should be aiming for more than that.' No one had ever said anything like that to me before.

My dad didn't even know what an 'A' was, I'm sure. He left school at fifteen and while he wasn't opposed to education, he just didn't understand it; almost was unaware of its existence, except that there was a building where I and my brother were supposed to show up every day at 9 a.m. When I eventually went to university, the first in the family to do it, he was proud, I think, in his quiet way.

Dad worked hard though, and he had opportunities. He was once offered a big important job in London. London in the late sixties was, to my dad, and probably lots of other people, a mythical place. It seemed almost impossibly distant, requiring a Dick Whittington-style odyssey to get there, but promising vast rewards. He didn't take the job, of course; he met my mother. It's possible he's resented her ever since.

In their wedding photo, still trapped behind glass high up on the shadowy landing, they aren't looking at one another. Dad is staring straight ahead, as though trying to make out the finishing point of a too-distant horizon. Mum is looking coquettishly to the side, eyes tiny under thick black lashes, her bouquet concealing the burgeoning bump that would become Alex.

Dad was a man of few words. 'Actions speak louder than words' was his motto, or would have been, if he ever said that much. His usual 'actions' included doodling over crosswords or tinkering in the garden shed or, in extreme cases of needing to escape the house, fishing with Alex.

Consequently I learned most of his life story from Mum, who would put on a fake posh voice and begin imperiously, 'Your Father always used to . . . ' or 'When Your

Father was young . . . ' It was clear she'd idolised him once, which must have made even more crushing the disappointment she suffered when he failed to deliver her into the glamorous lifestyle he'd seemed to promise.

'Hello Boy, Hello Girl,' Dad would call up the stairs every night, before sinking into silence.

My brother was delivered, so the story goes, by a stern-faced registrar and a trainee Polish midwife, and it took the efforts of both of them to pull him out with forceps. When he was finally dragged screaming into the world, the Polish woman apparently announced: 'It is Boy.'

'Yes, it is,' my father had laughed, and the name stuck. When I came along two years later (much more quickly, so much so that I was almost born into a hospital toilet), Mum and my father had both said immediately, 'It is Girl.'

They still loved each other then, I think.

★ ★ ★

One night Mum and I found each other, coming home.

It was coming up to Christmas and there was something about the coloured lights in people's living room windows that made me sad.

170

People tried too hard to make everything look jolly, in my opinion; there was something depressing about people dressing up their ugly houses in fairy lights and tinsel.

Number one had a fluorescent reindeer sleigh on the roof. Number three: a twiggy rose bush adorned with lights that weren't meant for outdoors and died with a crackle and a hiss the first time it rained. Number five: fake snow, from a can; stencilled words in the window: *Season's Greetings*. These words would stay there, slowly fading, well into the spring.

And everywhere, lights; and always coloured lights. I wanted to live somewhere where there were *white* lights. Laura's house had white lights. I wanted candles, and the smell of wassail, and instead of a tin of Roses next to the electric fire, its contents melting and sticking to the wrappers, real candy canes hanging from a real tree. Perhaps it was true what Mum was always telling me: I was a snob.

Most nights Mum would step into heels and click out onto the street and down to the pub. She went out, not so much for the drink, as for the life. She always suspected there was something going on out there and she had to check, just in case.

'There must be more to life than this,' she had sighed to me more than once.

'Yeah,' I would murmur because although

this was the kind of thing I knew people said all the time, at school, at work, on buses, and although I thought I knew what it meant, I didn't know how you were supposed to reply when your mum said it.

We stood in the street looking at each other in the way people do when they've seen each other out of their usual environment. Like when you see your doctor at the supermarket, small without his heavy oak desk and white coat, or when you see someone off the telly just sitting having a coffee, and you think for a second that you know them.

'Oi you,' she said. 'It's dangerous for you to be walking round the estate at this time of night.'

'Likewise.'

'S'pose we'd best walk together then.'

'S'pose so.'

She didn't ask me where I'd been or who with, just took my hand, linking fingers, and plunged it into her sheepskin pocket, like she used to when I was little.

★ ★ ★

One Sunday Dad taught me how to peel potatoes. First sharpen the knife; then use downward strokes.

'This way, if you slip, you'll only slice your

thumb off,' he said, 'not your whole hand.' He winked. 'Far less messy.'

While I did the potatoes he washed the carrots, scraped off their skins, shedding them onto an old newspaper at his feet. He looked like a sculptor, whistling softly with the radio, his glasses slipping down his nose.

Looking back, I can see now that my father was a man at odds with the modern world. Technology baffled him; twentieth-century society defeated him. He sought to prove himself to me by showing and sharing skills I didn't have, and often didn't need; by telling stories that he thought would make me look up to him.

'But Dad,' I would say, 'I can do that on the computer,' or 'they have machines that do that now, you know,' or 'they sell them in Asda already chopped and wrapped'. And he would shake his head and tell me that when he was younger than me he spent his Sundays wringing the necks of chickens, plucking them, scraping and cleaning out their insides.

* * *

She left, of course, for a while. We weren't supposed to talk about it. I didn't even note it in my diary.

For a week I became brisk and industrious,

173

in a soundless round of cooking, washing, ironing and organising. Alex retreated into his room, into his head. Dad didn't seem to change one bit.

I immediately assumed they were getting divorced. There didn't seem to be an in-between state, to me: there was marriage, and there was divorce. It would be okay; lots of people had divorced parents. Mari had never even met her dad, that's what she told me. She used to say even her mum didn't know who he was, but I knew that wasn't really true, I think she just said it for effect.

So why should it bother me?

The house became quiet when she left, me in my room, my brother in his, the two of us appearing and disappearing as we needed to, to make a Pot Noodle or to take out the washing. Dad in the living room with the sound turned down on the TV, peering at his crossword in flickering light.

Slowly all the things that had driven me crazy about her, all the ways in which she was different to Laura's mum, for instance; within a week of wearing her shoes, I started to understand them.

The truth is, she didn't *fit* with us. She was too colourful, too noisy. She was too much herself. Who wouldn't be driven crazy by

Dad's silence, and his piles of half-completed crosswords clipped from the papers, gathering dust? Or Alex's refusal to wash his hair, the weird smell from his room, his gloomy, tuneless guitar strumming?

And me: all my clutter and clatter. The make-up stains I left around the sink and on towels; my magazines everywhere; my superior attitude to everyone else in the family, my pretentious over-use and over-enunciation of words like '*act*-ually' and '*ult*-imately'.

Even so, it took me a while to see why she had to go and cause such a *drama*. Dad was so passive, so inoffensive, to me it was like saying you were trapped when the cage door had always been open. But slowly, as I adopted the routines of domesticity that came with no respite and (worse) no reward, I came to see how your own life could trap you, and you could be complicit in your own capture.

She left with only a small bag. With hindsight I see this was because she always knew she would come back; at the time, I began to imagine her as some kind of wandering spirit, an easy-going traveller, with gypsy blood and songs in her heart. I began to love her fervently in her absence and, while I wanted her back, I didn't want to be the reason why she couldn't be herself; I didn't want to keep her from a new, exciting world of possibilities.

Each night I would take myself up two flights of stairs, over the same pale green carpet and past the silently hanging photographs, into my room. I'd painted it myself, dark blue, walls and ceiling, and taken the blind down from the skylight, so that when I lay on my back and looked up it would all look like one sky and I would feel as though I was outside.

Every night I lay in bed and looked at the stars, wondering where in the world she was.

★   ★   ★

In the wings, holding the script, I felt like a writer. When the actors got stuck I mouthed the words to them, and they were my words, our words, and each one felt perfect on my lips. Of course some were Charles Dickens's words, and my actors were kids with mostly monotone voices and guileless expressions, but still the thrill — of my name on the programme, of the tremor of applause — was like nothing I'd known before. Even Alex, in the audience, had looked proud as he filed into his seat.

They came dashing off stage in a flurry of face paint and exclamations and I, not for the first time, felt torn between envy (should I have been out there, singing and performing, instead of back here, in my ordinary clothes, prompting?) and superiority (no one else could do what I had done; at least, no one else had been *chosen* to). I glanced across the darkening stage, over the bobbing heads, blonde, brown, black, ginger, anonymous to me, their inane chatter just a mildly distracting hum, and I saw your face; a wink, a smile.

You were mouthing something I couldn't make out. You started making hand gestures like on that TV programme — 'film', 'sounds like', 'three syllables'. I giggled, beckoned, mouthed with an exaggerated mime 'come here', and as the curtain fell and the applause subsided to the sounds of scraping chairs and cooing parents, you dashed and skidded across the confetti-strewn stage and scooped me up in a hug.

'Well done, well done,' you cried. Then with a flourish, 'A triumph!'

I laughed.

'Thanks, but . . . ' the buzz and hum of the other kids in my ear like the batting wings of moths, 'it's a thankless job, this writing lark, isn't it?'

You smiled.

'Oh dear. Sorry, sunshine,' a gentle thumb

on my chin, 'should I have pulled you onto the stage to take your bow?'

'God, no.' I conjured a shudder. 'I'm not one for basking in the limelight.'

'Maybe not, but you ought to have a reward. That's what I was trying to tell you before. I've got something for you.' There was that conspiratorial wink again, that twinkle, and you looked genuinely excited. 'I'll give it to you in the car.'

★ ★ ★

Under the streetlight, I looked down at the beautiful wrapping paper — silver, tissue-textured, no Christmas adornments — and felt both thrilled and dismayed.

'I didn't get *you* anything.'

'Don't be daft. Just open it.'

The gift tag read:

It's comforting to know that, in your hands, even an old classic can be improved. Keep the quill quivering! HM x

It was a book: *A Christmas Carol*, of course. A beautiful reprint of the first edition, a collector's edition, with gilt-edged pages and pencil-drawn illustrations. Its covers were dark green leather and a silk ribbon marked page one of the story.

I lowered my face to it: its pages smelled of old bookshops, of pipe smoke and cinnamon.

At home, the presents that waited under the tree for me would be predictable: money stuffed in a card; a jumper. Sweets or chocolate that I used to like but didn't anymore, hadn't eaten for about five years except at Christmas, but I would smile and say 'thanks' and let the sugar dissolve behind my teeth, under my tongue. Yum, yum, and a sickly grin.

Your present was perfect.

Diary: Wednesday, 13 January 1993

Long conversation with HM on the phone. Three things I learned tonight:

He's been setting some of my poems to music. Can't wait to hear them!

He used to have nightmares about abacuses (?!). Feels like that should be abaci or something, actually . . . where is Sister Ignatius with her Latin grammar when I need her?

When the Fates separate us in a shipwreck, we'll end up washed up on the same desert island. This is what he says.

Going to bed consumed by the biggest smile ever.

It was early, for me, for a Saturday. I'd been at Mari's but even Todd was too stoned to have a decent conversation with. I'd felt bored. For a while now I'd had a sense there was something more for me, I just didn't know where to look for it. When I tried to say this aloud, everyone either burst out laughing or stared at me, wild suspicion in their eyes.

It wasn't long after kicking-out time — kicking-off time, in places.

Curtains were drawn over pubs doing lock-ins. The streets were strewn with chip wrappers and cigarette ends. It was cold and my walk was brisk and jumpy; I stared down at my feet in their black laced-up boots, dodging broken glass. I hopped from foot to foot, even as I paused to pet a bony dog picking listlessly at the remains of a fish supper.

It was then that I saw her.

Or maybe I heard her, first — I don't remember. There was a low moan, as though from someone in pain.

I glanced down the alley and froze.

At first I thought she was in trouble, and I started to call out, but in the next instant found my own hand clapped over my mouth.

My mum was against a wall, her head turned to one side, her mascara smudged across the bridge of her nose.

The man kissing her neck was too small for her, in her heels. He was wearing a dirty coat, and his hair hung like pieces of rope on his shoulders. His hand was up her skirt.

I remembered a family summer, two weeks in a holiday camp, the four of us walking back from the sand dunes, rinsing off under freezing showers and laughing. The smell of frying onions and the 'clink, fizz' of different flavours of pop being opened. Cherry-ade, lime-ade. Pineapple-ade.

I turned away and looked up at the stars.

★ ★ ★

With one hand I scrabbled in the bottom of my bag, among sweet wrappers and hair slides, for coins; the other I held out over the road, a desperate flag to the passing taxis.

I recited your address to the driver as though reading lines from a play, and in minutes I was standing shivering at your door.

'Can I come in?' I tried to make my voice sound normal, but I don't know what I must have looked like, or what you thought, having me turn up uninvited in the middle of the night.

'I suppose you'd better, now you're here,' you said simply, watching the taxi turn around and drive back up the street.

It was only when you touched my cheek with your thumb that I realised my face was streaked with tears.

Your house was warm, and I sank onto the sofa.

'I thought there was more for me,' I said, 'but there isn't.'

You thought about this for a while.

'You're a bit young for a mid-life crisis, aren't you?'

I smiled weakly, in spite of myself.

'I don't know. I feel *old*.'

I was suddenly aware that I looked different to how you will have seen me before: this was my Saturday-night self, in clothes I wore to try to impress kids I didn't understand. I tugged miserably at the thick black tights, the laces on my boots. I wiped my eyes and a slick of charcoal make-up striped the back of my hand.

You brought me a cup of tea and my words started to tumble out, each phrase followed self-consciously by an apology or a retraction, hanging behind it like a shadow.

I was miserable, but I knew I didn't have a proper reason to be. I was sorry.

I felt lonely, but I was lucky to have so many friends. I was ungrateful.

I was sad, but I knew there were people

who had far less than me. *Just ignore me.*

'It's okay to be hurt,' you said quietly, 'and to admit it. No one can judge you or say you've no right to your feelings.' You stroked my head. 'That's just it, you see — they're *your* feelings.'

But I knew I was an impostor, a fraudulent visitor in the world of the miserable. On the sliding scale of happiness to unhappiness, I knew I was somewhere left of centre. Closer to Laura with her perfect home-life than to Mari who, for all her bravado, had the grief of an absent father and the problems of a dozen screwed-up, drugged-up kids who called themselves 'friends' on her shoulders. Further away still from the kid at school whose little brother was just killed in a car accident. He had real sadness now in his empty eyes, and no one knew what to say to him, which must have made it even worse.

'I shouldn't have bothered you. I'll probably be alright tomorrow. See?' I laughed, 'I can't even do teen angst right.'

'You should let your mum know where you are,' you said, reaching for the phone.

'She's not there.'

You frowned.

'Your dad, then.'

'He won't care. He won't even notice.'

'I think you'd be surprised.' You pushed the

receiver into my hand and I watched you dial, noticing with a little thrill that you knew the number off by heart.

I listened to it ring and, hearing a voice on the click, whispered to you, 'It's Alex.' Then, into the mouthpiece:

'It's me. I'm . . . err . . . I'm at Mari's.' I looked at you; you raised an eyebrow but said nothing. I turned from you slightly and lowered my voice, but knew you could hear me, of course.

'Yeah, well. Just tell Dad, will you? Yeah. I'll be back . . . ' I paused, glancing over my shoulder at your expressionless face. 'What? Yeah, I'm still here. Tell him I'll be home . . . in the morning.' I hung up carefully and passed the phone to you.

You smiled. 'Okay. Come on, kid.'

You headed for the bedroom and I followed; you handed me a T-shirt and left the room while I got changed, but you didn't offer the spare room and I didn't ask.

Climbing under the covers, you said quietly, 'What's this really all about, Fee?'

I thought for a while.

'I'm afraid,' I said. 'I'm afraid because I'm not important, I'm not special. I'm nothing.' And I started to cry again.

You put your arm around me, your breath in my ear.

'You ARE important, you ARE important,' you chanted, rocking me back and forth, 'a gift in a million.' And you held me until sleep took over.

* * *

I woke up at 5 a.m. and I smiled, because this was the time of morning you always said you woke up having dreamt something weird, then found yourself unable to get back to sleep. I waited for you to stir, but you didn't. Perhaps I was your cure. I looked around the room. Everything was in shadow.

I leaned into you and kissed your shoulder. Without opening your eyes you mouthed 'Morning' and pulled me closer. I kissed your mouth, and this time you didn't stop me.

I took your hand and placed it up inside the T-shirt, but you didn't seem to know what to do, it just lay there, like a stone. You were so unlike the boys I knew, the boys of Mari's parties with their hot mouths and insistent fingers.

You kept kissing me, our lips glued grimly together, as though you were afraid that if I pulled away I might see something I shouldn't see.

I opened my eyes and saw you in extreme close-up: your nose, your eyebrows. I closed them again and slid my hand under the covers.

You put your hand over mine, helping me find your rhythm, and I felt anger welling in me. *I can do it*, I thought, *I'm not a child*, so I bit you. I bit your bottom lip, a bite that said *stop it*.

But in a few moments we found our pace, and you made a soft noise, and I thought, *that's it*, I'm affecting you, that's what I want, and when you took your hand away and touched my face, it felt like trust.

* * *

Afterwards, there were more tears, I didn't know why, but you kissed them away and for that moment I felt safe.

* * *

You drove me home, holding my hand all the way, down by the handbrake where no one could see.

Your crooked smile when you dropped me off; almost shy.

I never told you; maybe you knew. It was my fifteenth birthday.

11

The second time I see her, I'm already anticipating that there will be a third time.

I've read my fairy tales, you see; I know these things come in threes. Once the second night has passed, second house has been blown down, second wish has been granted, a child listening to a fairy story waits with gleeful anticipation in the knowledge that the third time is coming, and this will be the time that the prince gets the girl, or the troll is defeated, and everyone lives happily ever after. The third time means something; it can't be ignored.

The second time I see her is innocent enough, and can't even be called an encounter since she doesn't see me.

I've disentangled myself from the bubble you and I have created and walked into town for a dose of reality, to clear my head. You offered to drive me; I declined gently. You protested and asked how long I would be gone.

'An hour or two,' I shrugged, 'that's all. And we have six weeks of holiday coming up, remember?' That is, you do; I have two weeks to take and a job I can turn up late for and come home early from without too many people even noticing. I'm looking forward to seeing more of you but I can't help feeling intensity creeping like a cloak around me.

It's a sort of sense check exercise; just seeing if the world is still there, where I left it. In a small way it's about seeing if I'm still there, too, because as much as I love being holed up in your house with you, I sometimes wonder if when I hit the fresh air I'll wake up and feel different, like after a hangover or a long flight.

Of course, not much in the city has changed: the same bustle and buzz, people laden with oversized department store bags, larger and probably more glamorous than their contents. Painted faces laugh at each other over coffee cups and clinking wine glasses. There is sun today, and a close-fitting heat, so people are outside, dipping into shops only half-heartedly, only for a few moments of air con, sifting listlessly through clothes rails before slipping their shades on and stepping back out into the glare.

It rains so often in this city that when the sun shines everything looks new and clean.

I pass a shop assistant on a break lighting a cigarette, her poise and outfit mirroring those of the mannequin in the window behind her.

She rolls up her sleeves, giving her milky arms five minutes of sun, and sucks in smoke with scarlet lips.

People are gathered around the fountains, kids on skateboards and teenagers necking. There's an end-of-term feeling in town today, and I can't help smiling as it spills over me, and I stop to listen to a cheery busker playing Beatles songs. It's at this moment, through the fine spray of the fountains, that I see her.

She's laughing, and she's with a guy about the same age as her, and both of these facts register immediately as relief. A normal girl; happy. Her name runs through my head like ticker-tape, *AliceAliceAliceAlice*, and I have to stop myself from calling it out. For an instant I want her to see me. Why would that be?

I watch her tossing back her hair, touching the boy on his arm, and I try to burn this new, carefree Alice onto my brain, by way of erasing the other girl who looked at me at my office with pleading eyes. But my feet are edging me in her direction.

The opening chord of 'A Hard Day's Night' suddenly pushes into my consciousness and, distracted, I stop and look around at the busker, and the crowd who have gathered and are dancing around him.

It's only a few seconds, I squint in the

sunlight and when I turn back, she's gone. Like a ghost: gone, but leaving traces, a change in the air.

★ ★ ★

I go to Mari's flat to pick up my post.

'You had a visitor,' she says. The ticker-tape is back, *AliceAliceAliceAlice*, and with it, a thudding in my chest. When you're afraid of something, at the slightest sign it's always the first thing you assume has happened. It's a protection mechanism: if I imagine it, then it's imaginary, ergo not real, so it can't have happened.

'Oh?' is all I can manage. Mari brings me tea.

'Dave,' she says.

'Oh.'

'I think you should talk to him, doll. He's in bits.'

I narrow my eyes.

'I thought you were supposed to be on my side.'

'It's not about sides. Jesus. We're not kids anymore.'

'Ha!'

'What does that mean?'

'Nothing. Forget it.'

'No, come on. Let's have it.' Mari holds her

190

head at a new angle, the spark of a challenge in her eyes.

I've only ever seen Mari angry with me once before. It was a few years ago, we'd come back to her flat from a night out and got stoned. One minute we were laughing then, seemingly from nowhere, she accused me of enjoying 'keeping her where she was'. I'd said something, it had been meant as a compliment; something about her never changing. She exploded. She said I used the fact that she was living in the same flat, that she had the same traits, the same friends, to make myself feel better about where I had got to in life. She said I acted superior.

I'd been confused: if anything, I envied her.

The next morning, she'd laughed it off: 'Jesus, doll. I was out of it. I was talking out my backside. Don't take it to heart.' And with a hug, that had been the end of it.

But now here it is again, and for the first time, something unsettling in her face: disapproval. There's a distance between us that is the size and shape of Dave. I imagine him coming here, sitting on this sofa, taking the cup of tea she's bound to have offered. Maybe something stronger. Mari sympathising. Promising to talk to me.

I take a deep breath.

'Alright. It's just — it's rich, that's all.

Coming from you.' There's more vitriol than I intended in the word *you* but I can't take it back now.

'What does that mean?' she says again, voice rising.

'You. You're the one who's . . . you've always led me into trouble. Egged me on. Revelled in it. Then when something like this happens, you judge me. Do you know what?'

'What?'

'You once accused me of wanting to keep you where you were. Keep you down, in some way.' She's nodding; it hasn't been forgotten, then. 'Well maybe you had it the wrong way around, Mari. Maybe *you've* wanted to keep *me* where I was. The boring little married friend.'

'That's not — '

'Well, fuck it. I can't stay married to keep *you* feeling wild.'

Mari flinches, but says nothing. I take a deep breath and say, a little more calmly, 'You only live once. Remember that? That's what you always used to say.'

'Yes, but babe,' she says, 'you have your life now. Maybe this is it. Your one life, your one shot. Don't throw it away.'

'It's done. It's thrown. Too late.'

'Just *talk* to him.'

'And say what? Why? I can't give him an

instruction manual to make it all better. It was never really broken.'

'So why are you where you are?'

Because I remembered, I think. I remembered what it was like to feel not just that nothing was wrong, but that everything was right. For some reason I don't feel able to say this out loud.

'I don't know. But I ought to work that out before I speak to Dave, don't you think?'

Mari sighs, 'Well, at least we agree on that.'

When I get up to leave, she stops me at the door with a hand on my arm.

'There's always a bed for you here, you know that, don't you?'

'Thanks for the offer,' I say, 'but I won't need it.' We hug, but something has shifted between us, and however hard we hold onto each other, we can't put it back into place.

★ ★ ★

'Dave's been ringing. I have to talk to him at some point.'

You and I are at opposite ends of your sofa, legs entwined. You're holding one of those huge wine glasses that seem to cover your whole face when you lift them. You look at me through your Rioja as though through a pool of blood, and say nothing.

'Morgan . . . can I ask you something?'

'Of course. I might not answer, but you can ask.'

'Why can't we talk about this stuff? About Dave, I mean. About what we're both doing here.'

'Who says we can't? We can talk.'

'So why don't we?'

You think about this for a moment, take my bare feet in your hands, bring my toe up to your mouth, softly bite it.

'I prefer it when it's just about us. Don't you?'

'Of course, but . . . '

'Aren't you happy here?'

'Yes,' I say slowly, 'but it doesn't mean there aren't things I miss.'

You drop my foot back into your lap, fold your arms.

'Okay. So talk. What do you miss the most?'

I consider.

'I miss Bella,' I say truthfully.

'The dog?'

'The dog. God. Is that weird?'

'Dunno,' you shrug, 'never saw the point of pets, myself. All that responsibility, you love them, look after them, then they die. Break your heart. Why do that to yourself?'

I draw my legs up towards me.

'Are you serious?'

194

'Damn right.'

'Some people get a lot of enjoyment from their pets.'

'Yeah, because they anthropomorphise them and project all these ridiculous emotions onto them that they can't possibly feel because, guess what, they're just animals. But no, they can't just treat them as animals, they have to act like they're their children or something.'

'Okay, while we're on that,' I take a deep breath, 'what about children?'

'What about them?'

'Well, you could say that about children. I mean, God forbid they should die before you, but even if they don't, they'll probably cause you loads of heartache. But people still have them, don't they? Millions of people.' I think back to that first rainy night in the restaurant, the night that started all of this. '*Normal* people.'

'Screw the normal people. Who wants to be normal?'

'Well, not you, obviously.'

'I've no interest in having children, if that's what you're getting at.' You lean over to the coffee table, pick up a newspaper, untangling yourself from me in the process. 'And from what you've told me, nor have you.'

'I don't know,' I say quietly, 'I mean, that's

what I told Dave, but . . . that was just easier than the truth.' I want you to ask me to say more but you don't. I go on anyway. 'The truth is, you were the only person I ever wanted to . . . do that with. And I felt like that chance had come and gone.'

You throw down the newspaper.

'We're not going to go down that road, are we? What happened to not speaking about it again?'

'Well, that was fifteen years ago. I thought maybe enough time had passed that I would be allowed to bring it up.'

'What for?'

'What do you mean, what for? I might want to talk about it. I've never . . . it's difficult, keeping a thing like that to yourself.'

'Best way if you ask me. Look, you make a decision and that's that. You have to deal with it and move on. You can't change it, and I don't think you'd want to, so what's the point in brooding?'

'Brooding. Great choice of word.'

'Fee, what's this all about?'

'I've been writing again.'

'Well, that's good.'

'And . . . thinking. Remembering. Stuff about us. Me and you. Only, some of it's a bit shadowy, and maybe if we talked about it . . . '

'The past, the past,' you say irritably, putting down your wine glass. 'All past. What's the point?'

'But the past is what makes us. It's why we're here.'

'The past is nothing but smoke and mirrors. Made-up memories and unreliable stories. You said it yourself. Shadows. The only thing that's real is right now.'

And you pull me towards you and that's all the talking, for now.

★　★　★

There's a strange nervousness, ringing someone you used to see every day and not knowing what to say. I look at the phone in my hand as though it's a bomb about to go off.

Dave and I rarely spoke on the phone — why would we? We were only ever apart with good reason, and when we did use the phone it was functional and often by text:

What do you want for dinner?

What time will you be home?

Can you just check I turned the iron off?

Phone calls are for people who live away: from a parent on the other side of the ring road, to the friend who moved to America. They're not for the person whose warmth was still on the duvet when you crept back under it with your cup of tea to the comforting sound of them running the shower in the next room.

You don't run out of things to talk about after years together; the things you talk about just change. I've used up all of my surprises, most of my stories, in the way everyone does: you gamble them all at the start, going all out to impress, maybe keeping one or two fascinating facts or funny anecdotes up your sleeve but more likely all your conversational cards are on the table in those first weeks and months. After all, you want to create the impression that this wit, this raconteur, will be a perfect first date/holiday companion/partner for life.

But suddenly we have a new topic: Us. Funny how couples only talk about Us when things are going really well, or really badly.

I'm assuming, of course, that Dave will want to talk about getting back together. After all, he's in bits, Mari said.

I prepare my lines as though writing a play: editing and refining, discarding clichés and hyperbole with a critical eye. Does anyone even dare say 'it's not you, it's me' anymore? I smile in spite of myself. Dave always argued that clichés become so for a reason — because there is some truth in them.

But my lines leave me when I hear his voice. He doesn't sound broken up. What was I expecting? Tears? I should've known better; this is Dave, he is tougher than he looks. I've only been gone a couple of weeks and yet there are things, important things, that I'm forgetting about him.

He's loving, and generous, and open, but he's also practical. He gets on with things. He won't have taken time off work as I have, won't have hit the gin bottle. He might be taking pills, I worry about that, wonder whether that's why his voice sounds so calm, and want to ask him, but I won't. He'll still walk Bella every morning and night, and the thought of them crunching through the leaves together, him speaking in the soft voice he uses only for her, sends a small pain through me.

Living in the city can keep you removed from nature, its colour shrouded by the buildings and exhaust fumes, its sounds obliterated by police sirens, the incessant click of hurried heels on pavements, the raucous chatter of nighttime revellers. So the park, only a couple of streets away from our house, kept us anchored to the changing earth, and Bella gave us a reason to be there twice a day.

In the park, the seasons are bold and

obvious, from April bursts of pale blossom to the rust-coloured carpets of autumn. The centre is marked by a war memorial fountain in which Bella habitually jumps and splashes.

'How come,' Dave used to laugh at her, 'when I put you in the bath it's like you're *allergic* to water?'

I know how Bella, the fresh air and exercise and all the routine of looking after her, will have kept him from dissolving, so I shouldn't be surprised he sounds like he's coping.

But I should also remind myself that this isn't exactly a social call: I've asked him not to contact me for a while, so he wouldn't have, not even through Mari, unless it was important.

I thought I had all my defences prepared. That's why I'm caught off guard when he says, 'You had a visitor.'

Here it is. The second I stop anticipating it, of course, here it is. I hold my breath.

'A girl. Alice somebody?'

Number three.

★ ★ ★

She went to my house. She saw my husband. Perhaps this is what helps me make the decision: the threat of two worlds colliding. I know I have to call her.

12

She asks me to go for coffee. What a civilised thing to do when you're about to tear someone's world apart.

This being the oh-so-cool Northern Quarter, it's not actually a coffee shop but a tea shop, as this is the latest trend. It's the kind of place you would absolutely hate: laden with ironic chintz, mismatched tablecloths and 'shabby chic' chipped-paint birdcages and picture frames. There are jars of different varieties of tea lined up on the counter, tied with spotty ribbons, and huge slabs of Victoria sponge and coffee cake. A smell of baking teases the back of the throat. A beaming girl in a gingham apron takes our money and cheerfully offers us a complimentary newspaper.

In here, every day is Sunday.

Alice perches on the edge of a sofa, the hard lines of her face incongruous among the cushions, but I choose a straight-backed, wooden chair and point it directly at her. I look at her coldly.

'Go on then — say your piece.'

She takes such a deep breath that for an

201

insane split-second I think she is going to burst into song. But the voice that comes out is low, and what she says is not what I expect.

'It's not me, really. It's Dennis. He's the one who thinks I should do this.'

Dennis is the boyfriend, it seems. I think about them laughing together behind the fountains.

'I told him about Mr ... about what happened, with ...' she straightens her back, 'with *Henry*.' She pronounces your name carefully, as though for the first time. It sounds foreign on her lips. 'And he said I should report him.'

When she says the word 'report' she meets my eye, an unblinking challenge. I sit back, fold my arms, an attempt to keep my thundering heart in my chest.

'And what is it he's supposed to have done, exactly?'

She emits a brittle laugh.

'I was fifteen. I thought I was ordinary, until somebody ... until *he* convinced me otherwise.'

A cruel observation flashes across my mind: *she looks pretty ordinary to me.*

Her blonde hair is darker at the roots, the ends dry from too much bleach. She's thinner than I am. Not athletic; she has the physique of the self-starved. Something about the hollowness of her cheeks, the shape of her collarbone. Her thinness is unnatural; she ought to be bigger. Her hands are constantly fluttering and I can see all of the bones in her wrist, like the way you can see a bird's skeleton on the underside of its wing.

She has placed a little tin of Vaseline on the table in front of her, and every so often dips her spidery fingers into it and runs them over her lips. She has small, pointed teeth.

'So you're going to report him for that? Doesn't sound like a crime to me.' But my voice breaks a bit on the word *crime*.

'No, but I'm assuming you don't want the gory details. You don't need them anyway — you were there before me, after all.' Her voice is light and a smile plays on her lips as though she's just told a joke.

'Okay, tell me in legal speak then. When you *report* him, what exactly is it you're going to accuse him of?'

'Now, let me think. According to my solicitor it's known as,' she speaks slowly, as though reading it out, 'sexual activity with a child.'

'A child? You just said you were fifteen.'

'A child in the eyes of the law, Fiona.'

I don't like the way she says my name. Her 'o's are soft and round, out of place here among northern accents. She must have been living in the south — the same change started to happen to my voice after three years in London, but I fought it. I want to ask her: 'Did you come back up here just for this?' Instead I ask, 'And you say this is your boyfriend's idea?'

She falters.

'Well, not his *idea* exactly, but . . . '

'Whatever you think went on with Morgan,' I say your name in a whisper, 'this Dennis doesn't like it and he wants — what? Some sort of revenge? Or is that what *you're* after?'

'I'm not after anything.'

'Not half.' I feel heat rising in my cheeks, I'm trying to keep my voice under control. 'Attention? Revenge? Money? Is it some sort of compensation you want, is that it?'

She sighs as though suddenly exhausted, runs a hand through her hair in a way that reminds me, perversely, of you.

'Look. Don't get angry. Please. I just wanted to talk to you. I just want to do what's right.'

'And why me, Alice? I mean, how did you know to come looking for me?'

'Once, he said I reminded him of someone. He said your name.'

'And you remembered, all this time.' *Of course you did,* I think. *I would have. I did.*

'What else did he say about me?'

'That you were . . . different.'

She doesn't have to say anything else. Any doubt I might have had, any hope I was holding onto that she was a fantasist, that she'd never even *met* Morgan (she wasn't in the yearbooks, I'd checked), much less been taught by him, been held by him — it starts to crumble.

'He's back,' I say suddenly; Alice frowns. 'I mean, I'm back . . . with him.'

'I heard you were married.'

'I was. I am. It's complicated. I moved in with him.'

'Wow.' She makes a soft whistling sound.

'So you see, these things you're saying, I don't . . . I *can't* hear them.'

She leans forward and rests her chin on her delicate hands, clasped together as though praying. She has the expression of a child trying to work out a puzzle.

'I wondered why you were being quite so . . . protective. Maybe this changes things. Maybe not. I still think I need you. And maybe you need me, too.'

She gets up and heads to the bathroom, leaving her words in the air between us, and her bag on the sofa. It's a battered satchel, clumpy and too full. *With what?* I wonder. A compulsion to search it, to tip it out, starts to rise in me so I look around to distract myself, and to place myself back in the reality that is other people.

A couple sit at the next table; they are married, wearing rings, but his body language has already left her. His knees point away, his eyes scan the room. He's good-looking, in an empirical way: the square jaw, the broad shoulders. She is leaning over a notebook, ticking off tasks, her bobbed hair neat, her face free of make-up. They aren't speaking. He looks as though he is wondering how he got here with her.

Another table is overrun by a huge family; the cantankerous old man at the centre of it is bullying his wife loudly to fetch him a more comfortable chair. She looks around desperately; the place is heaving. Her daughter's voice rises and rises over the noise made by her clutch of children, who are running in circles and keep knocking the tiny table, dishes holding muffins and flapjacks sliding and shifting like tectonic plates.

A student with headphones on scans a textbook, makes notes in the margin, checks her phone which 'beep, beep's every third minute or so, sips herbal tea, scribbles again, chews her pencil.

Alice is back, and smiling as though she is my friend.

'You know, for a long time I've wanted to meet you.'

'I can't say the same. He's never mentioned you.'

'I bet,' she laughs. Then says archly, 'but that doesn't mean I don't exist.'

How much does she have of you? I stare at the satchel, imagining you somehow wrapped up in there. I want to tear open its bulging seams. How much does she have of *me*?

Somehow the fact that you've talked about me is what troubles me the most. I'm beginning to realise that stories are rarely for their own sake; they are usually used for some other purpose. For what purpose did you use the story of me?

I'm torn between wanting to know everything and wanting to hear nothing.

How many times, where, when? How was it similar or different to how it was with me?

I want to know where I rank.

'Do you want to ask me anything?' she says quietly, as though reading my mind.

'Yes and no,' I say honestly. She studies my face.

'We should leave it. For today.'

'Alice,' I say, 'why am I here? I mean, what is it you want from me, exactly?'

'I want you to testify against him.'

I almost spit out my tea.

'You've got to be joking.'

'Nope.'

'Jesus. You did *hear* me before, right? I'm *living* with him.'

'Look, it's seven, eight years ago. There's no evidence, not really. It's my word against his. I need . . . I need backup.'

I suddenly feel like an older sister, oddly protective. I wish I could take myself out of the situation, watch from afar as a third-person version of me gives her a hug. But my overarching need is all about you; all about us.

'Just listen to yourself, Alice. Think about what you're suggesting. How serious it is.' I pause. 'If you do this . . . he'll be suspended.'

She looks at me, emotions passing over her face quick as light. Confusion. Pity. Triumph.

'It's done, Fiona. He was suspended three weeks ago.'

★　★　★

I stand outside the tea shop. I know I'm not ready to go home, wherever that is, but I don't know where I should go. There's a whirring in my head so loud, for a moment I think it's the traffic. I'm in two pieces, I feel like two people with differing views, neither one making a decision. I want anonymity; I want crowds. I want silence; I want solitude. Into this confusion God, or Fate, or whoever is the choreographer of the insane dance that is suddenly my life, sends the person most likely to throw me into more turmoil.

Matt.

He's sort of jogging towards me, one hand holding a briefcase, the other positioning a newspaper over his head to protect his hair from the rain that I hadn't even noticed. He's grinning and I have my back to the glass doorway so I can't avoid his smile, and short of turning and going back inside there's nowhere for me to disappear to.

One half of me, remembering Laura's pained expression last time I saw her, wants to slap him.

The other wants to laugh. Seeing his beaming face is a kind of relief. I long for the time when a flirtation with Matt was the most I had to feel guilty about.

'Hey,' he leans forward and kisses my cheek, 'how you doing, Fee? Good to see you.'

'You, too,' I say truthfully.

He looks over my shoulder through the glass into the steam and chatter.

'Listen, would love to chat but I need to get in there. I'm meeting someone.'

I suddenly have the sense of all the pieces

of my life connecting and a fear comes over me.

'Who? I mean . . . it's not . . . '

'It's not a woman, if that's what you mean,' he says irritably, 'it's a work thing. And anyway,' and in an instant, with a wink, the old Matt is back, the tease, the flirt, 'when did you get so virtuous? Marriage must really agree with you.'

Marriage. I look into his honey-coloured eyes and know we are complicit in our betrayals. 'She's pregnant', I want to spit at him, but the words sound hollow in my heart, before they even reach my mouth. His eyes say, 'we're the same, you and me'. Is it true? Are my fantasies just that — shadows I build to make the reality seem less sordid? Do we cheats seek each other out? Is there some invisible sonar, is that why he touched me the way he did when we danced? Did I encourage him, just by being what I am, this faithless creature?

'Hey, chill out,' he's saying, 'why such a serious face?'

'Nothing. It's just . . . well, what you said about marriage. Me and Dave are . . . kind of taking a break. I moved out.'

'Oh. Shit. Sorry, Fee. Laura never said.'

'Well, she wouldn't, since I haven't told her.' I sigh. 'We kind of had other things to talk about last time I saw her,' I add. Oblivious to my meaning, Matt checks his watch and smiles.

'Well listen, I really do have to go in there now.' I realise I'm blocking the doorway. 'But why don't you drop in on her this afternoon? I'm working late and she could really do with some girl time I reckon. Sounds like you could too.'

He kisses me again, cool lips on my forehead, and squeezes my arm, and for a second I want to grab him and bury my face in his collar, but I don't, I just say 'bye' and take myself off into the rain.

★ ★ ★

'How do they do that?'

'Who?'

'Children.'

'Do what?'

'Disappear like that.'

I'm at Laura's school. I'm always amazed by the way that children, even with all their mess and noise and clatter, can vacate a space in seconds; leave it ghostly.

She smiles. She's getting a bump. I feel a pang of envy, a surprise lurch in my stomach.

'I'm taking you for an early dinner,' I say brightly.

'Matt . . .'

'Actually he gave me the idea,' I confess. 'I've just seen him, in town.'

She bundles up the papers on her desk and runs a hand through her hair.

'Well, I guess that's okay.'

'Yep, you're free for at least two hours. I'll help you clear up.'

We slide in between yellow-topped desks, stooping to pick up an eraser here, a pencil there. Laura sits down, on a child's chair, Year Six driftwood on her lap.

'Matt,' she says again.

'Stop it,' I tell her.

'What?'

'Stop wondering what he was doing in town today, what he's doing this evening.'

'Am I that transparent?'

'Just think about you, for a change. Just for a couple of hours. Okay?'

'Okay.'

'Although I have to admit,' I take her handbag for her and link her arm as she flicks off the lights, 'I do have an ulterior motive for my visit. I need to pick your brains on something. Is that alright?'

'Of course,' she laughs, 'I hope I can help. I'm beginning to think that the more pregnant I get, the more brain cells I lose.' She makes a whistling sound. 'Even the ten-year-olds seem to be running rings round me at the moment.'

* * *

It was always obvious Laura was going to be a primary school teacher. She had patience and a love of children, and what's more they loved her too. They seemed to be able to sense in her a kindred spirit, one who had never really grown up, who still had wonder and innocence and could be silly at times. In turn, she loved their seemingly bottomless energy, and their honesty, both traits she tended to find lacking in adults.

Laura always tells me she loves teaching the class she does because they're old enough to have great conversations with. She says they're at that lovely point when their adult personalities are almost fully formed: 'everything's there except the crap stuff' she always says, 'that gets poured in last'.

'So how's school?' I say when we're settled. We're scanning the menus although I don't know why we bother: we always come to the same little Italian place in town and we both always order the same thing. When the waiter comes over and Laura mouths 'two minutes please', I know it can't be because she hasn't decided yet.

'What's this really about then, Fee?' She has a concerned look, head tilted, eyes wide. It strikes me if she wasn't a teacher she'd have made a great therapist. 'You said you wanted to pick my brains on something.'

'Yes, it's a bit of a weird one, I hope you don't mind?'

'Fire away.'

'Well. If a child were to make an, um, an accusation . . . against a member of staff. What would happen?'

She frowns.

'What kind of an accusation?'

'Oh you know, anything. Bullying, maybe. Verbal abuse. Physical abuse. Erm . . . sexual,' I add hastily. 'It might even be years later, say.'

'Well, it doesn't happen often, thank God.' At this point, incongruously, she taps the table as if 'touching wood', or maybe she is just keeping herself anchored to a world of solidity, where these things don't happen. 'But if a complaint was made, well, the teacher would be suspended immediately while the investigation took place. Then I guess it would go to court, and so on.'

'And if he — if they — were found guilty?'

'You're probably not asking the right person, honey. You'd need to ask a judge, or a lawyer. I can tell you they'd go onto List 99

214

— so they wouldn't be able to work with children again. Although I think you can appeal after a certain number of years.'

The waiter is hovering impatiently, and we both just point at our usual choices on the menu: salmon farfalle for me, cannelloni for Laura.

'Oh, and a bottle of Frascati, please,' I say with a 'what the hell' smile at Laura.

'You know you're on your own with that, don't you?' she reminds me. 'I'm not drinking.'

'Oh shit, yes. Better make it a half bottle!'

'Fee, I hope you don't mind me asking,' she waits for the waiter to move away, 'but why do you want to know all of this?'

I look at her. The friend I used to pass notes to, have sleepovers with, share our most private dreams and fears. It strikes me that the longer you've known someone, the further away you can drift, the more you have to hide. Maybe this is why people often find themselves baring their souls to total strangers on trains or planes. I want Laura to remember the uncorrupted me, the schoolgirl with all her wishes and fancies and wild opinions and as yet untested worldly cynicisms. I've always tried to show Laura only my best side, and this has meant concealing the rest.

'It's research,' I say, 'I can't say too much

about it, but . . . I'm writing a book.'

'Oh, Fee, that's fantastic!' Her enthusiasm temporarily floors me; her eyes are shining, she actually looks as though she might cry. 'I always knew you would do it. I think it's great you're using your talent.'

'Well, thanks, but you know, early stages and all that. I don't want to make a fuss about it.'

'So what does Dave think about it?'

The wine arrives just in time for me to take a deep breath and tell her we're separated, the only scrap of truth in a stream of lies. I trot out the clichés: 'I just need some space', 'we've drifted apart' and, wide-eyed, she accepts them. She's shocked, though: 'of all people', she keeps saying. It seems Dave and I had done a great job of convincing everyone around us, as well as ourselves, that we were a perfect couple.

'If you ever need to talk about it, you know where I am.'

'Do you know what, Lau? I really *don't* want to talk about it. I'd much rather hear about you. How are things with Matt?'

She suddenly looks panic-stricken.

'God, you didn't say anything to him when you saw him, did you? I mean, I'd hate him to think I was turning people against him, or something.'

216

'Of course I didn't. It's none of my business, I only care that you're happy.'

'Do you know what? I think it will be fine.' That hand on the tummy again, like a reflex. 'I know you're not supposed to use a baby as a sticking plaster and all that, but . . . he's been so sweet, and protective, since we found out I was pregnant.' Her grin is wide, definite. 'I think this will be just what he needs.'

Responsibility, sleepless nights, staying in, a dwindling sex life: he's going to love it, sounds right up Matt's street. But whether it's because I love Laura and it's what she needs to hear, or because of some impulse to defend Matt, or myself, I reach across the table, take her hand and say, 'I think you're right.'

13

I pull up outside the house and I feel your presence in there before I even go in. I suddenly wish, long, for a home of my own again.

When two people live together, they don't create their own spaces within the one home; they share every corner, every square foot, every nook and cobweb and piece of furniture. They breathe the same air; one breathes in, and when they exhale, the other inhales it.

The house I lived in alone, before I got married, is, in my memory, fresher, lighter. The space around me was mine. Not heavy with expectation. No words in the air, half-recalled arguments lingering like ghosts, no stale smell of bodies. My house was a place of thoughts, of quiet, except when I chose to bring noise in: music, friends, movies, chatter and the pop of the wine cork, the hiss of a joint being lit. Laughter.

I want it back.

I'm afraid of going inside and not knowing what to say. With Dave, I've had the kind of relationship where there were often silences.

They were not bored silences, the silences of long-married couples who sit at pub tables with blank faces, as if they have long given up even trying to think of conversation. I worried occasionally that they might turn into them, but until recently they never did. They weren't the awkward silences of acquaintances or people with secrets. They were the rarest silences: the kind you don't mind hearing.

But I always *talked* to you. I couldn't bear for us to look at each other soundlessly: because that would only happen, surely, at the end.

I'm not ready. That's all that keeps going around my head. I'm not ready, I'm not ready. To confront you. To confront you, or confront It?

I turn off the engine, ease back in my seat. I stare at the living room window, the open curtains. My hand rests on the car door handle, ready to open it if your face appears.

I'm torn between order and chaos; between peace and drama.

When I was a teenager, I fantasised constantly about falling pregnant and having to tell my parents. What would it be like? I envisioned wailing and screaming; maybe a single slap across the face. I imagined being thrown out, literally, onto the front street, in a scene where there was always rain or snow, their horrified faces at the window taking one last look then turning dramatically, haughtily, away. I saw myself giving birth secretly, bravely, in some backstreet room with a flickering light, to a beautiful dark-haired foundling boy, doomed to live a Dickensian life of squalor among thieves and addicts.

While other teenagers probably fantasised about running away with their favourite pop star, these were the kinds of stories I invented for myself.

When it happened, of course, it wasn't quite like that.

★ ★ ★

If I'm honest, there's something I've always liked about my own reflection when my eyes are bright with tears, mascara streaked down my face. I like drama. Perhaps everyone does, secretly.

I feel a nervousness that has been missing since those teenage years, and has been bubbling just below the surface since you reappeared. I look at my nails: bitten down, I don't remember when. Perhaps on this drive home. A jitteriness in my legs and I know, when I speak, there'll be a quaver in my voice. I consider how, in fact whether, to disguise these signs. Why are the symptoms of nervousness and dread so close to those of excitement?

I know that once I get in the house I will be swept up in . . . in what exactly? Well, just in you. So I need to be clear on what to do before that happens.

I could say nothing; carry on in our bubble and hope It goes away. Hope *she* goes away.

I could start dropping her name into conversation, make a cough sound like 'Alice', watch your reaction.

I could create a huge scene; shout and scream.

I could leave, and leave a dramatic note.

This is making me feel better. Because the thing is, although I like drama, even with the damage it causes, I also like order, and lists, and to be prepared for the possibilities.

What will you do?

1. You'll tell me it isn't true; this girl is a crackpot; reassure me. It will be over.
2. You'll admit it's true; you didn't know how to tell me; you'll ask for my help; you'll understand, of course, if I leave.

I take a deep breath, lock the car, and somehow my legs carry me to the house.

★　★　★

221

'Here she is,' comes your voice, then here come your arms, your lips, 'here's my angel.' And instantly I'm back in that place with no full stops, no pauses.

Every time I see you, after a separation however brief, it's like a surprise. It's still a surprise to me that you're here, that we've somehow ended up here, and I don't know how or why it's happened except that I'm sure there is a reason, whether via the machinations of a capricious God, or the movement of the spheres, there is a reason, a poetry and pattern behind it just out of sight, that maybe one day will be revealed, as though from behind a curtain ('Ta-da!' a voice off-stage will trumpet, and we'll sigh and say 'Oh, NOW I see . . . '), but for now we'll just accept it and be carried by its current.

In your arms, all my lists and order are meaningless. And most disconcertingly of all: my nervousness melts away.

The other thing that surprises me is just you. Your face, your way of moving. Each time I see you, everything is familiar but always in some way new and better. I wonder, is this a pure kind of love? I've heard kind aunties say to nieces and nephews, with dewy-eyed wonderment (and total sincerity), 'you get more beautiful every time I see you'

— and that's how I feel about you. Not more beautiful exactly — even I can't claim that's an epithet that fits you — just better. Better than I remembered, better than the last time I looked.

This is how addictions happen.

Tonight there are secrets between us, and this in itself is magnetic.

Knowing something about you, I feel a rare power. A tiny lift on my side of the scale.

'You look gorgeous tonight,' you say, and it's not a platitude, you mean it. You bring me to the mirror, to show me.

This is a favourite habit of yours: standing behind me, both of us looking at ourselves, and each other, in the mirror.

You put your head on my shoulder so our faces are next to each other. You love this, I know, seeing us together, seeing us as the world sees us. There's an odd sort of narcissism to us: we look for the similarities between us. Our skin is similar: fair but slightly sun-burnished. Your nose is more Roman, mine more snub. Your eyes, the colour of metal, reflect in mine. I wonder, not for the first time, what our children would look like. Count our imperfections, native or acquired: your crooked teeth, your scar. My dimples, my high forehead. I look young, though, next to you. You have thirteen years' more lines, after all.

In these moments I look better than when I'm alone; you know this. You like to show me the version of myself that you see.

'These are the photographs I keep in here,' you say quietly, tapping your temple, 'for later, in case you . . . for when you're gone.' Then you make a 'click, click' sound, like a camera, and smile, and I remember the first time you made me look in a mirror like this, years ago, when everything was unfamiliar.

'I'm not going anywhere,' I murmur, but my heart is pounding.

★ ★ ★

When there is something important to say, there is a line between before and after. Uttering the first words will take you over the line, where there's no going back. Behind the line, you can orchestrate what happens; you can predict the rise and flow of conversations, of events. The world is known. Over the line is the unknown — it's intoxicating, in its way — being about to take the first step, the veins thrill with adrenaline.

In a sick way, watching your face, being with you tonight, playing at lovers, I want to enjoy this delicate moment before the other side of the scale comes crashing irrevocably down.

Here we go again, I think: how strange to be sitting next to someone in the ordinariness of an evening, with a whole interior world of thought moving and whirring behind the eyes. How quickly I've shifted, I think, from hiding from my husband, to hiding from you.

'Is everything alright? You seem distracted.'

'I'm alright. What about you?' I try to keep my voice light. 'Anything you want to tell me? Any news?'

'Nope. I did a bit of gardening while you were out. It's looking good. You should see my clematis, it's really coming on. What did you do today?'

'How come I always end up talking about myself and you never give anything away about you?'

'Because you, my love, are far more interesting and enchanting than I am.'

'I'm serious.'

'So am I.'

'Why don't you tell me anything?'

You frown. 'Some might call me a good listener.'

'I call you evasive.'

'You say tomato . . . '

'Very funny.' Your kisses on my throat almost prevent me from saying, 'I mean it, I want to talk. Like we used to.'

'So, talk.' Kiss, kiss. Insistent. 'Tell me a story.'

'No, about real things.' I pull away; you look, not quite impatient, just fidgety; distracted, playful; with the bounce of a much younger man, a boy, even. A boy at Christmas momentarily bored of one present and waiting for the next to be opened. Staring at my neck, my shoulders, smiling, apparently fascinated.

'I'm serious, listen to me,' my turn to be insistent, batting you away as though swatting a fly, 'we only ever tell stories, or gaze at each other in the mirror and congratulate ourselves on our wonderfulness,' your giddy grin almost throwing me off-balance, here, 'or make fun of other people. Why don't *you* tell *me* something, for a change? Something about you, and what's going on with you.'

I take a deep breath. You're suddenly still, looking at the ceiling as though for inspiration.

'Ah,' you say slowly, 'I get it. I think I know what this is about.'

Your voice has changed pitch, it's lower.

'Do you?' Mine is warbling slightly; the blood in my ears, thud thud thud, a rush of something like guilt, as though it's me with the secret.

'Yep.' Sombre. The look in your eyes that always makes me breathe deeper. 'I think I know what you want to hear.'

You pull me towards you. Your hands on my back, your breath is warm in my ear.

'I love you,' you whisper.

Well.

Fifteen years ago, a week ago, or yesterday, I would have imploded with happiness to hear those words from you. But tonight . . .

I look at you, and calmly say, 'No, you don't.'

'Fee.'

'I'm tired.'

'There's something wrong.'

'Yes, there is. Ask me in the morning.'

'Shall we go to bed?'

'I'm tired,' I say again, but it's futile because your hands on me find a different answer: *yesyesyes*.

★   ★   ★

When the thing between us was still an affair, before we got here, every time we made love felt like it might be the last time.

It has to be the last time, I would tell myself, and sometimes I would say it, breathlessly, an incantation while we undressed, neither one of us believing it.

Tonight I have the same sense of teetering on the edge of something, of taking a last taste before everything changes. I turn the lights out, unable to look at your face, tired of trying to read it. Tired of thinking, I just want to feel you. You move over me, in me, expertly, until I'm enclosed. You're saying things I don't hear. I'm falling.

★ ★ ★

Afterwards, I wait until your breathing slows, the rhythm of you moments from sleep. My voice is small in the dark.

'I know about Alice. I know about school. The case. Everything.'

You hold your breath, a heartbeat. You switch on the lamp. Your face is ghostly, masked by shadows.

'Okay,' you say. If there was a flicker of panic, it's gone.

'Is that it? Okay?'

'Not much to say. It's not a big deal, really.'

The whispering voice that said love; the hoarse voice that made hot cries into my ear; both are gone, replaced by smooth control. Your everyday voice: authoritative, certain.

'But . . . they've suspended you.'

'It's just a formality. They have to do it. They completely support me. I'll be back there when I'm cleared.'

'*When* you're cleared?'

'Of course. Listen, you don't have to worry. The girl's a liar, everybody knows it. And she's had years to dream this one up. It won't be hard to discredit her.'

'So you're not worried?'

'Why would I be?'

'But . . . you didn't tell me. It *is* quite a big deal, getting suspended, whatever you say. And you didn't tell me.'

'Ah. I see. So it's not me you're worried about!'

'What do you mean?'

'You don't actually care what the outcome is for me. You're upset because I didn't tell you.'

'Well, that's not — '

'No, no, it's fine. I understand now. Look. You know me. And you — well, I thought you understood me.'

'I *want* to, but — '

'The ducking and diving, the keeping to myself — that's just me. I've lived on my own and looked after myself for too long to change. I'm more myself with you than with anyone I've ever met — but if that isn't enough for you, just say.'

'Of course it's enough. It's just . . . I want to really know you. Be part of your life.'

'Fee. You are part of my life. That's why you're here. Don't you want to be here?'

What I think is: *Why are you asking the questions suddenly? How did we get here?* But what I say is: 'More than anything.'

'Then take me for who I am. I'm forty-three, I'm not going to become anything else, now. Have I ever promised you anything?'

'No.' But a phrase rings through my head, from years ago: *If you trust me, I won't let you down.* Does that count as a promise? I shake my head and say again, 'No.'

'And I won't, either. And have I ever let you down?'

I start. Jesus. Can you read my thoughts now?

'Well, no.' *Not yet*, rises unbidden in me and is pushed back down.

'I'll promise nothing, precisely so you won't ever be let down. Because I would hate to do that to you. These are my terms, Fee.' You fix me with those concrete eyes. 'Take them or leave them.'

With this you turn off the lamp, the sudden darkness like a full stop, as if you don't expect a response or care what it might be.

What kind of a choice is this? I feel an itching need to get back to the point but I've been steered off course, can't even remember what the point was. I only know I want to be here, want to be near you, and these things are all happening anyway. Your life will go on, you'll exist in the world just as you did for years without me. I might as well be close by.

'I'll take them,' I say, and I manage a laugh, and you kiss me and in the dark it all seems alright.

★　★　★

But in the morning, awake but unable to get out of bed, the question that I didn't ask, can't ask, gnaws at my brain:

Did you do it?

The smells of breakfast drift into the bedroom as normal. It's early, and I can hear you whistling. I feel hung-over, even though I didn't really drink last night; the same foggy head, dry mouth. I think hung-over thoughts: *Did it really happen? Where am I, now?*

My nose leads me to coffee and bacon in the kitchen. Different people suit and belong in different rooms; the kitchen is your domain. You suit the role of chef, of host, of creator.

'Morning, sunshine.' You're dressed; wide awake. A faint damp sheen on all the surfaces and floor indicates you've been cleaning. You're washed and shaved. I feel oddly exposed next to you, in my pyjamas, as though I've turned up to a party wearing jeans and found that everyone else is in black tie and ballgowns.

I wonder how long you've been up. The cafetière is half empty.

'I'll make a fresh one now,' you murmur as though, as so many times, reading my mind.

'Are we going to talk about . . . ' I let the question drift, not really knowing what to call It, and disoriented by your breeziness, by the air of normality about the place.

You glance at the clock.

'I've asked someone over this morning. You've got about twenty minutes to get dressed.'

'Oh? Who? Why?'

'Imogen Cartwright. She's my defence lawyer.' You snake your arms around my waist. 'I thought meeting her might make you feel a bit better.'

★   ★   ★

Imogen Cartwright is the kind of woman who is always referred to by both names. She has a brittle smile and a firm handshake. She's dressed as though for an office, but she accepts your offer of toast and makes herself comfortable at the breakfast bar. I wonder how many times she has been here.

Sitting next to me, you hold the back of my head, like a ventriloquist with a dummy, as though at the command of your hand I might speak, or fall silent.

'So tell me about your meeting with Miss Webb,' Imogen says casually, brushing crumbs from her lap into her palm and sprinkling them back onto the plate.

'I'm sorry . . . who?' I'm conscious of having only been dressed a few minutes. I feel exposed.

'Alice Webb,' she says. Her eyes are emotionless.

I tell her about the encounter at my office, about the meeting in the tea shop. I'm telling her more than I've told you; as usual, you and I didn't get into the detail. You're listening intently.

'And I was thinking,' I know I'm starting to babble, 'maybe I could help. I mean, she sort of opened up to me. She practically admitted it was her boyfriend putting her up to it.' Imogen Cartwright and you exchange a brief glance. 'I could talk to her some more . . . I . . . I don't know. Maybe I could say something to make her change her mind. Stop it even going to court.' The words are tumbling out now, the two of you just watching me silently. 'She seemed to . . . want something from me.'

After a brief pause, Imogen says, 'Yes. To testify on her behalf, is that not correct?'

'Well yes, but that's not what I mean. There was something else. I think I could get through to her.' I sigh. 'I just want to help.'

Imogen Cartwright is probably the same age as me, maybe even a couple of years younger, but opposite her I feel like a clumsy child.

'Fiona,' she says, with another sidelong glance at you, 'I would *strongly* advise against you having anything further to do with Miss Webb. We know what we're doing, you know.'

'So, what is my role, then?'

'What do you mean?' She frowns.

'I mean, there must be a way I can help. I can speak for Morgan, can't I? Make him look good . . . '

Imogen looks from me to you and back again, then says, 'Given the, ah . . . the way the two of you met, I would advise that you remain in the background.'

There is more conversation, but I don't hear it. I sit staring past both of you, out of the window, into the reality of what lies ahead.

On her way out, Imogen turns to me conspiratorially. I sense that 'woman to woman' is not something she does comfortably, but she seems to want to try.

'You know, Fiona — he's made a good choice having a female brief. Jurors are less likely to believe that a woman could defend a . . .'

I nod briskly, providing a full stop, because she doesn't seem to be the kind of woman who tails off at the end of a sentence and I am afraid of the next word.

'Thank you. I'm sure you're right.'

★　★　★

The shift between us is small but I know you feel it. We carry on with the day, with few words and little physical contact. I edge away from you when we pass each other in the kitchen, I don't touch your hand when you give me a glass of wine. Your eyes are looking for mine but I'm always looking at a point slightly behind you. When evening starts to throw shadows into the house and we begin the ritual of flicking on lamps, drawing curtains, you finally say, 'Okay. Let's have it.'

'What?' I stand in the middle of the living room and turn on the TV. We rarely watch TV; I don't even know what any of the programmes are, they look like strangers to me. I stare intently at the screen as I flick the remote, watching numbers chase each other.

One, two, three. 'Why is there *nothing* on?' I murmur.

You take the remote from me gently, and with a hand on my shoulder guide me to the sofa.

'You want to say something to me,' you say. 'You're angry. Upset. I don't know. But just say it. Get it out in the open.'

I look at you.

'Can I have a cigarette?'

'Why are you asking permission?' You hand me the ashtray, pull out a lighter.

'I don't know.' The flame, the dry taste of smoke, soothe me.

'Fee,' you say quietly, 'come on.'

'Okay. It's just . . . ' *What? What is it that's so unsettling me?* 'You're so . . . cool about it all. I can't believe it's for real. I want to know what you're really thinking.'

'Do you?'

'Yep.'

'Well . . . I've had a bit more time than you, remember, to think about all of this. And the truth is,' you look up as though the way to form the words lies on the ceiling, 'I can't believe, won't believe that there can be a bad outcome. Do you know why?'

I shake my head. 'Why?'

'Because of you.' This isn't what I expected. I want to ask what you mean, want more of this, but before I can speak you laugh and say, '*And* because I'm a damn good teacher.'

I can't argue with this. You were bloody good. You were adored when I was at school. That rare thing, a teacher both boys and girls liked. You got kids from council estates excited about Shakespeare. You even made Drama cool; everyone wanted to be in your plays.

'Look at how hard I've worked,' you're saying, 'how many people I've helped, people's lives that in some small way I've made better. Pretty unfair, don't you think, that one spiteful, screwed-up girl and her idiot boyfriend could bring it all crashing down?'

I find myself nodding.

'But worse, Fee, it means I could lose you. All these years, I've wanted you, waited for you, wondered. And now I have you, here, I have a hope of happiness, and the worst thing of all of this is . . . '

Your words, your eyes start to drift, and instinctively I reach out. My hand on your leg seems to bring you back.

'The worst thing is, not only does someone want to take everything away from me, they want to use *you* to help them do it.'

'I'm not going anywhere,' I say for the

second time in twenty-four hours. 'I won't help her.'

You say I'm the only thing that's keeping you going. An amazing thing to hear: I'm needed. I realise this means more than when you said you loved me. I realise why I'd rejected it when you said it; the word 'love' felt borrowed in your mouth. I always thought you and I were somehow beyond the 'L' word anyway, the ineffectual four letters that everyone uses. Normal people. What we have is deeper than that, bigger than them: you need me. I make you feel safe. Without me, you say, you may as well give up, give them what they want.

'You have to trust me, Fee,' you say, 'especially after how I trusted you. Remember? Think of the trips we took. Remember?' Something high and desperate in your voice; your eyes boring into me, as though trying to excavate my memories. 'Jesus, think of the *risks* we took. Would I have done any of that if you weren't special?'

I'm cradling your head on my shoulder now; I want to protect you, this new vulnerable you, keep you safe.

'I know, I know,' I murmur.

'There are so few people you meet in life that you can trust, feel an affinity with. Even now; you're not the only one whose life has been turned upside down by us meeting again. I was doing alright; I'm in my forties, divorced, I was at peace with the possibility that this might be it for me, I might end up alone. I was okay with it. But when we met again, I couldn't stop myself. I think and feel all the same things you do. I know I don't say them, but I always thought we didn't have to do that. Not us. Not like other people. No big declarations; it was just *known* between us.'

'Yes,' I say, kissing you. 'Yes.'

'You're not going to leave me, are you?'

'No.' I stroke your hair, the side of your face. 'No, of course not. It will be alright. Trust me.'

14

Diary: Sunday, 14 February 1993

Happy Valentine's Day!

Love is in the air!! Hearts and flowers in abundance! Well, sort of. Mr Postman brought me a v. mysterious card yesterday. No writing inside, nothing, and the writing on the envelope looks like it's been disguised. It was really funny though, it has Garfield on the front and it says 'Tell me what you think of me, go on tell the truth, I can take it . . .' and inside it says '. . . however flattering it is!'

I wrote the poem below and sent it in a card . . . hope it arrived yesterday. Oh, but who did I send it to? Ha! As if we didn't know! I hope he likes it. Night night.

So many things I want to say,
Yet can't quite form them with my
   tongue
Or if I do, they come out wrong
Or never seem to find their way
To you, as in your freezing heart
A feeling lies in solitude
For fear of being misconstrued
You carry on to play your part.

So many things I want to say
Yet leave them all untold
While deep within my secret soul
Your force attracts, then turns away
From me, my love so bare and true
My mind so tired, my emotions lonely
To release, unleash, empower me only
Takes a word, a smile, from you.

It was a three-and-a-half-hour stretch of tarmac and pylons. Not a scenic route, apart from the few minutes when the motorway took a soft slow bend flanked by trees. We stopped for sweets, and argued about what tapes to play. I teased you for still having tapes. I put my sockless feet up on the dashboard, and you reached over without looking, to push them away. I did it again. And again. The third time I kicked your hand, hard. The fourth time you grabbed my foot, tried to pull it into your lap. I laughed and curled both feet under me, knelt on them.

'When you're old enough,' you said, 'I'll teach you to drive.'

★ ★ ★

We were on our way to London. I had passed it off as a 'St Vincent de Paul Society outing',

241

and although in a rare moment of parental interest Dad had mumbled something about it being strange he hadn't been asked to sign a form, I quickly persuaded him there were loads of us going, and we would only be away for one night, and these trips happened all the time, no big deal.

★ ★ ★

The closer we got to London, the slower the traffic became and the further away we felt from our old selves, our real lives.

In a jam, we kissed in the car. I suppose people might have looked through the windows but it felt as though we were in a protective bubble. There had been kisses, since the night at your house, but for me it was still a shock every time, and a sense I was watching myself from far away. The rush of blood to the head, the rattling words so loud I was amazed you couldn't hear them. A voice: *It's him, it's him, it's him, it's him*, like a drum. The hot crush of your mouth, the taste of cigarettes and sweet coffee. Your hand on my hand, placing it in your lap, me pulling away, going on like this for a while, you smiling as though I was being coquettish, you liked it, probably thought it was a little dance, I just didn't want you to hear the drum-voice in my head, or see or feel the shake in my hands so I would pull away and (eventually) you would let me.

* * *

'You check in like a pro,' I whispered at the reception desk.

It was the kind of hotel that made me want to whisper: a beautiful marble staircase, huge vases of lilies whose scent filled my throat. Muted music.

'What do you mean?' you laughed, signing a form.

'You're just very . . . casual,' I shrugged. I took the key card from you: it said 'family room'.

* * *

You were still allowed to feed the pigeons in Trafalgar Square, back then. We watched a young couple, dressed similarly in jeans and belted, black pea coats, sunglasses pushed back on their heads. He'd opened up a bag of crumbs and was surrounded by swooping and cooing birds; some resting on his arms, his shoulders, some appearing to peck at his hair. Behind the flapping of grey wings, I could see that he was grinning, and although his girlfriend was squealing and holding her arms up to her face, she was laughing.

'Bloody flying rats,' you tutted. 'Ugh. Filthy.'

'I don't know,' I murmured, mesmerised by the boy and his girlfriend, 'I think they're . . . sort of cute.'

'Do you disagree with me on everything just for fun?'

'I don't think I do. Do I?'

'Yup.'

'I don't.'

'There you go again.'

'Ha. Maybe.'

You smiled and linked my fingers with yours and I suddenly realised how far from home we were. I gazed across the square at the face of Big Ben in the distance, car horns and the chatter of unfamiliar accents and languages resounding in my ears.

I suddenly had a sense of being at the heart of the world. *When I grow up*, I thought, *I'm going to live here.*

We strolled, still hand in hand, looking askance at the people on open-top buses — 'Tourists!' we scoffed — not us; we belonged here.

It was as though I'd only in that moment realised that places existed all the time without me in them; that all over the world there were places where I could be, where *we* should be. Places we, you and I, *should* go to.

'Istanbul,' I shouted, 'we should go to Istanbul.'

What a waste it seemed: life happening elsewhere. *But just for today*, I thought, *I am in it. Today it's my life, and it's full of possibilities.*

You didn't question my outburst, didn't even look surprised, just squeezed my hand and said, 'One day we'll go to Istanbul, sunshine.'

★   ★   ★

Us in the mirror.

'Look how good we look together.'

I nodded approvingly.

'Yep,' I said, 'in London, we look good.'

Still bright in my mind, fifteen years on, what seems like a slow-running cinema reel of you laughing in the bedroom as I sang in the bathroom, my head dizzy with you, putting on lip-gloss that would soon be kissed away.

★   ★   ★

It was one of those months between winter and spring, when the air feels clean and everything is just below ground, waiting to

245

push through. We lay on our backs in Hyde Park.

'You remind me of someone I used to know. Have I ever told you that?' I shook my head. 'She was a writer, too. She wrote poems.'

My heart caught in my throat. You called me a writer. I rolled onto my side, rested my head in my palm.

'What was she like?'

You smiled, right into the corner of your eyes, and for a moment I hated her for being the cause of that smile, but I wanted to hear.

'She was like you. She was . . . different.'

'In what ways?'

You laughed.

'Well, she liked Fleetwood Mac when everybody else was into Rick Astley and so on. She cared about everything, except what people thought of her. I love that.'

'Where is she now?'

You shrugged.

'I don't know. She . . . she moved away. She had her whole life ahead of her. Like you, she could achieve anything. I doubt she even remembers me!'

How could anyone forget you? I wondered, and rolled back into the grass.

★ ★ ★

Back then not only could you feed pigeons in London; you could smoke pretty much anywhere, even inside, without being frowned on. Imagine that! I can't actually believe now that I ever wasted time smoking outside, in parks and in the street. If I'd known what was coming I would've gone immediately into a café, a pub, onto a train, to light up, just because I *could*.

But you were frowning at me.

'Why do you smoke?'

I thought about this for two long drags, looking at the white tails left by aeroplanes in the sky. Finally I replied, 'Because nobody tells me not to.'

'What if I told you not to?'

I looked at you.

'But *you* smoke,' I pointed out. 'You smoke *loads*.'

'That's different. I'm . . . '

'What? Old? A hypocrite?'

You ignored this.

'And drugs?'

I groaned.

'Jesus. Don't give me the Just Say No talk, please.'

'I know you aren't going to like what I'm about to say, Little Miss Independent. I'm not sure I like it, to be honest. It's just . . . sometimes I want to put you in my pocket and take care of you. There!' You exhaled dramatically. 'I've said it.'

I made a yakking sound into the grass, chanting, 'Gross, gross, gross.'

But you were wrong; I did like it. I liked it a lot.

★　★　★

We went out, because nobody knew us in London. I looked older, dressed up, you looked younger, somehow.

We held hands, my nerves high in my throat.

I let you lead me, trusting you, all the time looking down. The pavements looked cleaner, in the dark, in the rain. Taxis edged past slower than we could walk, horns occasionally and for no apparent reason blaring. Coloured lights from the buildings above reflected and bounced in the puddles. I jumped on them, trying to capture them, splashing my shoes, making you laugh.

Nobody gave us a second glance, everyone pressing forward on their own personal missions, with fast feet, hard eyes.

I pressed my face against the window of a Chinese restaurant, eyeing row upon row of featherless ducks, hanged and burnt-looking, waiting to be eaten. I shuddered.

'Do you want to go in?' you said into my ear, brushing a raindrop from the end of my nose, and then you were ushering me into the steam and the warmth. We draped napkins big as bed sheets across our laps and I played with the chopsticks, making them dance like skinny bodiless legs across the table. I flicked through the menu with disinterest, let you order for me; eating was a necessary but temporary diversion from my real business, of talking to you, being close to you. Restaurants were just a place where we could sit still, sit opposite each other.

You wanted to know what was going on at home; what was the source of my most recent exasperation.

'It's like with our kid,' I blushed, corrected myself, 'I mean, my brother, our Alex. Alex,' suddenly afraid I might sound common, but you hadn't seemed to notice. 'He comes and goes at all hours, there's always some girl or other on the landing, queuing for the bathroom, wearing one of his skanky old T-shirts and no knickers. Ugh.'

I was exaggerating a bit — they usually were wearing knickers — but I liked the fact that you were amused.

'My point is,' I went on, 'do they even notice? Well, *she* does, and you know what she says? 'Better he does it under my roof than in an alley somewhere, or in the back of a car.''

'Well, she might have a point there. And he is a bit older than you, so . . . '

'He's seventeen,' I grimaced, 'and why does he have to *do it* anywhere? Ugh, ugh, ugh.'

'Sounds to me as though you have very cool, liberal, dare I say it maybe even a little bit hippy-ish parents, and most of the kids in school would kill for a swap. But you, naturally, would rather they were hard-line puritans who sent you to bed at 7 p.m. with a gruel supper and no TV.'

'First of all: they're *not* hippies, they just don't give a shit.' I had never sworn in front of you before, I was pretty sure — I checked your face — no reaction. 'Second of all: *please* don't talk to me as though I'm some typical teenager with textbook, predictable reactions to everything.'

'Would I dare?' you smiled.

'I'm telling you. I know everyone thinks their family is weird and says 'oh, they don't understand me', but mine really is, and they really don't.'

'I know. I get it.'

I also wanted to say, of course, and you. *You. You're the proof that I'm not the same as the others. The fact that you're my 'crush', if we must call it that (everyone seemed to).*

Not Mr Hill, the anaemic Biology teacher who looked barely out of school himself and had all the other girls in giggles every time he walked down the corridor. Laura was chief of his fan club; she raved about him. He left me cold.

You had something about you — it's an overused phrase, one that we all nodded knowingly around and pretended to understand. But no one else really did; you had something about you and I wasn't surprised that not everybody could see it.

Of course they couldn't — it was for me. It was the Something that connected you to me; the light in your eyes, like a secret, waiting for me, whispering that you were mine.

★ ★ ★

In the hotel room, the bed loomed between us, too big, too well made. I tugged at the covers so tightly tucked under the mattress, and I pulled the very top one onto the floor. Sitting on it cross-legged, I reached up and dragged a pillow down too.

You raised an eyebrow.

'What's this?'

I shrugged.

'I just don't like the bed.'

You bounced on it, patted it as though

encouraging a puppy.

'It's comfy,' you said.

'It's too . . . big.' It looked like the kind of bed that would expect something from me: a performance maybe, one I hadn't had time to rehearse. It was a movie bed, a grown-up bed. I was happy on the floor. Slowly I peeled off my socks.

'Then I'll come to you,' you smiled, but there was a touch of annoyance in your voice.

'Whatever.' I suddenly wanted water; the Chinese had been too salty, the wine too strong, the air-conditioning too dry.

Then you were kissing me, and there was no time for water, and anyway I liked it, I liked that part, always. I made the sound that I could never help making, 'mmm,' as though I was eating something good, and you smiled into the kiss because you thought you knew what *that* meant, and you fumbled with the button on my jeans.

I helped you. I got undressed quickly because in truth I just wanted it over with, I didn't want the next part, not tonight. I just wanted a quick kiss and a cuddle and to go to sleep here on the floor. But I didn't know how to tell you that, and anyway you mistook my speed at undressing for excitement, which made you smile even more. You didn't even wait to get your own clothes off, you just unzipped your trousers and climbed onto me.

I made some more noises because I knew that would make you finish faster, but I stared at the skirting board the whole time, and once you were breathless and still I said, 'You can go and sleep in the bed, I don't mind.' You did, leaving me on the floor.

I got up early and packed my bag while you slept so that we would be ready to leave, then made you a cup of tea and brought it to you. I stroked your hair and you woke up and murmured, 'You're an angel.'

That was my favourite part of the whole weekend.

★ ★ ★

When I came home from London, Mum was home too. She was sitting at the kitchen table drinking tea, like a visitor, so I went upstairs and looked in their bedroom. Sure enough, her clothes were hanging back in the wardrobe, her eyelash curlers and hair tongs were sitting on the dressing table.

'So you're back,' I said later.

'I never went away,' she said simply. I looked at Dad; he nodded and looked down. *So this is how it's going to be,* I thought. *We're just going to pretend it never happened.*

253

★ ★ ★

The best way I could think of to close the weekend off was to lock myself in my loft room and get stoned, but I couldn't get hold of Mari. In a way I didn't want to see her; she knew me too closely. I wanted to be with someone I could pretend with.

Todd. He was clearly pleased to hear from me and appeared at the bottom of the stairs so quickly I thought he must have run round from his house.

He'd brought his little biscuit box.

'Come to Mama,' I smiled, feeling terribly grown up and cool. Todd's eyes were shining.

I lay on the bed looking up at the sky while Todd rolled the first joint.

'Are you sure your folks won't mind?' he asked nervously, looking at the door.

'Advantage of living in the loft,' I said, standing on the bed and reaching up to open the skylight. Cold air whooshed into the room, 'and of course of having completely disinterested parents.' Secretly, of course, I didn't want either of them to come up the stairs. I didn't know what their reaction would be; apart from anything else, unlike my brother I never had 'friends' of the opposite sex over.

We were listening to Nirvana, but Todd was

flicking through my albums. He seemed impressed at all the 'really cool *old* stuff' I had: Joni Mitchell, Bob Dylan. Funny; I had always thought that stuff made me *not* cool. I smiled, the marijuana working its magic and sending happy little swirls into my brain. I felt as though I was watching them. It was also making me chatty, giddy.

'D'ya know where I've been this weekend? *London.*' I said it reverentially; *if you only knew what I was doing while I was there*, I thought. 'Have you ever been to London, Todd?'

'Me?' he inhaled. 'Nah, never been anywhere, me. I mean,' hurriedly, 'I go to Manchester, like, all the time. Hacienda and that . . . '

He trailed off and stared at me. His eyes were chocolate-coloured, and like a dog's; round and baleful. His hair dropped in curtains around his face, decades away from turning grey. He looked untouched.

'Why are you looking at me like that?' I brought my hands up as though to brush something from my face. Todd was grinning.

'You're not like the other girls. You know that?'

'Hmm, so I'm told,' and perhaps he thought my smile was for him, instead of belonging somewhere else, across town, or in

London, or in an English classroom, because he leaned in a little too close and I had to feign a coughing fit, which turned into laughing.

'You know what it is,' he was saying, 'that attracts you to people?'

'Err, usually a fit bum,' I giggled. I was the funniest person alive right now.

'No, no, I mean you know like when you fancy someone and, erm, you're not really sure why you do? I mean . . . do you know what it is that causes that?'

I tried to be solemn.

'No,' I said. 'No, Todd, I don't. Tell me!'

'It's the smell. Not, like, perfume or whatever. It's pheromones, or something. You don't even know it, you're not conscious of it, I mean, but that's why you like people.'

'Oh. Okay.' But then I was off again, until I thought I would die laughing, and eventually I started to fall asleep, my eyes too heavy and my head too thick, even though my shoulders were still shaking. And I was thinking of you, and your smell, of Aramis and cigarettes and coffee, and I thought, sometimes it's perfume, sometimes something else. And Todd said sweetly that he should leave, and said something serious about friendship that made me suddenly want to cry.

So when he kissed my forehead a chaste

goodbye, I smiled with my eyes closed and whispered, 'Nice smell.'

★ ★ ★

There are two, or maybe more, sides to every story. Sometimes people will try to muffle every version of the story but their own. 'Where they burn books,' Mrs Syms, our History teacher, once said, 'sooner or later they end up burning people.' She told me she'd seen it inscribed at a concentration camp. I didn't know why anyone would want to visit such a place, but Mrs Syms was the kind of woman who seemed to want to surround herself with other people's suffering. She was kind, and interesting, and was the person who made me understand the importance of the past.

This was about the time that Mari found the letters. It turned out her dad, the missing dad who had served as the template for all her expectations of men, had been writing to her for years, and her mum had been hiding the letters from her.

'All men are the same,' used to be Mari's line; 'selfish bastards, all of 'em.' The funny thing was, this never seemed to bother her, it was just a fact that she'd accepted. She even seemed to *like* men; she had several close male friends. She just had no expectations of them. So she'd never seemed particularly hurt by her view of the world. But after she got hold of the letters; this was what did it. Having to rewrite years and years' worth of your version of events; this is how your heart gets broken.

She never shouted and screamed at her mum. They were too close, she said, had been through too much together. In spite of their strange co-existence, meeting only ever in the crossover place of day and night, one eating breakfast, the other tea, with brief words and even briefer hugs, they were close. In spite of their seeming independence, a relationship more like sisters than mother and daughter, or more like friends than sisters, no, not even that — more like co-lodgers — in spite all of this, in the way of family they were all the other had. They were very ordinary letters, Mari said, telling her what he'd done at work that week. Hoping she was being good at school. They never suggested meeting up, never explained why he'd left or said sorry. But they were regular, and carefully written. She said she only read them once, but she kept them, in a shoebox on the top of her wardrobe. And when she moved into her flat, the shoebox came too, and was placed on top of another wardrobe, and is still there.

What I never understood was why, if her mum hadn't wanted Mari to see the letters, she had kept them at all.

'That's easy,' Mari said, and I suddenly realised why there had been no recriminations over the whole thing, 'because they're part of him. She still loves him, of course. The letters were meant for me, but she took them and kept them because they were all she could have of him.' She shrugged. 'How could I be mad at her for that?'

Diary: Monday, 12 April 1993

Laura is sleeping over tonight. We've had cheese on toast and we're in our PJs now, writing our diaries. She's been talking about Mr Hill — she's got it bad for him, bless her. She swears he stares at her in assembly, giving her the PPs (piercing, passionate looks, in case you were wondering!). She's probably right — why wouldn't he? She's gorgeous.

I didn't mention HM. I said I still like him, yes, when she asked, but nothing else. She knows we're friends, which we are — good friends. According to him. He hasn't asked me to keep the other stuff secret, but I keep it to myself anyway. I haven't even told you everything, Dear Diary! Ha ha. (Prying eyes and all that.)

The whole thing with HM just feels so different

from the rest of my life, I have absolutely no idea,
if I did want to talk about it, where I would begin
or what words I would use.
    Ten-ten, TTFN.

15

I dress for court as though for a funeral.
Black skirt, black tights. I want to be in
shadow, today.

My hair, disobedient as ever, won't lie flat.
Or rather, on one side of my head it is too
flat; limp against my temple, resistant to the
coaxing of the brush. On the other it skips
out at chin level, a jaunty curl I can only tuck
behind my ear. I stare at myself in the mirror.
For at least fifteen minutes I'm convinced
that today's outcome somehow depends
solely upon my ability to control my hair. My
eyes fill with frustrated hot tears and I brush
them away impatiently and slick concealer
under my eyes.

You are surprisingly upbeat. Whistling,
even. Behind me in the mirror, you straighten
your tie, bare your teeth to check for stray
crumbs. Is your confidence completely
unshakeable? What would have to happen to
make you weak, make you crumble? *Losing
you,* you would probably say, and I would
smile and nestle into your shoulder, only half
daring to believe you.

'Shall we go?' you smile, as though

suggesting a visit to the shops. I nod and follow you numbly out to the car.

* * *

The court building smells sterile, like a hospital. The people in its halls look lost, dazed. Most stare into space. The clicking of heels down wooden floors echoes around the vaulted ceilings of the hallways. I sit on a plastic chair, my hands clasped.

I can't help but wonder what Alice is doing now.

* * *

I scan the courtroom desperate to see a friendly face, and dreading seeing a familiar one. I have an aunt who's been known to pop up in the public areas of court cases completely unrelated to her. And what about the jury? They could be anyone.

I suddenly remember reading somewhere that in the earliest courts the jury comprised one member of each zodiac sign. That's why there are still twelve jurors today. The reason was to represent every facet of the human personality and therefore assure the defendant of a fair trial. As they file in I look at their faces, try to read from their clothes, the way they hold themselves, whether they are the type of people who would find you guilty. *Am I?* I wonder, but I don't have time to give myself an answer because we are beginning.

I hadn't thought about seeing some of my former teachers here. I know you've aged, but some of them look ancient. Mrs Syms — my beloved History teacher — is grey-haired now, and seems smaller, her shoulders bony. I don't like looking at her, and don't want her to see me. I sink further down in my chair.

One by one, a procession of witnesses trot out the same mantra. Lines repeat themselves as though from a higher source: well-respected. Unblemished record. Previous good character. Moral.

When Sister Agnes, the head teacher, takes the stand, I glance at Alice. She looks as though she might faint. A couple of jurors, their faces inscrutable until now, lean forward perceptibly. Who wouldn't be interested in the testimony of a nun?

What's more, Sister Agnes seems to want to take the opportunity not only to defend you but to attack Alice. When asked how she remembers the plaintiff, she scoffs, 'Hardly a model pupil.'

Sister Agnes is still a physically slight, unimposing woman, but her voice seems to boom around the courtroom and her stare and her words are like knives. Even Imogen Cartwright has to ask her to stick to the point. When she finally leaves the dock I could swear she casts Alice a triumphant glance.

Your part is brief.

'Have you ever invited a pupil, past or present, to visit you alone at home?'

'No.' An unflinching lie.

'Can you explain how this young woman could have provided an accurate description of the inside of your house?'

'Yes, I think I can.' You smile disarmingly at the jury, address your answer to them, patiently, as though talking to a small child. 'Alice had an aunt who lived just along the road. It's a fairly new estate, all the houses have a very similar layout,' you shrug. 'Alice was at her aunt's reasonably frequently as far as I can make out. She could probably give you the exact dimensions of the rooms.' That smile again.

'And the decor? Your furniture?'

'Not sure.' You stroke your chin as if puzzled, as if unrehearsed. 'I suppose it's possible she may have seen photographs. I have a few family photos on my desk at school. Nieces, nephews, that sort of thing.'

Imogen opens her mouth to speak but you chip in, 'Of course, I suppose she may have looked through my window one time on a visit to her aunt's.' At this you look directly at Alice, a lingering look. A gentle look. With a soft laugh you finish, 'But I'm not suggesting she was *that* obsessed.'

'But you do think Alice Webb was obsessed with you?'

A sigh, the hands through the hair. 'I'm afraid so, yes.'

*   *   *

She had a crush. She'd become something of a teacher's pet, hanging behind after class, signing up for extra lessons. You didn't worry too much about it at first — you were pleased because it marked a turnaround in her behaviour, which previously could at best be described as 'rebellious'.

Down in what increasingly are looking to me like stalls in a theatre, I catch sight of Sister Agnes nodding furiously.

The allegations; this is the first time I've heard what they actually are, in detail.

Three counts of sexual activity with a child.

Once in your car. Twice in your house.

Described in detail, not by Alice in person, but by a statement written by her and read out. I hear her voice in it. I listen carefully for your voice, for any piece of you in the descriptions, but to my relief I don't hear you.

Letters are produced but they're quickly discounted as nothing can be proven from them. You admit when questioned that it was 'ill advised' to write letters to a pupil. You were trying to support her, you say. To 'reach' her.

You were concerned; Alice had stopped turning up for her extra tuition. She was troubled, but she was bright. You wanted to help her. That's why the letters said things like: 'talk to me' and 'we can sort it out'.

One of them was signed with a kiss; all with your initial or initials, but never your first name. That, you say, would have been inappropriate.

⋆　⋆　⋆

Drinking champagne seems wrong, somehow. We're an odd collection: me, you, Imogen Cartwright, Mr Addison. Mr Addison: star witness! Mr Addison, I mean Bill, Bill Addison, I should call him by his first name, of course, as I silently top up his glass like a waitress. Instead I still see him as my Geography teacher; see chalk in his hand, remember exercise books tossed disdainfully across desks, bored scathing comments from his weasel lips hanging in the air.

I don't think he recognises me. Why would he? I don't suppose he would be expecting to see two former pupils in one day and, besides, he's engrossed in his own self-importance. I'm just the girl holding the bottle, the girl in black, in the background. Bill Addison, greedy champagne slurper, is too busy swallowing praise: yours, and Imogen's.

'Now, now,' he blusters, 'it was nothing, really.'

His testimony was key. He was the colleague you had confided in — shared your concerns with about this poor, troubled pupil whom you feared was getting 'too close'. His words, careful and clear as though rehearsed, were: 'If there was something going on with the girl, why would Henry have told me his concerns about her?'

It had annoyed me that he kept referring to her not by name, but as The Girl. *Alice*, I kept thinking. *Alice Alice Alice.*

What an odd foursome we make, laughing and supping our bubbles; looking out over the freedom of the garden.

The dry taste of champagne in my mouth, the smell of freesias, transport me to a summer day only two years ago. I look down at my severe black outfit, feel uncomfortable in the thick tights. Is it so long since I was wearing white?

Our wedding, over the course of its planning, had become a thing that got out of control, grew legs ('and hair and teeth,' Dave used to laugh). Well-meaning aunts and friends had done their 'bit' with table decorations, flowers, candles, favours. It had all seemed odd to me; beautiful, but odd, like wearing jewellery that doesn't belong to you.

The wedding was a little idyll. It exceeded my expectations in every way. Everyone says it's the best day of your life and this is the whole problem with marriage, surely? Everything that comes after the wedding, this day of hyperbole, of almost overwhelming *pleasantness*, is bound to disappoint.

Even my parents — usually surly and uncommunicative, often with people generally and almost always with each other — were merry and sociable. I actually saw them hold hands. We were both products of so-called 'happy marriages', Dave and I, or at any rate, we both had parents who stayed together. Mine seething with barely concealed resentment, mother raging and occasionally leaving, father saying nothing; his so calm and level-headed and fair about everything, you could easily believe they were self-medicating.

But everyone was at their best that day; the

whole event was suffused with a kind of warmth I'd never experienced before.

Wedding days are always remembered, like childhoods, as warmer and sunnier than they really were. The photographs are always flattering, and deceiving; they don't capture the moments of stress; everyone is smiling; there's no way of knowing from the pictures that the bride can barely breathe, laced into her corset, unable to sit down, much less eat a meal.

But there is a moment I remember with total clarity, exactly as it was. Just after the meal that I couldn't eat, Dave and I slipped away from the party for half an hour, walked in the gardens behind the hotel.

There was the overwhelming smell of freesia (*meanwhile, in today's new world, I hover in the conservatory, stare through glass at your garden*). And there were sweet peas, and lily of the valley. Sweet, old-fashioned flowers.

As we walked, fingers interlinked like shy young sweethearts, I suddenly wished everyone else would go home. Everything had changed for us now; we were public property. I felt as though we had made our vows not just to each other but to all of these people. They were our witness; they owned pieces of us. It terrified me, made me want to run away.

Of course, the evening would roll on and be wonderful, twinkling with candles and stars, and I would forget my fears. But for that half an hour, while it was just us, it was just Us. Us in beautiful clothes, showing our best side to each other, but still Us. And we were Ours, away from the camera flashes and the kisses, we were ours, and each other's. And I knew that moment was perfect, and would never ever come back.

And now I find myself staring out of a window, clutching a half-empty bottle of champagne, wondering how the hell I got from there to here.

'Anyway,' Addison's blustering voice snaps me away from my memories like a command, 'it wasn't me who was the star witness. It was the girl's mother. Where did you get her from, Imogen? What a coup!'

Imogen Cartwright smirks. She hadn't had to do too much. She'd questioned Alice about the problems she'd shared with you. A picture emerged of a vulnerable girl with a troubled home life. A violent father and a mother too weak, or too drunk, to leave.

'And why did you tell Mr Morgan all of these things?'

Alice was silent for a moment, looked down. In her navy skirt suit she looked like a child who'd raided her mother's wardrobe.

'Alice. Why did you confide in Mr Morgan about the things that were going on at home?'

'I felt he was . . . my friend.'

'Anything else? Something you might have mentioned in an earlier statement, for example?'

'I don't remember.'

'Let me see if I can help you out.' Imogen lifted a piece of paper and looked at it as though for the first time. In the mechanical voice that signifies quotation marks she said, ''I told him stuff, coz I knew he had a weakness for girls with problems.''

There was a strange, barely perceptible shuffle from the jury, and the air in the courtroom moved. It was as though you could hear their minds beginning to change.

From this point Imogen Cartwright was relentless in depicting Alice as a conniving, sexually aggressive, devious girl who had set out single-mindedly to seduce Henry Morgan and in the process wreck his career. The picture didn't sit well with the pale young woman in the dock, who occasionally shook her head and whispered 'no', but otherwise looked beaten. I stared at her bitten-down fingernails. I stared at my own.

As Mr Addison rightly pointed out, it was Alice's own mother, however, who would prove to provide the turning point.

Alice had looked horrified when the woman with bleached blonde hair and a haggard expression took the stand.

'Lies,' she said simply. She had a lisp that meant she spat at the microphone with every 's'. 'It's all lies. All that about her dad hitting me? A load of rubbish. It never happened.' Her bold, unblinking eyes were the only resemblance she bore to her daughter. 'You won't find a single person, apart from Alice, who'll say that it did.'

'But Mrs Webb, why would anyone invent such terrible stories?'

'That's just it. That's our Alice,' she sighed, 'always been a storyteller.'

I started as though hearing someone call my name.

From that point on, it was like watching a building be demolished in slow motion. A psychotherapist's report citing Alice's anorexia, self-harm, some delusional tendencies; the minor criminal convictions and failed money-making schemes of Alice's partner Dennis. What had seemed a huge boulder in your path settled to crumbs and dust; just the word of a girl, a troubled girl, her head in her hands.

'Unreliable witness . . . '

'Attention seeking, dangerous and plausible liar . . . '

272

'Any conviction would be unsafe . . . '

'In view of Mr Morgan's previously unblemished character . . . '

'No case to answer.'

16

You're an avid reader of newspapers, most days. You're the only person I know who reads every section. Sport, Gardening, Travel. News, Reviews, Business. You even look over the classifieds, although to my knowledge you've never bought anything from them. Picking up a Sunday paper after you've had it is like sifting through rubble. As neat as you are in every other way around the house, when you read you leave a mess. Pages lie open, folded backwards and over themselves, in the wrong sequence. Articles you've paused on are partly obscured by coffee-coloured rings and your doodles, your scribbles.

But today you turn the pages slowly, meticulously; today you are scouring them only for your story.

'No case to answer,' you murmur, flicking through the pages, 'that's what will be written.'

'Therefore it's true', is the unsaid post-script to your comment; 'what's written is true'.

I look at the entertainment section, scan

the reviews. Maybe we should go to the theatre this weekend.

My mobile rings; Mari's name flashes up. I pause, then pick up with a breezy 'Hello!'

'Hello . . . ' she says hesitantly, as though not sure she's got the right number. 'Are you okay? Where are you?'

'What do you mean, where am I?' My voice is too high, too happy, too sing-song. But I don't know how to stop it. 'I'm . . . here.' I can't bring myself to say 'at home', it still doesn't sound right. I get up from the table, smiling at you, and wander out of the room. You aren't looking at me, you're still studying the papers.

'Are you okay?' she asks again. 'I saw the news.'

'I know, it's great, isn't it?'

'Is it?'

'Of course.' I try to keep the frown from my voice. 'No case to answer. The whole ridiculous thing thrown out.'

'Fee,' she says slowly, 'he wasn't found innocent . . . *she* was found unreliable. There's a difference.'

'Is this why you called?'

'I don't want to hear this', I want to say. I want to eat breakfast and make plans for the weekend. I'm done with all the analysis.

'No, not really,' she sighs, 'I miss you, babe.

275

Wanna get together and throw back some wine? Sit up all night talking about nothing?'

A strange feeling, like fear, comes over me. As a general rule I love nothing more than an all-nighter with Mari. We've always tended to stay in rather than go out; maybe it comes of beginning a friendship in the days when we were too young and too skint to go to the pub; maybe we've been trying to keep the spirit of the old parties going all these years. Most likely we just find being 'out' too noisy, too distracting; we've always had far too much to say to each other to risk it being drowned out by other people's chat, by the clink of other people's glasses.

The thing is, general rules don't seem to apply anymore. I glance back down the hallway into the kitchen. You're drinking coffee, looking out of the window now, the papers abandoned on the table. The thought of leaving you, even for a night, fills me with panic. Other people, people outside of these walls, represent danger now. Even Mari, my surrogate older sister.

'I don't know,' I say; met with silence from the other end, I have to keep talking. I've always found it hard to say no to Mari. 'I mean, I'd like to, but I'm kind of busy, I've ... I'm ...'

'Don't worry,' she sighs, 'I get it.'

'It's just . . . ' Hopeless; I have no excuses.

'Just let me say one thing, babe. It's lonely, you know? It's lonely when no one knows what's going on in your life.'

And with that, she's gone.

        ★   ★   ★

You're back at school. I'm back at work, and already the summer seems like a distant idyll and the blot on it that was the court case is receding. 'Forget it ever happened' is your mantra, the only thing you ever say about the case, and it's as though everyone has. The world kept turning, after all.

We've settled into a sort of domestic routine, albeit one still flavoured with romance. We leave each other notes. I can't remember which of us started it; it just seems something that is right for us to do. On the days I leave the house before you, I put one in your coffee mug, or in your trouser pocket. I lean into the steam of the kettle, for warmth, chewing the end of my pen, thinking. You leave them in my make-up bag, or sometimes under the windscreen wiper of my car.

I leave kisses; you write 'BOO!' in big letters or sometimes just 'Good morning'. Sometimes you might write a line from a song, illustrated in your painter's hand with carefully coloured-in quavers and clefs.

Already we look back at the summer weeks in the same way we look back on all our past times together; they've become pages written about somebody else. Funny how when recalling those times you always encourage me to go to the good parts. Your memory's terrible, or so you say. As the autumn gloom and chills encroach on our evenings, we curl up and you murmur, 'tell me again about the time we . . . ' and 'remember when . . . '

You sow happy thoughts in my brain, making way, pushing out the bad, the sad.

You assume, of course, that I kept a diary all those years, 'prolific little scribe that you were'.

'On and off,' I shrug. 'It's not very organised. Scraps of paper, here and there. Notebooks. And I don't know how much of it to believe myself, to be honest. Can there be a more unreliable narrator than a teenage girl?'

As soon as I've said it I regret it, as a shadow passes over your face, but you quickly laugh.

'Good to see you haven't forgotten everything I taught you. When reading any text, always consider the context it was written in.' You pause. 'I'd love to see them.'

'I thought you said the past was the past.' I

feel suddenly protective towards my teenage self, her thoughts (and pretensions) etched onto paper, part deep truth, part self-imposed censorship.

'Yes, but I enjoy anything you write.'

'You're never seeing them.' I try to end this with a laugh but it comes out cold. You frown.

'What, are you worried I'd try to destroy the evidence?'

This strikes me as an odd thing to say; we stare at each other for a few moments. Eventually I'm the one to break the silence.

'Perhaps you were right before and we should leave the past where it is. I sometimes wonder . . . '

'What?'

'Well . . . perhaps we should be talking about the future. Why don't we?'

'Because, sunshine, at my age there's not as much material. I'm afraid the future is a narrow field of interest for me.'

'Come on,' I say irritably, 'you're forty-three, not ninety-three.'

'Okay, so let me ask you — why do you want to? Isn't it amazing enough that we've got here? Can't we just enjoy what we have?'

I shrug. We've got here as a result of my decisions, not yours — you haven't changed anything, you haven't left anyone, you're still in your home. And although I left mine, I haven't fully, not really, not in a committed way.

'What is it you want?' you tease, filling up my glass. 'Your name above the letterbox?'

You joke but I still have my post redirected, not here, but to Mari's, from where she in turn redirects it here, in bundles every few days. In fact my only contact with her since our conversation just after the court case has been her handwriting on the letters that drop onto the mat. 'Please redirect to:', all her letter 'E's written like capitals, and a cross through my old identity, and your address, underlined. We haven't spoken, or met, in weeks. How many weeks? I count them on my fingers.

I still have things, stuff, as well, at home. Home? Dave's house? What should I be calling it now? I still have a key, still feel the door is open. I know I could walk back in. So have I actually made any decision? Is it so amazing that we're here?

'I just feel in limbo,' I sigh, and what I really want to say is: 'we're still just two people having an affair'. Like millions of people, holding a secret the same as millions of secrets.

I wonder why I've only told Mari about you; no one else. Well, I know why I told her at the start; I thought she would understand (which she did), and I thought she might even find it amusing (which she didn't, not really) and therefore convince me it wasn't a big deal, it wasn't serious.

I told her because I knew she wouldn't judge me, so I wouldn't have to judge myself.

Some friends, while they'd never judge you, act as a sort of mirror, reflecting the truth back at you. Is this why I haven't told Laura? Or is it because secrecy keeps a thing special?

'Don't tell anyone' is a powerful phrase. On this friendships are forged, wars won, lives saved. It binds. It says: no one else would understand. It's this I haven't been able to let go of. I regret even telling Mari, which is why, looking at her handwriting on my bills, counting time on my fingers, I suddenly realise why I haven't seen her.

Maybe it's time. Time to make it real. Time to hold up the mirror.

I'll call Laura.

My phone starts to ring while I'm rummaging in my bag for it, and when I see Laura's home number flashing on my phone, I pick up with a smile.

'You must be psychic. I was just about to call you.' But I'm surprised to hear Matt. His words, and his voice, are broken.

'It's Laura. And. The baby. Hospital. Please come.'

★ ★ ★

Hospitals make me feel queasy. It's the colours: the pale green walls, not mint or apple or lime, just a very pale green, a poorly colour. The white sheets: boiled, starched, regulation. Egg white. The sand-coloured floor tiles.

Laura looks small in her bed, overpowered by flowers. Lilies, her favourite, and roses and gerbera. I add my own bunch, busying myself making the leaves symmetrical in their vase, waiting for her to wake up.

When she does, it's with a smile and a 'hey'.

'How are you?' A useless question, but she tilts her head as though really thinking about it, as though it's something she hasn't been asked before. Finally she says, in a matter-of-fact voice, 'Empty.'

I look at the red rim of her eyes, the remnant of tears only for the lost baby, or something else as well?

'What happened?'

'He wasn't there,' she says. 'When I fell. He wasn't there.'

'Where was . . . ?' but I don't have to finish,

282

because suddenly I get it.

'Oh, he told me where he was. Racked with guilt, I suppose. And he didn't stop there. He told me everything.'

She's said this sort of thing before. Since she first told me she knew about Matt's infidelities she's referred to them countless times but always in an oblique sort of way, as though to a vague phenomenon she thinks might be happening but is detached from and has no interest in proving or disproving.

But something in her voice is different this time. Although she looks small propped up on her pillows, she sounds stronger. Sure.

'What will you do?' I ask. I move to stroke her hand but think better of it; she doesn't look as though she needs hand holding.

'*Do?*' She looks puzzled. 'Carry on, I suppose.'

★   ★   ★

I find Matt outside chewing on a vended plastic cup, long since drained of coffee. I raise a 'What the?' eyebrow.

'Too right I've told her everything,' he says. 'Time for a clean slate.'

'Jesus, Matt,' I say, 'she's in hospital. What are you trying to do to her?'

He shrugs.

283

'I know it sounds bad, it just . . . it just seemed like the right thing to do. I couldn't bear the thought that if I lost her, she would . . . she would be gone and I'd never have told her the truth.'

'And how was she?'

'Surprisingly strong.'

I nod. *That figures*, I think. That's Laura in a nutshell: surprisingly strong. She's practical. She's always had the ability to weigh things up logically. She'll be hurt, now, but she can measure the hurt; she can process it. The unknown hurt of being without him; this is what will terrify her. Perhaps losing the baby, and going through this new pain with Matt, will even bring them closer together. *It was a risky move, though*, I think, looking at him, remembering the story you told me once: the heartbroken wife in the lake.

'You told her about the other women, everything?'

'I think she already knew, on some level.'

'Matt,' I say, 'we all already knew. On every level.' I sigh. 'At least it shows some sort of respect for her that you admitted it.'

'There's one thing I didn't tell her,' he says, and I immediately know what he's going to say. 'I didn't tell her about the time that we . . . you and I. You know.'

'Well, nothing happened,' I say, suddenly

unable to look him in the eye.

'I know, that's maybe why I don't feel so bad not telling her. And you're her best friend.'

'You know, over the years, I've wondered if I imagined it. If I misread the signals.'

He laughs. 'You didn't misread it, Fee. And even with all the things I've done, to be honest that's one thing I'm not ashamed of.'

'You ought to be, for Christ's sake. It was your engagement party! And as you say, I'm her best friend.'

'I know. It's just ... there was always something about you.'

'Don't start.'

'No, no, that's it. The old Matt, done and dusted. I'm a reformed character. That's what I'm trying to tell you. I won't even flirt with you anymore.' I swear his eyelid flickers as though he's trying to suppress an uncon- scious wink. I smile ruefully. 'And that's not all. I'm going to marry her.'

'You do realise that announcement isn't so dramatic when you've been engaged for five years?'

'Yep. And I don't care. I don't care about drama. Sometimes you realise what's impor- tant in life, Fee. As horrible as all this is,' he waves his hand down the corridor and then around his head as though trying to bat away a fly, 'it's been the wake-up call that I needed.'

★ ★ ★

I go back into the ward to say goodbye and Laura has the glazed look of someone just about to doze off. The half-closed eyes that make those around them tread softly and lower their voices.

'Congratulations,' I whisper, 'I hear you're getting married.'

Laura smiles.

'Yeah, I heard that too. Thanks.' She stares at me. 'I feel sort of guilty, like I can't be happy about it. I don't really know how I'm supposed to cope . . . with *this*.' She motions listlessly towards her stomach. 'This wasn't in the plan, you know?'

I nod.

'Well, maybe there's a different plan. You just can't see it yet.'

'Maybe.'

'Sorry, that was a pretty useless thing to say. I know nothing can make this better.'

'It's just good that you're here.'

Her eyes start to close and this time I do grasp her hand, and she gives it a squeeze in return. Just when I think she's fallen asleep, she whispers, 'You know what it's like, don't you? *This*, I mean.'

I hesitate, 'Well, not really.'

'To lose a . . . you know.'

'Well, that was a bit different.' I shift in my seat.

'You never really . . . ' she draws a slow and painful-sounding breath, 'you never really told me.'

'Ssh. Try to rest now.'

'I feel like I'll never rest again.'

But in spite of herself she yawns, and her eyes stay closed, and I watch the rise and fall of her chest slowing down as eventually sleep comes over her.

★ ★ ★

I nudge her gently awake as visiting hours come to a close and the light gets lower.

'You'll be okay, won't you? You and Matt, I mean.'

'*We* will.' She narrows her eyes even more until they're almost closed. 'What about you?'

'Well, Dave and I — '

'I'm not talking about Dave. I mean the other one.'

I look at her.

'How do you know?'

'I just know *you*.'

I laugh; that's true. I haven't given her enough credit.

'Ask me again when you're home, and better.'

'I don't know if I'll ever feel better. Not really.' That matter-of-fact tone to her voice again. She takes my hand. 'But, you promise you'll tell me?'

I hesitate. I can't escape the feeling that the reason I haven't told anyone else about you is because I *know*. I know what they'll say, and I know they'll be right.

'I promise.'

* * *

You're working hard, these days, and late, some nights. You did warn me this would happen. More management-type stuff, you said. Kind of a promotion.

'I'll have to put the hours in,' you say, 'especially now.'

'I thought you said everything was the same, nothing has changed.' I sound whiny but I can't help it; without you here, I feel completely lost in this house. And for the second or third time in as many weeks, you're telling me you'll be late home. As usual you tell me casually, while cooking dinner, while not looking at me.

288

'Nothing's changed for *us*, is what I meant,' you frown, 'I mean, we're okay, aren't we? At least, I hope you wouldn't let that stupid . . . well, you wouldn't let all of that get to *us*, would you?'

I give the only answer that question can accept: 'of course not'.

'But at school, obviously it's different . . . all I'm saying is I'm grateful for how they've supported me, so I might have to do a bit extra here and there. Not have to, in fact — *want* to. It's the least I can do, don't you think?'

Again I have to agree. I know I'm being too sensitive; I try to make light of it. Sliding my arms around your waist from behind and leaning into your back, I murmur, 'Just come back to me as early as you can, okay?'

★   ★   ★

The phone wakes me in the dark. Your phone. I blink at the clock: 2 a.m. We both scramble for it, me rolling on top of you, almost entirely over you, but it's on your side so you reach it first, reject the call, switch it off. You turn back into the pillow, wordlessly, as though to go back to sleep.

'Who the hell was that?' I ask.

'Wrong number.'

'How do you know, when you didn't pick up?'

'Go to sleep, Fiona.'

Fiona, not Fee. That means: end of conversation. With a loud 'humph' noise I get out of bed, pull a cardigan from the chair around my shoulders and stalk out of the room.

★ ★ ★

In the morning, you whistle as you make your coffee. Take it into the bathroom with you.

Your phone, on the kitchen worktop, sitting there like a clue to an unsolved crime.

I pick it up, hands trembling, and start to scroll. Missed calls, received calls. Nothing. All call history erased.

★ ★ ★

I visit Laura as soon as she is home and, keeping my promise, I try to contain you in a few sentences.

It's weird, because I was at school with Laura so she has a certain view of you, different to that of, say, Mari or someone who hadn't met you. I tell her about then, about now; I tell her everything as quickly as I can.

She looks at me with wide eyes.

'I always thought . . . it was Todd. I thought you were going out with him. Everything that you said happened . . . I thought it was him.'

'Todd was my cover, I suppose,' I sigh, 'we were never boyfriend and girlfriend.'

'Mr Morgan,' she's shaking her head. 'I'm not totally surprised, I have to say.'

'Don't tell me,' I say, 'he had an affair with you, too, right?' It's a weary joke but a tiny beaten part of me is afraid she will turn to me and say yes.

'No, but . . . I heard there was a girl. Years before . . . years ago. And . . . Helen Platt. I remember her. That was taken as fact, right? You. This girl, Alice.'

'What are you saying?' I frown.

'I'm saying, who knows how many, since . . . and now.'

'So girls threw themselves at him. That doesn't prove anything. And who hasn't got a past, especially when you get to your thirties and forties?'

Gently, she puts her hands on my knees and says, 'We're not talking about someone who's just got 'a past', Fee. Or someone who's had or is even still having lots of partners. God knows,' she smiles ruefully, 'I know enough to write a book about that. We're talking about a man, Fee — and children.'

291

In a small voice I say, 'But he's with me now. I'll . . . I can help him. I can . . . *save* him.'

The words recall a note in my make-up bag that I'd forgotten, even though it's only weeks old; a page from an exercise book, your handwriting saying 'Save me?', the question mark, everything.

A plea I've never answered.

A note I'd forgotten. I guess we pick and choose the messages we receive.

'He's my template, you see,' I tell her, 'he was the first . . . and the last. Everything in between just feels like it was a pretence. A waste, even. Nothing was ever going to live up to him. It didn't matter, doesn't matter, what he's done, what he's like. He's what I measure by. He's all I know.'

'You should've talked to me before,' she says quietly, studying my face. 'You've been lonely.'

To my own surprise, I find myself saying, 'Yes.'

I'm reminded of the last phone call from Mari, a few weeks ago now. *It's lonely when no one knows what's going on in your life.* Her plea for company. The times I've let her calls ring out since then. I suddenly realise: maybe it wasn't about me. I look at Laura, her sadness, her surprising wisdom. People's lives are going on, I think. What if I hadn't answered the phone to Matt, what if all this had happened and I hadn't known about it? With a final, gentle hug, I start to gather my things together.

'Thank you,' I say to Laura. She looks puzzled.

'What for?'

'For making a few things clearer.'

17

It takes Mari a long time to answer the door, but somehow I know she's in there. I knock gently, as though afraid of causing pain.

When she answers, Mari has a look I've never seen her wear before: the look of someone who's cried a lot. Not recently, maybe not even today, but the traces of hours of it are on her puffed eyes, her pinched lips.

She walks back to the living room, gesturing for me to follow her, and sits in a well-worn spot on the sofa.

'He died,' she says.

'Who?' I want to ask, but stop myself when I see the letters she's clutching.

'Your dad,' I say. Not a question.

'My dad.'

The grief has bowed her. The jut of her chin is gone. Her hair, usually spiky, sits flat against her temples, its cheerful red incongruous with her unpainted face.

'Jesus, Mari. I'm sorry.' I'm sorry that he died, sorry that I wasn't here, sorry that I've been so wrapped up in my world that it's been weeks, maybe months, since I asked about hers.

'I never even knew him,' she's saying, turning his letters over in her hands, 'not really. But now I miss him. That doesn't make sense, does it?'

'I think it does,' and I hug her, because I don't know what else to do.

'Thank you,' she mumbles into my hair. After her shoulders have stopped shaking, I pull away and say, 'Mari . . . can I stay here tonight?'

'Yes, please.'

★   ★   ★

'I'm quitting,' she says, peeling the cellophane off a packet of cigarettes, and unlike the hundreds of times she's said it before, I believe her. Still, she says, 'I really am. Soon. But for now, for a while, I just want to pretend.' She looks at me, her eyes shining. 'I want to go back.'

I nod. I understand.

★   ★   ★

Within a few hours we've both smoked ourselves hoarse and burnt our throats with neat spirits. No time for wine, or beer, tonight; we are serious about getting drunk.

It's okay, though; we've been laughing.

Crying a bit, too, but finding the occasional space to laugh. We lie on our backs, a battered sofa each, our heads at opposite ends, our feet close enough to extend to the occasional playful kick.

Old stories, old conversations, play out before us like cinema reels. We dig out questions we've been meaning to ask.

'You and Todd,' she says suddenly, and I groan a 'not that again' groan, which makes her giggle. 'No, seriously. Why not? You two could've been the perfect couple. Coulda been, like, childhood sweethearts. All that rubbish.'

'Yeah, and you could've married The Tobacconist.'

'Very funny.'

'I mean it!' I touch her foot with mine. 'Remember the time you gave me sex advice?'

She spits out her whiskey laughing.

'The only sex advice I ever gave you, kid, was not to have it.'

'I know. More responsible than you looked, weren't you?'

'I always did feel sort of responsible for you,' she says quietly, 'not sure why.'

I look up at the ceiling and watch the reel unfurl.

* * *

It was before a party; we were fourteen and sixteen, drinking cider and kohling our eyes. 'Once you've done it, you can't get it back,' Mari was saying. The two years she had over me seemed like eons of wisdom. 'You can still have fun. You can be the 'everything but' girl. They'll respect you more that way.'

'What about you?'

She laughed.

'I'm the 'everything' girl, kiddo. Unfortunately. It's too late for me — I was spoiled a long time ago. But once you become that person, people look at you a certain way. Damaged goods. So what I'm saying is, don't rush anything.' She paused, looked at herself in the mirror. 'Christ, I sound like your mother!'

'Yeah, except my mother would never give me such good advice,' I said. 'Or any advice, in fact. Mari?'

'Mmm?'

'Is that why you like The Tobacconist?' We always called him The Tobacconist, instead of by his Christian name; I don't know why, it was just a habit we started and couldn't shake. It made us laugh for some reason.

'Pah! I don't *like* him. I just work there.'

The main thing I remember about The Tobacconist, it's funny, is that he didn't eat much, but he loved cheese. He was older than

Mari; early twenties, looked thirty. He wore a small fluffy beard. He'd inherited the shop from the grandfather who'd raised him; he was an orphan.

He ate a different cheese every day, Mari told me. He was stringy thin.

'Maybe it's a sort of eating disorder,' I would frown. Mari scoffed; she considered most illnesses a kind of vanity, and reserved the greatest of distaste for the psychological variety.

'A man with an eating disorder,' she'd say incredulously, 'I mean. Ugh. That's just wrong.'

And she shuddered and rubbed her hands together, looking rapidly around as though for a place to wash them; to wash the idea off her.

The Tobacconist (what was his name? It began with K, I think. Kevin? Keith, maybe) loved her, of course. Why else would he have employed her to work every single day — albeit for only a couple of hours each day? The shop was hardly busy; there wasn't much call for a real, old-fashioned tobacconists' on our estate.

Mari worked there not just for the money, but for the smell, she told me. She loved the smell, especially of the pipe tobacco.

'You love *his* smell, you mean,' I'd tease.

And she'd wrinkle her nose and say that the smells of Wensleydale; of Brie; of apricot-studded Stilton, cancelled him out. But in her smile I could tell there was something, not just the shop, the smell, the money, it was him; he kept her going back.

'You know what I'm saying,' I said quietly. 'He — he looks at you a different way, doesn't he? He thinks you're . . . better. *He* doesn't see you as damaged goods.'

She was shaking her head, but she was smiling.

'Just you stay *undamaged* for as long as you can, kid,' she said. 'As long as you can.'

★　★　★

Back in the present, she's murmuring, 'Kendal. That was his name.'

'God, no wonder I've forgotten it. Really? As in mint cake?'

'Yep.' She sighs, 'But anyway — you and Todd. What happened? Or more to the point, why didn't it happen?'

'Everything you said. Damaged goods and all that.'

She sits up.

'What?'

'It didn't happen,' I say slowly, 'because of him. Because of Morgan. By the time I realised Todd liked me, and that I might have liked him, it was . . . too late. That's how I felt, anyway.'

'Todd wouldn't have known.'

'Maybe not, but I would have. *I* knew.' I put out my cigarette and announce, 'After tonight, I'm quitting, too.'

'Yeah, yeah.'

'No, I mean it. And I'm going to cut down drinking, and eat well, and go to the gym.'

'Gonna give up everything that's bad for you, are ya?' Mari narrows her eyes.

'We'll see . . . yeah, maybe I will. Maybe I'll be good and go back to my husband.' I'd not even considered this until saying it aloud, and am surprised to hear how familiar, how warm, the word 'husband' sounds in my mouth.

'If he'll have you.'

'That's not funny.' My turn to sit up on the sofa. 'Shit. What if he doesn't?'

'Well, you can't expect him to have just waited around for you.' She must see something in my face because she adds quickly, 'But he will, babe. Course he will. But the thing is . . . ' She trails off, and for a minute she's so still and so silent I think she's fallen asleep. Just as I'm considering taking the burning cigarette out of her hand and throwing a blanket over her, she says, 'Well, maybe you should be on your own for a while. Without either of them.' She flicks away the teetering cone of ash, and somehow it lands in the empty glass on the floor without her even looking. 'You could always stay here.'

My head is in my hands.

'I think I'm getting my hangover early,' I say, looking at the clock. 3 a.m.

'You don't have to take the safe route, you know. I've always said follow your heart, follow your dreams, all that crap, haven't I?'

'Yes,' I laugh, 'but if it's that easy, how come I've got what I thought I always wanted and I'm not blissfully happy? How come I suddenly don't know which way to go?'

'Because maybe Morgan isn't it, babe. The only way to know is to watch, and listen, and trust your gut. You know what they say,' she smiles, 'you only live once.'

* * *

I must have drifted off, because it's 4.30 a.m. when Mari shakes my shoulder with the reproach, 'Come on, kid — we're supposed to be on an all-nighter. Like the old times.'

'Jeez,' I rub my temples, 'I don't remember signing up to that, but then right now I don't remember much.' I consider the half-empty glass of rum by my feet and think better of it, stumbling into the kitchen for water.

'Remember that dumb ex of mine?' Mari calls.

'Ha! Which one?'

'Very funny. You know, the married one.'

'Oh yes, the married one. The one we don't speak of by name anymore.'

'Exactly. The one whose tyres I let down.'

'Hmm.'

'Well, I did more than that, you know. I never told you.'

I sit down next to her, cradling my glass. 'What? What did you do?'

'I sent stuff. To his wife. Photos, letters.'

'Jesus, Mari.'

'I know.' She's laughing but it's a nervous laugh. 'I had to. I had to do something, you know? It was spiteful, I suppose. I mean, I really hated her. I'm not proud of it.'

I picture her, running her tongue along the glue, sealing her evidence in a brown envelope, writing 'Mrs' coupled with his name on the front in her broad, curly handwriting. Or maybe she disguised her handwriting.

'This was after she found out about you?'

'Yep, and after he told her it was all over, when it wasn't. It was spiteful, of course it was — I did it so there would be no way back

302

for them. But I also did it because I knew it would make him hate me. So there would be no way back for *us*, either.'

She lights a cigarette; her eyes are filling with tears, but I know Mari well enough not to make a fuss, not to offer her a tissue. I know to pretend not to notice. *Still in pain*, I think, *after all these years*.

She goes on, 'Because I would always have been tempted, you know? It would never have ended. And at best, sooner or later, I'd become the wife, and I'd be at home and I'd be the one he was cheating on. He'd be taking photos of someone else, writing letters to someone else. And I couldn't have dealt with that.'

'So you made sure that could never happen.'

'Exactly.' She tries to blow a smoke ring, makes herself giggle. She wipes away a tear. 'Best damn thing I ever did.'

⋆ ⋆ ⋆

When there are only questions, you flit from place to place looking for answers. A few days after seeing Mari, I leave your door and take the train back to my parents' house for a long overdue Sunday lunch.

I stare out of the window watching the

landscape unfold behind the reflection of my eyes. Houses line up, identical apart from their gardens and their colour, the subtle ways people set themselves apart from their neighbours. Outer paintwork white, ecru, magnolia, beige. Shades of sameness. Desolate industrial estates slide by, barren chimneys, empty car parks. Miles and miles of inactivity.

I like listening to people's conversations on the train. A young man, bright with the freshness of college or university, talks to a much older man (not his father, but an uncle? A family friend?) about accepting a job offer and turning another down. All around me, half-heard stories about choices. It strikes me that everyone's life is a series of choices, of crossroads, and later, of What Ifs? And Whys? Why did I take the route I took, what if I hadn't, where would I be now?

As my stop nears I'm overwhelmed by an urge to get off the train and get on another, go in a different direction, go somewhere I've never been, see what happens.

What if I disappeared? Suddenly for a moment I can see why people would do it. What if I just threw away my phone, took money out of the bank then cut up my cards, got on a train somewhere and never looked back? What would happen to me? Who would

I meet? Where would I end up?

But the choices we make are not just the ones we take note of, like taking a job or not for this young graduate, like getting married or not, moving city or not. We make them every day, because every day we choose not to disappear. We choose to go on, and keep living the same life. And this is actually the most momentous choice of all.

What was mist is becoming fog now, and the way it half shrouds the buildings makes them eerily beautiful, as though they are hiding something.

Every day, I think, looking around the carriage, people do make the choice to disappear. And some of them are noticed, and missed; and some aren't.

It's a short walk from the station and the familiar streets make it seem even shorter. I'm annoyed by the litter, the overgrown gardens. I feel sad for my parents, that they never moved from here, and relieved that I managed to escape. Then I feel immediately guilty about it; what makes me better than the people round here? I appear in the doorway and am greeted, of course, with tea, and the usual question: 'No Dave today?' and disappointment when I shake my head.

The moment, for me, when Dave and I stopped falling in love and 'landed', was when

I first took him home to meet my family. We had got to the point where you realise that even with the day to day humdrum of putting out the bins, and weeding the garden, life together is better than tolerable. Life together might even be good. We were only weeks away, as it turned out, from his marriage proposal, so he must have been thinking the same, and amazingly my family didn't put him off.

In short bursts, of course, other people's families are more than bearable; they can even be entertaining. In short bursts it's easy to cover the cracks, and especially on a first meeting everyone is on their best behaviour. Consequently on days like this I loved them as well.

Today is no different. We're a family at our best on Sundays, no interruptions apart from each other. My brother and I become kids again, teasing, nudging, laughing. His wife, Jill, looks on with amusement at a side to Alex she's never seen. She's good for him, I think. She's quiet and studious and she looks at him in a way that makes me feel warm. I like her but she's always been a bit guarded with me, as though I'm a living reminder of the world she pulled him out of, a bridge to an earlier, less civilised time. I want to reassure her, take her arm and whisper 'don't worry, I don't want to go back there either'.

Our nostalgia is more than rose-tinted of course; it's downright false. I know neither of us remembers getting on this well when we were kids, but we're playing roles that make everyone comfortable. 'Remember the time you?', 'Remember when we?', we chuckle and snigger, even though we both know it wasn't funny at the time, not funny at all.

For years I've felt that I've moved on and everything at home had stayed the same, and I thought that's why I always resisted coming back, and felt uncomfortable when I did. But it dawns on me that they have moved on. Mum and Dad have become people again, not just parents: Dad shows me his new shed, Mum talks about painting the bathroom, but also, of course, about the darts team and her plans for a night out with the girls when they win the league. They seem to have fallen into contentment together, at last. I even see him squeeze her shoulder while she stirs the gravy; she smiles and doesn't shrug him off.

Dave is everywhere in this house. The chair he usually commandeers; the window he looks out of into the garden while he chats with my dad about the football, about the weather. The imprint of him is on my parents: at a glance I can still see the pride on my dad's face when he walked me down the aisle two years ago and shook Dave's hand; the way my mum always blushes when he compliments her cooking, always over-feeds him, sometimes ruffles his hair as though he's a beloved puppy. Shortly before we got married, Alex and Dave went out for a beer, for a 'boys' night', and I remember looking at Alex in a new way, shoulder to shoulder with my husband-to-be. He wasn't a boy any more, he was a grown-up, going for a grown-up drink, talking 'man to man', and I felt proud of my brother, proud of Dave.

I found out later that Alex had tried to give Dave the 'if you ever hurt my sister . . . ' talk, but they'd both ended up laughing. Perhaps somehow they realised that if anything it was going to end up being the other way around. Anyway, they'd staggered in drunk, Alex slurring to me what a 'good bloke' Dave was, which was high praise from Boy, who'd inherited Dad's scant conversation skills.

My husband has a knack of putting people at ease, I realise, and of bringing out the best in them; and that includes me.

The house feels a little emptier because he's not here.

After dinner, Jill carries the plates into the kitchen and Mum and I start the washing up while Dad and Alex retire to the sofas.

Gender stereotypes are alive and well in this house.

I fill the sink with hot water and plunge my hands into it, swirling them to make more bubbles. Mum picks up two tea towels, throwing one to Jill.

'What are our husbands up to in there?' she asks her.

'Charlie's looking for something on Tele-text,' Jill laughs.

'Who the hell uses Teletext these days?' I ask. 'Mum, you really ought to get the internet.'

'What do we want the internet for?'

'Well, y'know, to keep in touch with the world.'

'What's so good about the bloody world?' she sighs, then smiles, 'I have all the world I need here.'

We form a little conveyor belt, washing, drying, putting away, in comfortable silence until Mum says, 'You go and see if the boys want a brew, Jill love.' Once we're alone, she says to me,

'Now then. What's going on?'

'What do you mean?'

'No Dave? What's that about?'

'Nothing. He's . . . ' I can't think what to say.

'Well, whatever it is, sort it out, will you? We like Dave.'

'Oh, well, as long as *you* like him . . . '

'We assumed you did too, given that you married him.'

'Fair point,' I sigh, 'but my track record in relationships isn't that brilliant, is it?'

'I don't suppose I set you the best example.'

At this moment Jill calls from the living room, 'Charlie and Alex would like tea please, Tina!'

'And you, my love?'

'I'll have a coffee, please. Shall I come and give you a hand?'

'No, no,' Mum's eyes not leaving my face, 'me and Fiona can manage. Stay where you are.' She lowers her voice and says to me, 'You're like your mother, that's the trouble . . . flighty.'

'Well, it takes two to make a marriage work, Mum.'

'I could have been a better wife, though. And a better mother,' she laughs, a brittle sound, and looks at me closely. She places an awkward hand on my arm. 'I'm sorry, you know. I should have been better, when you were . . . young. I should have protected you. I thought you were so . . . grown up.'

I laugh, say 'so did I', and take her in a brief hug.

'Well, you're all grown up now.'

'That's true.'

'So sort it out. Right,' she puts away the last plate. 'Pudding?'

★   ★   ★

Later, as the world outside turns dark, I doze on the sofa, stomach full of chocolate pudding and custard, resentful of the train I have to catch, sorry for the first time I can remember to have to leave these people, leave this life.

18

When Dave and I began, we would pass time making lists. He had teased me about the list thing, said I was a control freak, but soon our lists became a ritual, a game, a fairly crude way, with hindsight, of probing for personal detail before getting involved. Top Ten Songs, Top Ten Films, Top Ten Foods. Like a game of Snap! for the personality; trying to find a match. By the time I met Dave I'd been through so many short-term, ill-advised relationships that I just wanted to say 'Snap!' enough times with someone that it seemed possible to live together.

You don't want to play the list game.

'It's childish,' you say. *You would've humoured me when I was fourteen*, I think.

'Too much like giving something of yourself away?' I ask.

★   ★   ★

I don't know why I start trying to call Alice. I've no idea what I'll say if she picks up.

I'm not surprised when it rings out. 'Hi,

this is Alice,' her machine tells me, 'leave a message.' I hang up.

★ ★ ★

This age of texts, of emails, of instant messaging, instant contact, has added speed but removed romance and excitement. I wish for the prolonged anticipation of the post: letters from Laura, from Mari, when I was at university. Laura's three or four pages with fortnightly regularity; Mari's sometimes a gushing tap, sometimes a two line update on a postcard, those ones from the local corner shop, all bleached at the edges where they've sat on the shelf for years: 'Everything much the same here, kid. Miss ya! x'

Letters from you, at school, in plain envelopes, handed under a desk or brushing by me in the corridor.

Now that we have all the technology, we're losing our language. We shorten words, don't bother talking. And there are more ways to cheat, and more means of being found out.

★ ★ ★

There have been a couple more late night calls, each time shrugged off by you as 'a prank' or a 'wrong number'. You've taken to setting your phone to silent. I've taken to staring at it, as it idles in your hand while we watch TV, willing it to become separate from you, watching it and wishing for it to give up its secrets. But I haven't been able to get near it: for weeks you've kept it close as a talisman, as you lounge on the sofa, as you cook, as you lean over exercise books with your red pen. I've been trying to remember whether you've always done this, and I just haven't noticed, until now. Until the doubts started to take their insidious roots in my brain.

You've even been picking it up and taking it with you as you move from room to room. Have you always done this? I don't think so.

'Waiting for a call?' I've asked occasionally, trying to keep my voice casual, leafing through a magazine. You've shrugged, or changed the subject.

I don't know what makes you less vigilant today. It's been a relaxed day; we've just talked, and lazed around the house, with no plans except for a meal out in the evening. We've laughed lots, and made love, and the gnawing, needling feeling I've had for the past few weeks has all but subsided. So when you announce you're off for a shower, leaving the precious phone blinking on the coffee table, I actually hesitate before picking it up.

The sound of the shower is like a meter

running. I'm trembling, breaths short and shallow in my chest.

With one eye on the door, I pick up the phone, press my thumb to the arrow keys. Scroll quickly.

There's no name on the text message, just a number. It reads:

I wish I was your cigarette
Between your lips so warm and wet
Take a breath
Don't fear, sweet death
will take you, but not yet.
And a kiss.

I look at it quickly, then press the red button. Stop. Then I look at it again, for longer. Then I consider sending it to my own phone, so that I can look at it some more. No.

My brain buzzes.

Someone is writing for you. It's not even very good. What is it supposed to mean, anyway? Is it supposed to be clever, or deep, or something?

Have you kept the message because it means something, or because it means nothing?

The shower shuts off; I count the seconds out in my head, picture you stepping out, grabbing a towel, running your fingers through your wet hair, rubbing steam from the mirror so you can look at yourself.

Staring at the little screen, I blink as I notice another message. How had I not seen that? With a trembling thumb I open it: *When will we get 2 spend a whole night together?* and a string of kisses, like bullets.

I feel faint.

Even though I'm going to confront you, so you'll know soon enough what I've done, I put the phone back exactly in its place. I *am* going to confront you — aren't I?

If I ask if you are cheating, I know what you'll say. Never a straight answer. A teasing smile will play on your lips and you'll say 'depends on your definition of cheat'. I glance at the overstuffed bookcase, wondering crazily if I've got time to look it up, imagining confronting you with the dictionary, because you never could argue with black and white, on the page.

When you're back in the room, wet hair, beaming smile, I try for what seems like hours, days even, to say nothing, to let it go, but I suppose it is just minutes.

The moment before saying something that you know will take you from here to there — will change everything — is like holding your breath. Suddenly it seems to me that our relationship has been just a string of these instances. Like going to a cliff edge, taking in

316

the view for just a moment, then leaping off, only to find that when you reach the bottom, even though you've survived, there's another ledge right in front of you.

Is this how it's supposed to be? When will there be no more drops?

You move towards me and I move away, panicking, trying to keep a distance between us. I know if you touch me I'll bottle it. You lean forward again and I lean back, as though the space between us is not space at all but an actual, solid thing, a boulder, a block.

Your face creases into an amused frown, and as you reach for me a third time, I blurt, 'I've done a bad thing.' I didn't know until the words came out that this was going to be my opener; that I was going to come to you penitent, instead of accusing.

'Oh dear, oh dear,' your voice low with mock gravity, 'what might that be then? Confess all.'

I can see how this will play out. Why did I start off penitent?

'I'm sorry', I will say. Perhaps through tears, perhaps just sniffing, and blinking, as though even my tears haven't the energy to roll out.

You will give a long pause and a dramatic exhalation of breath. Maybe you will do the running your hand through your hair thing.

'It's alright', you will say. Beatific smile. Arms outstretched. Grateful, I will take them and bury my silly head in your shoulder. Thank God, thank God, you haven't had enough of me yet. You are still putting up with me.

'Thank you', I will say/sob/whisper.

You are so patient.

And I, so untrusting, with my black heart, will nestle into your arm.

Not tonight. Not this time.

'I looked in your phone,' I say, 'I looked in your phone while you were in the shower, and I read your messages, and . . . ' I falter because I'm not sure what comes next. I swallow the 'I'm sorry' that's waiting in my throat and look at you.

'Okay,' you say slowly, 'okay.' You are staring at the phone, but you don't pick it up. I can tell by this that you know what I've seen, what I've read.

I'd expected that if you had something to hide you'd be angry, and the fact that you're not confuses me, and gives my own anger nowhere to go.

But remembering the kisses at the end of the texts, bold letter 'X's screaming 'wrong' at me as though marking me in a test, I press on.

'So who is she?'

'She's a kid,' you say simply.

'A kid,' I repeat, 'and *you're* forty-three,' and you bounce back, blue-grey eyes unblinking, unflinching.

'She's a kid at school with some . . . problems.' You are calm. I breathe slower.

'*Have you learned nothing?*' I want to scream.

'What's her name?'

'Tess.'

'How old?'

'Why's that important?'

'How old?'

'She's year ten, so, fourteen or fifteen I suppose.'

'And why would she send you a message — messages — like that?'

To my amazement, you laugh.

'Like I said, she's a bit . . . troubled. I haven't the heart to have a go at her about this sort of thing, so I just ignore it.' You pick up your phone and, saying 'ignore it' again, still smiling, casually delete the messages. The messages you've kept for four days.

'Is it her that's been ringing? Late at night?'

'I've no idea.'

'No idea? So it might have been? You said they were wrong numbers. Which is it?'

'Look, Fee, is this going to take long?' The exasperation creeping into your voice pleases me; it feels like I'm having an impact, it feels like progress. 'I want to get ready for dinner . . .'

'We're not going out,' I say. 'We need to have a talk.'

'We can talk over dinner.'

I ignore this.

'How many?' The question is quiet, calm, necessary. You look confused.

'What? How many what?'

'You know.' '*You fucking well know*' I want to say, but I need to keep control and I know swearing will drag volume out of my lungs.

You lean back in your chair with a bored sigh, the shift from confusion to indifference visible in your eyes.

'How. Many?' I stand up. 'How many?'

'Fee, sit down. You're being — '

'What? What am I being?' I'm shaking.

'Dramatic. Childish.'

'Childish?' I laugh uncontrollably, and razor blades slice through my chest, my throat and out of my mouth. I think I will never stop laughing. 'Childish! Ha. You are *brilliant*.'

'What is it you want from me, exactly?' There it is, the smooth control, the perfect contrast to dramatic, childish, hysterical little me. My laughter subsides to a sigh.

'I want to know. That's all. Me. This Tess

girl. Alice. How many others? If you care about me — if you've ever cared — just tell me.'

You are silent. Words scramble up through my body, over the hard, tight knot in my stomach, and when they reach my mouth they taste of where they came from, they taste of bile and regret.

'I left my bloody husband for you. I left my *life.*'

'I didn't ask you to.'

The sound that comes out of me is a short, sharp scream, just an echo of the howl that I've got whirring about inside.

'How fucking many, *Mister* Morgan?'

★   ★   ★

Fights have a rhythm, like everything else, and in between bouts of shouting there are often quiet phases, where the words are soft, even affectionate.

'You're not a man to grow old with,' I say, shaking my head, trying to lose this realisation, but once it's said, it's out there, it must be true.

'You're just saying that because I'm already old,' you smile but it's a weak joke, and it's as though we're both staring, shocked, at my words as they hang in the air.

'I love you.' Only the second time ever you've rolled out the magic words, and there's more, 'No one will ever love you like I do.'

'You've hurt me. You don't hurt people you love. That's Rule One of loving them.'

'That's not true, is it? Come on, Fee, you of all people know life isn't like that. Life isn't all black and white.'

'Sometimes it is.'

'Okay then. *How* have I hurt you, exactly?' Two words unsaid, underneath: 'prove it'.

'What, just like that, put it into words, define it? What do you want, exact times, dates? It's about feelings, for fuck's sake. I can't put it all into logic because if I do, you'll say something more logical and you'll beat me down. And you'll lie, and I'll believe you, because I want to, desperately. Anyway,' I lower my voice, try to keep it steady, 'I'm not just talking about now. I mean then. You hurt me *then*.'

'Ha!' Not the reaction I expected. 'I gave you the attention you needed, right when you needed it. I looked after you. I gave you what *you* wanted, remember?'

'No! I don't remember, not really. That's the problem. I remember pieces . . . and some of them are great, and some of them really hurt. The past . . . you can't just forget it . . . it's there, it's in us. All the time.'

'Past, past. A million years ago! Is this because of Jean?' I start; Jean? Who? Oh, the woman from the disco . . . so that was her name. You go on, 'Christ, Fee, so I had female friends. Friends my own . . . ' (you stop yourself saying the word 'age', but I hear it, I hear it). '*You* were running around with that Todd boy and God knows how many others, and I never said anything.'

'No, because you didn't give a toss.'

'Bullshit.'

'Anyway I'm not talking about *Jean*. That's not it. You . . . you took advantage of me.'

You start to laugh, a horrible, clanging laugh like pans being knocked together.

'Oh, spare me. You came after me, and you got what you wanted. *That's* what happened.'

Suddenly there isn't enough air in the room; it's as though your laugh has consumed it all. I have to sit down. I suddenly feel very tired.

'And the . . . you know. You *know* what. You weren't there for me.'

'What the hell are you talking about? Just say it. Go on, say it out loud.'

I shake my head violently. You know I can't.

'You weren't *there*,' I say quietly, 'and after that . . . I had a shelf life, didn't I?'

'What?'

323

'I had an expiry date.' I look at you, my eye a challenge.

'I have no idea what you're talking about.'

'I saw your diary!' The words burst from me, and you look genuinely shocked, and in an instant I realise that you possibly *don't* know what I'm talking about, that maybe you haven't been obsessing over every detail the way I have for all these years, and whether that's because there were others or not, maybe that's the problem. You don't know that I'd picked up the navy leather-bound book from your desk, in your office, and flicked through it, thrilling to the sight of your handwriting, as I always did, and shivering when I saw my initials. I'd been excited that you were making plans with me, until I saw what you'd written.

Still, I continue, 'You marked my time.'

'Fee, I really don't . . . '

''17 January. FP 16th birthday. 25 May. FP last exam.' Ring any bells?' You shake your head. But in my head, swimming before my eyes, your handwriting, and next to each of these entries two words, and a question mark: 'The End?'

'I didn't make it that far though, did I? I didn't even last past Christmas. The thing is, Morgan, what I don't get is, if you were planning, if you were *diarising*, the end of my

usefulness to you . . . what am I doing here?
Now?'

'You really don't know?'

'No. I really don't.'

You sigh, and you suddenly look like an old
man.

'Then I guess you choose which messages
you read.'

★   ★   ★

I rattle round the house picking up the things
I'll need. It's a standard collection, could be
anybody's: toothbrush, phone, purse, underwear, contact lenses, old letters. I picture my
possessions shrinking with each house I leave;
picture all the things that are still at Dave's,
then all the things I might leave here, a
pyramid of belongings and me, at the top,
without them. Next time I leave somewhere, I
think, I'll probably just be in the clothes I'm
standing up in.

I head for the door.

'So that's it, is it?' you say quietly. 'That's
it, you just walk away?'

'I have to.'

'Oh, yeah,' your voice thick with scorn,
'back to your easy little life, back to
normality. Back to *sleep*. Is that really what
you want?'

What I want is to trust you. What I want is to wrap myself in your arms and never surface. What I want is for everything in the world that isn't you and me to just not exist. But I don't say any of these things.

'It doesn't make a difference,' you're saying. 'Whatever it is you think you can do to me, to us . . . you can't, you know. Or you won't.'

'Why not?'

'Because of . . . this.' You wave your hand between us. 'Because it's Us. And it always will be.'

And as usual, you don't have to say any more. I know what Us means, I know what it feels like.

'Believe what you want, but those will be the last words you ever say to me,' and as I slam the door and go out into the night, I know this will only come true if I do something to make sure of it.

19

I had heard about you, of course. You were Alex's favourite teacher. He talked about you, said you were *cool*, at a time when everything bored him. Came home and recounted jokes you'd told. He sold the idea of you to me for three years before I even got there, so when I saw your name on the timetable I was given on Day One, I felt pleased.

Day One, and this new place almost knocked me over with its strangeness, its size, its bustle. There's not really a way around it, but moving from Top Class to Bottom Year is scary, especially when half of the 'kids' around look like adults. I felt small. Laura tells me now that they have days, even weeks, when year six kids can visit for 'adjustment time' before they join the 'big school'. I'd laughed and dismissed it as mollycoddling, but thinking back now, I probably could have done with it.

Day Two, jostled in the corridor, I dropped my things. I was scrabbling on the floor, picking up the yellow sheets of paper on which were printed my timetable and a map of the school, picking up my pencils and lip balm and hairbrush, when the crowd parted like the red sea and you were kneeling in front of me.

'It gets easier, don't worry,' you said, and you smiled, and winked, and then you got up and were gone.

I didn't know it was you, of course, in that instant; I thought it might be, from Alex's descriptions, but I wasn't sure, until as you marched off and barked something I heard a boy taller than you stammer in response, 'S-sorry, Mr Morgan.'

Day Three I was in your class. At the end I was the last to pack up, and you looked at me and said, 'See? You've settled in already,' with that same smile, and I realised that from a sea of faces you'd remembered mine, and I blushed and nodded gratefully, and I fell a little bit in love with you there and then, that day, aged eleven.

Within the space of three days I saw your name on my timetable and then I saw you, and I started to formulate a plan to get your attention. This is what I've told myself.

But now I wonder, was it you who saw me? Saw my chewed nails, my one rolled down sock and grazed shin, saw my clumsily lined eyes and my freckles. Saw something that you liked, but more than that, something I might become.

For three years from then, it was clever, it was gradual, but it was always me. I was different, alright.

★   ★   ★

Memories don't come back chronologically; they come in snatches. Flashes of colour, of feeling. Pieces of time.

Some of these pieces, these movie clips, are so hard to watch that I try to switch them off as soon as they surface. They are unbidden, they'll come when they will; if I try to summon them, all I get are fragments, like half-overheard scraps of conversation whose meaning is lost.

★   ★   ★

But when it's least expected, a replayed scene can scald you with its clarity.

Three-and-a-bit years after our first meeting in the corridor, I found myself at your door in the middle of the night, in tears, and then in your bed, in the morning, everything I knew about to change.

Everything was in shadow.

I leaned into you and kissed your shoulder. Without opening your eyes you mouthed 'Morning' and pulled me closer. I kissed your mouth, and you didn't stop me.

I took your hand and placed it up inside the T-shirt.

You kept kissing me, our lips glued grimly together.

I opened my eyes and saw you in extreme close-up: your nose, your eyebrows. I closed them again and slid my hand under the covers.

You put your hand over mine, and in a few moments we found our pace, and you made a soft noise, and I thought, *That's it, I'm affecting you, that's what I want,* and when you took your hand away and touched my face, it felt like trust.

This was something I knew, this was something I could do. Lying alongside each other, our bodies straight lines, fingers fumbling and fiddling. I was practised in this. In fact for some minutes I felt *I* was showing *you* something.

But when you rolled on top of me, the world shifted.

You were heavy; you leaned forward and my breath caught in my chest. I couldn't let it out. I was pinned. Your mouth hot on my ear, 'Are you okay?'

But what could I say? My saying nothing was your permission, I suppose.

Then suddenly there was pain in a part of

me I didn't know was there.

I thought I heard myself say 'no', but it might have just been in my head. It's such a small word, after all. Easily missed.

And how could you hear it when your breathing was so loud?

Everything that was you was bigger, louder, rougher, stronger than me. I felt tiny; as tiny as the word I now couldn't muster. 'No'. It was invisible. Felt myself dissolving.

I willed the softness of the pillows, the mattress, beneath me to swallow me up, but they didn't. They were beaten, by the hardness of your body, your mouth a gag over mine, your hands clamped to my wrists.

Is this how it's supposed to be? I wondered.

And all the time a voice in me chanted *Now I have you, now I have you*, trying to soothe, trying to give me the one comfort, the one thing that would make it okay, but it didn't stop the pain, and I didn't really believe it.

And when I closed my eyes, all I could see was your handwriting, in red pen, and the words: 'It's been done before; see me.'

Afterwards, there were more tears.

★　★　★

I waited. Well, of course I did; it was a waiting room, after all.

The flowers on the reception desk were a bit too fancy, I thought. No wonder the place cost so much. They were those huge red ones that look plastic and have long protruding bits, like yellow tongues. I stared at them, almost expecting them to start singing, you know, like the plant in that film. It would have been a relief from the silence.

The clock above the door had a second hand that seemed to spin round without stopping. Eleven o'clock came and went. A nice lady with a clipboard came out and said my name, and I just looked at her.

'We're waiting for someone,' my mum said, and squeezed my hand. I can only remember her doing that two or three times, ever. I suppose she must have done it more when I was tiny, but I don't remember.

'You're being very brave,' she whispered, her head almost touching mine. I tried to smile, because I thought that's what a brave girl would do, but my face wouldn't follow my instruction. Mum went back to flicking through a magazine, it was full of pretty houses where the sofas matched the curtains, and from time to time she would point to something and say, 'Ooh, *that's* nice.'

By quarter past eleven the lady with the clipboard was kneeling in front of us and saying something. Mum looked at me and said, 'I think we should go,' and for a second I thought she meant *go*, leave the building, go home, and I would've, I swear to God I would've thrown my arms around her neck and hugged her, and I would've flown from that place like a bullet from a gun, I would've run down the street, arms and legs pumping until I couldn't catch my breath. But she didn't mean that; she meant 'I think we should go in'.

So we did, we went into the room where I was to go behind a screen and take the bottom half of my clothes off, and they asked me to lie on a bed, and they gave me a small piece of material, a 'modesty sheet' they called it, and I had just enough time to think about how absurd that was, under the circumstances, before they put something over my face and asked me to count to ten, slowly.

'One.'

'Two.'

'Three.'

And while I was asleep, they made me not pregnant anymore.

★ ★ ★

Only a few weeks before, because once the pin was out of the grenade, things moved at startling speed, I'd sat on a school toilet, skirt around my hips, trying to direct my pee onto an innocuous-looking white stick.

I stayed in the cubicle while I waited three minutes as directed for the result. I left the stick face down on the cistern while I looked at my watch.

And when the blue lines appeared, as I somehow knew they would no matter how much I willed them not to, all I could think of was getting through the day and getting to you. I fumbled through my lessons in a daze, watching the clock, occasionally touching the stick that lay wrapped in paper at the bottom of my school bag. When the final bell rang, I ran to your room, your office, on trembling legs.

★ ★ ★

'You can't be.'
   'Apparently, I can.'
   'I mean, we've been . . . careful.'
   'Not every time.'
   'Well, but . . . oh, shit.'
   'Yes. Thanks.'
   'You can't be.'
   'I am.'

'This is bad. This is very, very bad.'

And seeing you come apart like that, I was suddenly terrified. I'd been weirdly calm, believing, no, *knowing*, that when I came to you, you would fix it, make it all alright, make me feel safe.

I actually thought you would fold me in your arms, that you would smile, even, and be happy!

I thought you'd have a plan. I thought you'd tell me not to worry, say okay, it's not ideal timing but that you'd support me. We'd work it out, build a life together, and when the baby, *our* baby, was a bit older, I could go to uni as I was supposed to, as planned, and you would look after her (she was a girl, I don't know why, she was always a girl, in my mind). You'd look after us both in fact, and it would be fine, better than fine, it would be wonderful.

I thought you would kiss me and hug me and have a plan.

So the sight of your face, crumpled and confused, scared the life out of me.

I was suddenly aware I was in your office, in school, aware of the walls around us, the classrooms stretching out along the corridors, the bricks and the breezeblock and the roof crushing down on us. I saw us as though from outside myself, me in my school uniform, you in your shirt and tie, which you were loosening as though from the neck of a man who was choking.

Instead of holding me, you were shrinking from me, repeating 'this is bad' and I sank to the floor, bowed by the grim dawning realisation of what you wanted me to do.

★   ★   ★

I don't know why I was so convinced she was a girl. I think I envisaged her as a little version of me, but better. She was mine, and they took her from me. You — you just paid for them to take her.

You sold me an alternative future: university. Education, illumination, the joy of learning. In your version everything looked like *Brideshead Revisited*.

In my (real) version I would live in a room with damp in the corner and let boys traipse one after the other through my door and under my bedclothes. It would never make me feel better.

★   ★   ★

You'd amazed me by saying I had to tell my mum. It became clear later, of course, why: she could be recruited as my chaperone for

The Thing That Needed To Be Done, as you came to call it.

I asked her to come up to my room. She sat on the bed, fidgeting. We didn't really do woman-to-woman chats. Her eyes scanned the room, and I followed them, over the bottles and pots that cluttered my dressing table, the records scattered on the floor, the book and mug on the windowsill. 'You ought to keep things a bit tidier, you know,' she muttered, frowning. I looked at her, wondering how to say these words to a woman I didn't feel I even knew.

In the end she said it for me.

'What's this about, Fee?' she demanded. She hardly ever called me Fee. I said nothing. I was staring at her so hard I felt my eyes might burst. 'You're not going to tell me you're pregnant or something, are you?'

I made a sound like a gasp but no words came out.

She was businesslike. 'Have you missed two periods?'

'Just one.'

'Oh, well, you're probably not pregnant, then. Periods are irregular at your age,' she frowned. 'I did say you should've gone on the pill.'

She did, as well. Even offered to take me to the clinic. It was when she'd read my diary

(she never admitted this, but it was obvious, there was no other reason she would have brought up such a personal subject, or even tried to speak to me on my own. She'd read some account of a party at Mari's and jumped to conclusions; it had seemed ridiculous to me that she thought I was at any risk of getting pregnant. Yes, there were encounters in the dark, but we just kissed, touched, felt each other, sometimes we didn't even undress. It was innocent, teenage stuff and I'd laughed when she'd falteringly asked me had I thought about contraception.)

'Mum, it's not like that these days. You can find out really early.'

But in my mind whirred the thought, *Maybe she's right, maybe I'm not*, even though the blue lines, clear blue lines, clear as sky, screamed *Yes*.

'What does he say?'

'Who?'

'Todd, of course.'

I suddenly realised I had thought I could somehow have this conversation without mention of the other essential piece of the jigsaw: The Father.

'I haven't told Todd,' I said, truthfully.

It's not as though I lied — in fact I did try to tell her it wasn't him ('you don't have to protect him' she kept saying, and I kept thinking, *You're not listening, you're not listening*), but I suppose when I didn't offer any other names she carried on assuming.

One thing was for certain, she wasn't going to let me tell Dad.

'He'll make you tell him who it is,' she said gravely, 'and if you told him, he'd . . . '

She'd looked into the distance with a strange expression that told me that her ellipsis would lead to something so fundamentally un-Dad-like that she couldn't picture it. Maybe violence, even, against the boy (man!) who'd taken his daughter's innocence. Something in her eyes made me think she would actually like that. Drama, action. A reaction. In a way, I felt the same. My dad as hero — imagine: however misguided, however much I would have hated to see you hurt, would have railed and screamed and sworn I'd never forgive him, the image of Dad-Hero was something so exotic it was impossible not to find it captivating.

★   ★   ★

You never actually said you would come, but I sort of assumed you would. I made sure you knew where and when it would be, like planning an event, a show, a rendezvous, not

339

the ending of a life. Date and time. Venue. Be there or . . . don't.

I knew it was risky, but I also knew Mum wouldn't make a fuss, not there in the clinic. Mum cared what people thought of her, especially doctors and, funnily enough, teachers. She always put on a special posh voice when she spoke to them.

But you didn't come.

⋆　⋆　⋆

It was weird because you were attentive, afterwards. You called me every day for a week. I didn't go to school and Mum didn't push it, but nor did she talk about what had happened. She made me tomato soup with little pieces of buttered white bread floating in it, the way I liked it.

On the phone, your tone was light and friendly. You regaled me with school stories: the cringe-inducing assembly with third-year pupils playing faltering guitar; the teacher — pupil football game featuring a controversial sending-off.

'Mr Dawson was hilarious,' you laughed, 'he swore *very* loudly, then off he flounced, taking his headband with him.'

'Great,' I said.

You didn't ask me how I was.

'I'd like to see you,' you said during the last of these calls.

'Okay.'

⋆　⋆　⋆

You picked me up in the car and pulled in only a few streets away. This time you weren't bothering to take me anywhere pretty. *A back street*, I thought, *this is what I'm worth, now.* You left the engine running and I listened to it hum and rumble. I sat in the passenger seat, staring straight ahead, perfectly still. I felt like an ice sculpture, hard, cold and brittle. I felt like if you touched me, I would shatter. But I knew, somehow, that you weren't going to touch me. You took a deep breath.

'We should cool it for a bit. Let the dust settle.'

'What?'

'We can be friends.'

Friends?

'I don't even know what that means.'

'Look, this . . . ' you gestured vaguely in the direction of my middle, 'this was a wake-up call. A sign, maybe. Things have gone . . . too far.'

I looked around the car, scene of so many kisses, conversations, hurried un-fastening and fastening of buttons, jokes, hands on knees, cuddles, even tears. This enclosed space with its smell of leather and air-freshener, once a magical place to me, a place that meant nearness to you, a canopy, a shelter, a safe place, was now just a car. Determinedly impersonal, no trinkets, no tapes or empty wrappers, not even a speck of dust. Everything clean and empty. No traces of evidence.

'What's done can't be undone,' I said quietly, wondering how many times I'd thought that and not said it aloud.

'I know, but we can make it right, from now on.'

'By not being together.'

'Well, by . . . I mean, we'll still see each other.'

'At school?' I said through gritted teeth.

'I haven't done right by you,' you said in a low voice. 'Let me try, now. For once. Let me be a decent man, for once, please.'

'Do what you want.' *I won't beg*, I told myself, *I won't*, but the threat of tears stung my eyes and burned my throat and I felt like I couldn't breathe.

'It's not what I want, Fee. It's about doing what's right for you.'

In the shadow of the car I could see tears, or maybe sweat, something on your face that you brushed away with the heel of your hand, and in that moment I wanted to reach for you, but I feared being brushed away just as easily.

I was also brimming with anger and couldn't trust what I was going to say or do, so I sat in my stifling silence and just let the tide of rage wash over me, drown me, until finally the struggle subsided and I was floating and numb and blissfully indifferent to everything. For just a split second, a heady, wonderful second, I didn't care, didn't give a blind fuck about any of it.

This was the second in which I was able to choke out the words, 'Take me home, please.'

★ ★ ★

When I got in I staggered to the attic and threw myself with a great heaving sob onto the bed.

You said it was 'good timing', just before the Christmas holidays. A couple of weeks' 'distance', you said, was what we needed. All I could see ahead of me was just that — distance.

I should come back in January and concentrate on my exams, you said. Something baleful and pathetic in your eyes, your voice: 'forget about little ol' me'.

The previous Christmas, the world had seemed shiny and interesting. Now everything was dark and ruined. How much can change in twelve months and how mercilessly the turning seasons remind you of what happened last time they showed their colours. I now knew that every Christmas, every winter, I would be doomed to remember and to mark this sorry anniversary, the best and the worst times wrapped up together in foil paper and twinkling lights, forever.

20

My thoughts, for a while, are full of revenge.

When someone hurts you, the instinct is to hurt them back, right?

That's what my mum would say when we were kids. 'If anyone ever hits you, hit them back.'

My dad would mumble something like 'you can't counter violence with violence', and Mum would shoot him her most withering look, he'd go back to silence and Alex and I would be none the wiser as to what was the correct response when the fists and insults that populated adolescence on our streets came flying.

That's why I'd needed Mari to rescue me that day; I'd just stood, mute and unmoving, when a group of girls launched themselves at me for no reason beyond not liking the look of me.

That's all I kept thinking: *Why? What did I do wrong? This makes no sense.*

And this makes no sense, now.

★   ★   ★

345

I remember reading somewhere that one of the suggestions given to unhappy couples by Relate (formerly Marriage Guidance, name changed so as not to exclude non-married couples who can of course be equally miserable) is to spend a whole month apart. No contact. No phone calls. No visiting hours. No letters, but you are allowed to write things down: divide a piece of paper into two. Make a list of all the things you love about your relationship on one side, and on the other all the things you hate or are unhappy with.

Now when you get together at the end of the break, voila! Everything will somehow be okay.

I always knew lists were a good thing.

If the lists match? Or if your positives match his negatives, or vice versa? Will that help? Be each other's bright side, so to speak.

The truth is, no one really knows what happens at the end of the month. What they don't tell you is that most couples don't last the whole month. Don't make it, one way or another.

What is it they say? If you love somebody, set them free. If they come back, they are yours forever. If they don't, they were never yours to begin with.

What is it you say? Cliché? But Dave would

argue clichés become so for a reason.

It's been longer than a month, for me and Dave, when we meet for a drink. And as far as I know, neither of us has made a list.

★ ★ ★

'How've you been?' he asks.

He looks good; he looks better. Better than me, and better than I remember him ever looking before. He's had a haircut; his shirt is untucked, but neatly pressed, and he has the remains of a tan. He's been away, I think. Where? Who with? He looks brilliant. He looks relaxed, and his smile is simple, with no agenda behind it. Nothing hidden.

'I'm sorry,' is all I can say. I wish I'd made more of an effort; thought more about the details, what perfume to wear, what jewellery.

'No wedding ring,' he observes sadly, and in spite of his expression I smile, because I can't remember the last time I felt as though Dave had read my mind.

'I want to wear it again' is what I want to say, but instead I change the subject, toy with the menu, ask about Bella.

'She misses you,' he says.

'And you?' I want to ask 'do you miss me?' But I don't, because neither answer would make me feel better.

He's going on, with a guilty, lopsided grin, ' . . . she's getting fat, though. I think I've been spoiling her.'

'I doubt it,' I laugh, 'you exercise the legs off that poor dog.' Eventually I say, 'I miss her, too.'

He looks in my eyes and I find myself panicking, thinking, *Don't say it, don't, don't be nice to me, please.*

'You could come home,' he says, and then, hurriedly, 'I don't have to be there. I mean, just try being at home for a while. See how it feels.'

'I have a few things to sort out,' I say. 'I don't know if I should . . . come home, until I'm done.'

'It's up to you. I'd just like to know that you were there. And if you leave again, well . . . '

'I can't promise anything.'

'It's up to you,' he says again.

★   ★   ★

When we get up to leave, wrapping scarves around ourselves, draining our glasses, Dave reaches into his inside pocket. For a strange moment I think he's going to produce a ring again, propose again, and we can go back to the beginning, and it will all be alright.

348

I close my eyes for a second and when I open them he is holding out an envelope.

'What's this?'

'Something for you. Take it.'

'Why?' I say simply.

'Because I didn't know if I'd get to say what I wanted to say, or know how to. And,' he smiles, 'because I know you love letters.'

* * *

I open it, alone in the car. It's only one page, Dave's handwriting neat as a child's. It looks as though he's copied it from a book, three or four times until it was just right, but the words are all his:

Here are the things I miss:

The way you play with and smooth down your eyebrow when you're bored, or nervous;

Your out of tune singing in the shower, especially when I catch you using a shampoo bottle as a microphone;

How you love to eat fish but if you get a whole one on your plate in a restaurant you have to cut the head off and cover it up 'so it can't look at you';

Oh, and

You.

349

* * *

The school seems smaller, but it has the same smell, of disinfectant and central heating. And it's harder to get into; I have to show the curly-haired receptionist two forms of photo ID, tell her my maiden name and have her look me up on the computer to confirm me as an alumnus before I get so much as a smile from her.

'And who is it you're here to see?'

'Mrs Syms, please.'

'Is she expecting you?' Her hand hovers over the phone.

'Um, no. But . . . she'll be pleased to see me, I'm sure.' I try my most winning smile.

The receptionist, dubious, looks me up and down, glances at the clock and makes a clucking sound with her tongue. Finally she sighs, 'You might just catch her. She'll be in her room. It's — '

'Up the stairs and on the left. I know. Thank you so much!' I scuttle away before one of us has a change of heart.

I take the stairs with no words in my mouth. I had thought that by this point I would know exactly what I was going to say, but through the entire journey here my mind was resolutely empty. My palms feel clammy. I recall the one and only time I was ever summoned to the head's office — I can't even remember what for, talking in class, probably — and I feel the same weight in my legs, the same dread.

If she's not there, I tell myself, I'll leave it. It's a sign. I'll have tried, at least. I'll sort this all out some other way. This makes me feel better; I move quicker, turn left, and see a light on in Mrs Syms's classroom.

She sits at her desk, head bowed over a laptop. I suppose they all have laptops these days, but she looks out of place in her teacher's uniform of plaid skirt and polo neck, tiny glasses perched on her nose. She is squinting slightly. Just as she did that day in court, she looks old.

I open the door and, because I don't know what to say, I cough.

Mrs Syms looks up with slightly narrowed eyes that say, 'I recognise you, but . . . ', and a question mark of a frown. What does she see when the recognition flickers in her eyes: the fifteen-year-old me, gauche and talkative and precocious? Or does she vaguely recall my face from the court, from behind the pew-like bench; does she see the same scarf pulled around me, the same restless hands?

Is she trying in this moment to put the two 'me's together — to work out what my being here means?

Finally she says my name, seconds before I open my mouth to do the same.

'Fiona,' she says, her voice warm, a long emphasis on the 'oh', 'how *are* you?'

We talk. The potted histories people give when recounting fourteen or fifteen years, condensing years into minutes, show what has been important to them. Or what they think it's important for others to hear, which is not necessarily the same thing.

So I tell Mrs Syms about university; she's delighted I studied English, always said I was a great reader, a great writer. In fact, as I recall I used to frustrate her; I was so good at putting together elegant and pithy arguments in my essays that I wasn't as thorough on the facts as my classmates. But she could never mark me down. I always had the language to conceal lack of substance.

I tell her about my career, such as it is, and she kindly shows interest, and when I'm apologetic about not having ended up doing something cerebral, or something worthy, she makes comforting noises, pats my arm.

I tell her I'm married. If she notices I'm not wearing a ring, she doesn't mention it.

'Children?' she asks, because this is what people ask when you're married and over a certain age.

'No, just a Labrador,' I smile, which is how I always answer.

And now I know that what she wants to ask is: 'why are you *really* here?'

I'm overwhelmed by a desire to ask about her, to delay the difficult things I have to say, of course, but also because being here, in this building, and being with Mrs Syms, brings back good memories. This place reminds me of a time when everything seemed simpler, and everything seemed possible.

I feel sorry that she's spent most of her life being interested in others, working hard for them, putting her heart into it, before sending them off into the world, to never see most of them again, much less be thanked, or be asked once in a while: 'how are *you* doing? What's new these days in *your* life?'

This woman's kindness, her genuine interest in me, me, one of thousands of children she's taught yet one she remembers; this kindness fills me with sadness. She's looking at me, still, in the way she did then, as though I'm full of promise.

Tears rush to my eyes, and I know when they spill I'll be forced to tell her why I'm here. She hands me a tissue and waits.

Not for the first time this year, I realise that it only takes a few minutes to change everything in your life. Life hinges on these moments: the things you choose to say, or not say; nothing changes as a result of feelings alone, only of actions, and the reports you make to the outside world.

It's been years since I went to confession at church, but the experience of it is suddenly bright in my memory: a matter of moments during which a whole gamut of emotions rattle through the heart; fear, remorse, relief. And best of all: the abdication, at least partially, of responsibility. The sense that now I've said it out loud, I've shared it, now someone else can deal with it. Someone else can do what needs to be done.

I find myself hugging Mrs Syms as though she were my mother, and sobbing into her neck.

'There, there,' her soothing voice, her nurse-like hands patting my back. 'You've been hurt, I know. But it's alright now.'

'I'm not crying because I'm hurt,' I tell her, 'I'm crying because it's over.'

★　★　★

In what I'm coming to think of as the 'business end' of the conversation, once the tears had been mopped up, my nose blown and mascara smudges wiped away, Mrs Syms told me she'd recognised me, that day in court. Hundreds, thousands of children, she said, but some faces, you remember. More than you'd think. She said she'd wondered why I was there but didn't imagine I was with you. This made sense; we'd taken pains, on the advice of Imogen Cartwright, not to arrive or leave together.

I'm driving away from school, my hands unsteady on the wheel, driving where? Home, I suppose.

Mrs Syms, her kindly voice still in my ears: 'You know I have to do something with this information you're giving me, don't you?'

'I don't want to . . . go to court, or anything,' I'd said, 'I don't even want to see him. I can't.'

'Well, maybe a statement or something will be enough . . . do you have anything written down?'

'Yes. Yes, I do.'

★ ★ ★

I have found making friends, as a grown-up, uncomfortable. I guess that's why my two best friends have been the same since childhood. Well, youth. (When does child-hood end and youth begin, anyway? There are markers for adulthood — at eighteen you're mostly there, at twenty-one, definitely — but what about leaving childhood? Surely you're not a child at seventeen — so when does it end? I've been thinking about it a lot since meeting Alice: 'A child in the eyes of the law, Fiona,' she'd said, and I can't stop thinking about how I'd hated the way she said my name. The funny thing is, she'd looked like a child herself, with her tiny hands and make-up-free face.)

It's harder, as a grown-up. Even at university I struggled a bit, and that's a place where it seems everyone's desperate to be your friend. Like another playground but with beer and flirting.

So to say I find myself wanting to befriend Alice seems strange, especially given the circumstances. But isn't that how relation-ships are formed — when you feel a kinship with someone, when you find yourself wanting to see them again?

I know we won't ever be friends, of course. But I also know I have to see her and I'm grateful when finally (because this isn't the first time I've tried her number, not sure of what I would say if she picked up) she answers the phone with an exasperated, 'What is it?'

'I need to see you,' I say, 'just half an hour.'

★　★　★

'Thanks for seeing me.' We're in a pub in Manchester and I realise it was a bad choice, too close to the Christmas markets, too crowded, too noisy. As much as I generally try to ignore Christmas, it can't be avoided here: a huge inflatable Santa waved jauntily from the top of the town hall as I hurried past the throng of shoppers, wrapping my scarf around my neck, pulling it up, covering my mouth and nose against the biting cold.

'How have you been?' I ask, swirling my straw around my glass, ice clinking. It's hot in the bar, the windows steamed, but Alice keeps her coat on.

'Not great, actually,' she says flatly. 'Being branded a fantasist and a liar can put you on a real downer.'

I tell her I've left you and left no way back.

I tell her I've been to the school.

I tell her I wanted her to know all this but I don't know why.

She doesn't say much, just nods occasionally and murmurs the odd 'okay'.

'I hope you'll be happy,' I say finally.

'Why?'

'What?'

'Why say that to me? You don't know me.' Her eyes glitter.

'I know, but . . . ' I stare at the bottom of

my glass and I'm relieved when she gets up to go.

'I'm meeting Dennis,' she announces, squinting at the hazy windows as though looking for him. 'We're buying a Christmas tree today.'

We squeeze through the revellers, the after-work crowd, and out onto the square.

'Alice?' I call as she starts to walk away; she looks around without turning her body. 'One more thing.'

'Yes?'

'I'm sorry I didn't believe you.'

She looks at me for a long time, then says, 'You did believe me.'

21

Alone in the house, I'm claustrophobic. Itching eyes and nose, heavy head, everywhere too warm and not enough air. The blanket of central heating, the inherent insulation of being at home. Can't move for . . . stuff. Just want silence, and space. I long for a white canvas, a blank page. Close my eyes and wish that when I open them again it will be the same, smooth blank space as behind my eyelids. Just colourless, blind space, occasional blobs of light drifting by but nothing that I have to look at, no accusing, loving, questioning, hurt, imploring, wistful, pathetic, angry, sad eyes looking at mine.

I open the windows but I'm afraid of the night creatures. Afraid of moths, especially, fluttering their dull hairy wings, drawing stupidly to the light, buzz, frizz, then flitting away. Absurdly afraid, since it's winter. I hate things that fly. Dave thought I would like butterflies, though. He once took me to a bloody butterfly house. I couldn't believe it. I screamed when one landed on me, and cried on the way home. How could he have taken me there?

'But' — he was perplexed — 'they're butterflies. They're — '

'What?'

'They're beautiful.'

'They're just pretty moths,' I said.

I hate them but I could never catch one or kill one. Hope the dog eats it. But of course: Bella has gone with Dave. I used to joke that if we ever split up there would be a bitter custody battle over the dog. He has taken her out of our home, taken her to stay with my mother, said she would be too much for me, as though I'm frail or ill. 'You know how boisterous she gets,' he said.

I don't even know where Dave's staying: presumably *not* with my mother; presumably somewhere he can't have a dog. I haven't asked, and he hasn't told me. Just said he'll be back in a flash if I ask him.

If it's dark they might not come in. I take off all my clothes, turn off all the lights. No, the other way around. Don't want to look at my own body. Close the curtains, open the window. The sudden rush of air sprinkles cold bumps over my bare breasts. Shiver as my sweat turns cold.

Lie on my bed, staring at the window. The ghost of a missed child with me all the time now. A child that was never even a baby, just a collection of cells, that's how you put it to

360

make me feel better. But I still feel her, imagine soft kicks low down in my tummy; feel her newborn mouth tugging at my breast, feel her crawling and grasping around my heels. Feel her head on my shoulder as I carry her to bed.

The curtains waft, waving to the creatures of the night, beckoning. Moth. Vampire. Incubus. In you come.

⋆　⋆　⋆

I did exactly as I was told, from January to May. I came back to school and I studied and I played the part of a good girl. In class I kept my head down.

At first I looked for you all the time, made excuses to walk past your classroom and glance in, just to see you. But as the weeks passed it seemed as though it was you looking for me. I had my hair cut shorter. I started to wear glasses; this gave you an excuse, apparently, to stop me in the corridor. You did a little half-jog to catch up with me.

'I like the glasses,' you said. 'You look clever.'

'I am clever.' You laughed at this.

'That's true. And the hair. You look nice.'

'I am nice.'

'Yes, you are. Lovely, in fact.'

361

I walked away.

On another occasion, I burst from the girls' toilets surrounded by my 'followers' as you called them, in a mist of Dewberry perfume and cigarette smoke, and you were there.

'Bloody hell, girls, you smell like jam,' you said. Some of the others sniggered, because you'd sworn, I suppose. 'Jam and old ashtrays.' You looked at me and I held your stare but didn't say anything.

'Get to class, all of you. You're late,' and you were gone. Gradually, I stopped writing about you, until this last diary entry, in tipsy, looping letters, the remainder of the book blank pages, empty lines, as though time from this point had stopped:

Diary: Thursday, 26 May 1994

Disco was good.

HM has a new girlfriend. Jean or Joan, or something. She seems nice.

Danced to Climie Fisher with Sean S at the end of the night. That was cool.

Signing off.

Fee.

By 3 a.m. I'm wondering how many entire nights' sleep I've missed this year if I count up all the hours I've lain awake.

I get out of bed and drag out the suitcase from the spare room, the one bursting with diaries, letters, photos, memories.

I'm looking, this time, for something in my own hand, and I won't be distracted by other people's faces and words until I find it.

Here it is; your address on the front, no stamp.

The letter begins:

Dear Older Person,

which makes me smile, in spite of myself, because that's what I used to call you, and you called me Younger Person, or Kid. At twenty-two, fresh out of university, my handwriting looked bigger, more confident, than it was at fourteen, and than it is now. Sloping and curling with a smile behind it.

Remember me? I wonder!
I told a couple of uni friends — acquaintances, really — about you. About Us. I thought they would find it funny, I thought it would make me seem cool. Turns out, they didn't, and it didn't. I was shocked.
They told me that I should 'do' something. Tell someone. About 'what you did'. But naturally, I don't see it like that.

They say to me, you should have a stance on this.

A stance. As though this is a political issue, not something I lived.

I know my stance on capital punishment (against), a woman's right to choose (for).

This? You? I don't know.

So this is it, my darling. This is my stance. Just this letter.

Because I didn't have the guts to face you again.

Because I felt weak for saying nothing.

Because I was not strong enough to speak out, in the self-serving belief that others would be strong enough to not be affected.

Because I was vain enough to think that I might be the only one.

Because in the sad broken part of my heart I could never face you and see anything less than adoration there.

Because this is the only way I knew how.

Because I could be kinder to you this way.

Because maybe this would meet with your approval. Haven't I done well?! Look at me: still a writer.

I dare you to come back, now. I'm twenty-two; not old, but I've lived a bit.

This makes me laugh. I look at the pages as though watching a character on TV. I wonder: what did the twenty-two-year-old me know that the fourteen-year-old me didn't? I keep going.

I've uncovered truths, seen reality. You weren't so experienced, so worldly, after all. I've met people better travelled and not as old, would you believe! I've been back to London — I lived there — and I see now that we may as well have been on the open-top bus that day. We were tourists. I thought you were so clever, so knowing. You weren't; you'd just read a guidebook and knew you could impress me with a half-decent hotel and being able to follow the Tube map.

I know you thought they were all layabouts, or stoners, those kids I hung around with. But you were wrong. They were — we were — just kids, that's all.

If you came back now, I would be:
Tougher
Less pliable
Sexier!
I would put you through the mill a bit.
I would eat you for breakfast, now.
There I go, still wanting to affect you, one way or another. But the truth is, if you

came back I would probably just go back to being the overawed, devoted schoolgirl I tried so hard not to be. Remember? You saw through my bluff and bluster, of course, but played along — it suited your game, to give me more credit than I was due.

The truth is, I still want to please you.

The truth is, I won't even post this letter.

Yours, as ever,

Fee Fi Fo Fum

I start to fold the pages, put them back in their envelope, as predicted, never to be posted. Then I notice a PS:

You spoiled me for everything and everyone that was to follow. Why couldn't you do what you were supposed to do, and leave me alone?

I sit back on my heels, stare at the page. It seems the twenty-two-year-old me knew even more than I do, now.

★   ★   ★

I like snow. It demands to be looked at. It stops things, doesn't it — when it's thick, I mean, when it comes down properly, in cotton-wool balls. When it's thin and half-hearted and turns quickly to slush, turns grey, it just riles people; sends them, like the hands of a clock on a winter afternoon, hurtling forwards into miserable gloom.

Thick, white, *proper* snow has the opposite effect: people slow down. People smile; they play.

'Can't go anywhere today,' they say cheerfully, and their clock tick tocks happily back to childhoods, to sledges tugged up roads usually heavy with traffic, to mittens and snow angels.

A sense that there might be, once it's melted, something clean under there.

Wrapped in a blanket, I creep back to the suitcase. I find an envelope, my home address (childhood home — isn't that what everyone really means by 'home'?) in solid, impersonal type; postmarked London. I'm puzzled, genuinely don't remember what it is until I open it.

Dear Confused of Manchester,

It opens. Ha! I look at the date; I would have been fourteen. I remember it now.

Thank you for your letter. We get so many

letters to our pages every week that unfortunately I can't print them all in the magazine. Hopefully you will find this reply useful nonetheless.

Your feelings for Mr X are perfectly normal at your age. In fact, they're better than normal: they're great practice for when the 'real thing' comes along! These feelings show that you are sensitive, that you have the capacity to harbour strong affections for people, and these qualities are not only normal but essential to living a fulfilled life.

However, I'm afraid I have to bring you back down to earth. You say you feel an affinity with each other, but the truth is you don't really know this man. You don't know anything about his home life, for example. He could be married, or have children.

(I remember the teenage me sitting on my bed, biting my nails, turning this very page over in my hand, shaking my head, puzzled, angry. *No, no. You've got it wrong. You didn't read my letter. You've got me mixed up with someone else. You've sent me the wrong reply. Look again.*)

He's kind to you, and takes an interest in

you, and that's his job. But that has to be as far as it goes. If he were to take things any further, he would be risking his job, his family life and possibly face a criminal conviction.

Could it be possible that you've misconstrued his good intentions in helping you, and mistaken them for altogether more intimate feelings which in fact don't exist? Sometimes when we feel so strongly about someone, it is hard to imagine that they don't feel the same in return.

The best thing you can do is spend less time with Mr X, particularly outside of lessons. You may be making him feel uncomfortable or even putting his reputation at risk if people are gossiping, as your letter implies.

Please continue to work hard at your studies, particularly in English, as it sounds as though you have a talent in that subject. Soon you will be preparing for exams, and you need to apply your energy to that, and spend time with friends of your own age.

Best of luck for the future.
Kind Wishes,
Jessie.
Extreme Teen Magazine.

I now know what people mean by the phrase

'you have to laugh'. Unable to do anything else, now, I tear up the advice and throw it in the bin.

★ ★ ★

Dave is coming back home but he doesn't want to know anything, he says. I want to tell him, but that would be selfish, of course.

This is my penance, I tell myself. *To carry this. To carry* you.

There are things I must tell him about, of course. Like the pregnancy. Now that I've written it down, remembered it, properly, perhaps I can also say it out loud.

He's remorseful. He wants to make up for the things he thinks he's done wrong, but how can he, when all he did wrong was to not be you?

How can he fix me when he doesn't even know the ways in which I'm broken?

★ ★ ★

I'm curled up on the bathroom floor. I come in here often. The bathroom is the only room where you can have privacy when you're married. My head is on my knees as though trying to overcome a dizzy spell; I'm shaken with silent sobs.

When you cry and try not to make a sound, it hurts. Hurts the lungs, the throat, the head.

Splash my face with cold water; the shock of it erases the tell-tale red blotches. Wipe away streaks of mascara. Blow my nose.

Put on a bright smile, a front.

Wearing the coat of a wife, I'm back.

For the first time in I don't know how many months he watches me in the bath.

Sits on the floor, leaning against the toilet. His feet pointing one way, mine the other. Chatting. Then staying silent. Like we used to, in our first home, a rented house with a green bathroom with a worn carpet and a blackening patch in the top left corner.

Today everything is white and modern, and clean, and ours.

He watches me wash my hair. I use a heavy ceramic jug, wash slowly, tipping my head back and rinsing, smoothing down the hair, following the path of the water with the stroke of my hand, pressing. Tip, pour, press, squeeze.

Water drips back into the bath, expired.

'No one will ever love you like I do,' he says quietly.

'I know,' I say. *That's what Morgan said, I think.*

* * *

We will be alright, I think, Dave and I. I know you will scoff at that. If I can be mended, if what our marriage should have been can be recovered, we will be alright. I aspire now to be one of the 'ordinary' people you so enjoyed looking down on. Because when I tried to scramble up to join you on that lofty plane of yours, it was they who never stopped trying to hold my hand.

* * *

'It's nearly Christmas,' Dave says, as though I could have failed to notice the tinkling carols in the shops, the lights adorning the streets, the adverts for turkey and sparkling wine and party dresses.

We are curled into each other on the sofa, almost like old times, except that my limbs feel awkward, I can't quite get my elbows and knees into the right place to be comfortable. I feel changed out of my normal shape, somehow.

'I was wondering if we'll be spending Christmas together?' He's almost shy, like when we were first dating and he asked me to go away for a weekend.

Yes, I think, yes.

'And with the new year, maybe a new start?' He looks at me hopefully and I know without anymore words what he means.

A baby. A chance to start again and to become something more than the sum of us. To do something that's both ordinary and extraordinary. I look at Dave and try to visualise the child we will make. I can't, but maybe in time a picture will form. A new focus, watching the dates and taking folic acid and waiting for a result, the beautiful clarity of that 'yes/no' moment. The chance, finally, to say the words 'I'm pregnant' and have everybody respond happily, the way they're supposed to. Everything, in fact, just the way it is supposed to be.

★ ★ ★

I look out for you but I don't see you everywhere anymore. Car registration plates now are just that. Your initials have disappeared from view. I don't hear your songs, smell your aftershave. I don't have your taste on my lips. I taste only of mint and water.

I smell the fresh roses that my husband has arranged artlessly on the bedroom window-sill. Your words are burnt out and the memory of them is in shadows.

The thing that remains is this: my promise to you. Here is my book. Here is my paltry revenge, light in your hands.

A second copy sits on my shelf. Final destination undecided, but it's there, and you should know this. You can wait, now, for the knock on the door, the phone call, the visit that will make your cleverly constructed little world come apart.

'Write something for me,' you used to say, and I did, I always did. That was how this started: a chronicle of us, but also another attempt to win your approval. But it's funny how memory, and experience, can make a fool of your intentions, and now everything is different.

Here is my book.

What's written is true.

We do hope that you have enjoyed reading this large print book.

Did you know that all of our titles are available for purchase?

We publish a wide range of high quality large print books including:
Romances, Mysteries, Classics
General Fiction
Non Fiction and Westerns

Special interest titles available in large print are:
The Little Oxford Dictionary
Music Book
Song Book
Hymn Book
Service Book

Also available from us courtesy of Oxford University Press:
Young Readers' Dictionary
(large print edition)
Young Readers' Thesaurus
(large print edition)

For further information or a free brochure, please contact us at:
Ulverscroft Large Print Books Ltd.,
The Green, Bradgate Road, Anstey,
Leicester, LE7 7FU, England.
Tel: (00 44) 0116 236 4325
Fax: (00 44) 0116 234 0205

Acknowledgements

Thank You

To my parents and step-parents, for your love and support, and to Stephen, the brilliant big brother I will always look up to.

To the amazing friends who have encouraged me, I am fortunate that there are too many of you to name, but you know who you are. I will repay you each individually, probably with cake.

To my fellow Hog's Back Writers, for listening to and believing in this book.

To Caroline Ambrose, Dionne Pemberton and everyone involved in the Bath Novel Award, for plucking my manuscript out of many hundreds and setting me off on this fantastic path. I'll always be grateful.

To Juliet Mushens, agent extraordinaire, for your warmth and wisdom. I'm proud to be on your team.

To Gillian Green, Emily Yau, Ellie Rankine and all at Ebury, for your belief and commitment and for helping me to make this the best book it could possibly be.

To Gethyn, my greatest love.

SPECIAL MESSAGE TO READERS

THE ULVERSCROFT FOUNDATION
(registered UK charity number 264873)
was established in 1972 to provide funds for research, diagnosis and treatment of eye diseases. Examples of major projects funded by the Ulverscroft Foundation are:-

- The Children's Eye Unit at Moorfields Eye Hospital, London
- The Ulverscroft Children's Eye Unit at Great Ormond Street Hospital for Sick Children
- Funding research into eye diseases and treatment at the Department of Ophthalmology, University of Leicester
- The Ulverscroft Vision Research Group, Institute of Child Health
- Twin operating theatres at the Western Ophthalmic Hospital, London
- The Chair of Ophthalmology at the Royal Australian College of Ophthalmologists

You can help further the work of the Foundation by making a donation or leaving a legacy. Every contribution is gratefully received. If you would like to help support the Foundation or require further information, please contact:

THE ULVERSCROFT FOUNDATION
The Green, Bradgate Road, Anstey
Leicester LE7 7FU, England
Tel: (0116) 236 4325

website: www.foundation.ulverscroft.com

An English Literature graduate and winner of the Bath Novel Award, Joanna Barnard is presently training as a counsellor. A Northerner currently exiled in the South of England, she misses flat vowels, friendly bus drivers, and chips with gravy.

Follow her on Twitter —
@JoannaBarnard76

PRECOCIOUS

They say your school days are the best of your life. But everybody lies . . . Fiona is (un)happily married when a chance meeting with her former teacher Mr. Morgan plunges her headlong into an affair. But as their obsessive relationship grows ever darker, Fiona is forced to confront her own past. She first drew close to Henry Morgan as a precocious and lonely fourteen-year-old, and their relationship was always one which she controlled — or did she? Are some of the biggest lies Fiona has told been to herself? Has Henry Morgan been the love of her life, or the ruin of it?